WHICH CHILD

The sensational psychological thriller

SHANE SPYRE

Published by The Book Folks

London, 2024

This book is a work of fiction. Names, characters, businesses, organizations, places and events are either the product of the author's imagination or are used fictitiously. Any resemblance to actual persons, living or dead, events or locales is entirely coincidental. The spelling is US English.

ISBN 978-1-80462-178-3

www.thebookfolks.com

PART I

Sarah

CHAPTER 1

The girls were four years old when I was asked to choose between them. I guess I always knew this day was coming. They might have looked the same, and sounded the same. All of them had come into this world at the same time together. But they were all unique. They were different people. And contrary to what others might say, no mother can love each of her children in the exact same way…

"Excuse me. Is this seat taken?"

I looked up from my book. It was one of the other mothers, searching for a place to sit.

I shook my head and moved over to the edge of the bench.

"Thank you. I appreciate that."

I lowered my head briefly, but had a sense the conversation wasn't done yet.

"Are you the mother with the twins?" she asked.

I forced a smile, and closed the lid of my book. "Twins. I only wish."

"Oh, I'm sorry. I thought you–"

"No. You're right…" I inhaled deeply. "The girls are mine. But there's four of them, not two."

"No kidding."

"And… Here they come."

I stood up and walked to the edge of the playground. "Purple," I whispered. "Red. Yellow. Blue…"

The children ran by us.

"We named them after flowers," I explained. "And now they have ribbons in their hair, matching the color of their flower. It's the only way we can tell them apart."

"Shall I guess what their names are then?"

"No, that's alright."

I stared at the woman on the bench. Sizing her up. Trying to understand who I was talking to.

She had unremarkable features. She was thin, pale, wearing a maroon skirt that went down to her ankles and dark gloves on her hands. She had short chestnut hair.

I'd say she was about forty.

"So, which is your child?" I asked, gazing back into the playground. "Boy or girl?"

"I don't have any children," the woman answered.

"Oh." I walked back to the bench. "So, why all the interest?"

It was her turn to force a smile.

She stood up and walked back to where I had been.

"I don't have to explain myself to you."

And right there. That was the moment.

The tone in her voice signaled an inner calling. A distant ringing of the bell.

An alarm.

I turned swiftly, in search of the girls.

"Don't make a sound."

Pain.

Sharp, hard, fast.

From her hand to my spine.

"Is that what I think it is?" I trembled.

She pressed it further. "What do you think?"

I think it's a gun.

* * *

There are certain moments we find ourselves in that alter our life path.

Later I'd realize, there were no coincidences here. This woman knew me. Somehow, sometime, somewhere.

This woman knew my girls.

"No one needs to get hurt," she explained to me.

We were both sitting back down on the bench. Watching the children play as if nothing had happened.

The gun was in her purse.

"What do you want from me?" I whispered.

She took her time to respond.

It was enough that I could actually feel hot tears begin to pour.

"You have four children," she said.

I grimaced.

"I want one."

"How dare you," I hissed.

"You have four, I just want one," she repeated. "If you don't cooperate with me, then I promise you, a lot of people are about to get hurt."

I shook my head, searching for a way out.

"Surely, there must be something else you need. Money…? I don't have much, but…"

"I just need one of the girls."

"But why? What are you going to do to her?"

"I'll look after her. I can promise you that." She stood up and went over to the railing.

The girls' colors went by us one last time.

"I need an answer, Sarah."

"What answer?"

"You have four, I want one. Now, which child will you give me?"

CHAPTER 2

Seven years have gone by since that day, and the universe is now split. I think about the alternate realities I could be living in, as if they were no different from my own. In one I have three daughters. Their names are Violet, Rose and Daisy.

In a second, my girls are named Daisy, Rose and Poppy.

In a third, it is Violet, Daisy and Poppy.

But those are worlds I will never know. All I have is this one, which is the true reflection of what happened that day in the park.

"Come on now, girls!" my voice carried through the hallway. "You don't want to be late for school!"

Violet was the first into the kitchen, as usual. I could tell it was her by the purple-colored headband seated in the middle of her hair.

"You know *I'm* never late," Violet declared proudly.

"Yes, I know of course you aren't," I said handing off the packed lunch with her name on it. "But still, you must wait for your sisters."

"I really don't mind walking alone," Violet said dryly.

"You say that now," I said giving her a kiss on the cheek. "But I know you girls can't bear to be apart."

Violet scoffed and walked on ahead to wait by the front door.

Two minutes passed before Rose casually slinked into the kitchen. I knew it was her, by the red-colored artificial flower pinned above her ear.

"Do my eyes look tired?" she asked me.

However, it was not her eyes I took issue with. "Is that lipstick you're wearing?"

Rose blinked a few times. "It's cherry. I'll… rub it off before class."

"Please do." I handed her the lunch bag, which she set down on the table and started rifling through. "Hey! What are you–"

"I'm just checking, because… ah-ha." She held out the punnet of blueberries.

"Yes?" I replied.

"I told you already, I don't like blueberries, I like strawberries."

"Oh, what's the difference, seriously?"

"It shouldn't be that hard for you to remember, should it?"

I sighed and snatched the punnet from her fingers. I went to the fridge and opened it. "I don't think we have any strawberries left. Will these do?"

I turned around offering Rose a bag of red grapes.

"Thanks, Mom!"

She took the grapes, kissed me on the cheek, and hurried to the front door.

As I turned away from her, I saw Poppy standing at the edge of the kitchen.

I could see it was her, by the blue feather clip clamped above her eye.

"Sorry, I'm late," Poppy said softly. "I don't feel like going to school today."

I approached my child and put my hands to her shoulders. "How come? Are you not feeling well?"

"It's not that."

"So, what is it?"

She put her head forward, and I leaned in.

"I'm getting bullied."

My jaw dropped. "What? Since when?"

Poppy shrugged.

"Who is bullying you?"

"The girls in class."

"Why? What do they do?"

"They just call me weird. And they make me sit at the back."

"What about your sisters? Don't they stand up for you?"

"No."

I took a deep breath.

"Violet! Rose! Get back in here!"

"No," Poppy murmured.

The other two casually breezed through.

"I hope you're driving us now," Violet remarked.

"Some girls have been picking on Poppy. Were you aware of this?"

Violet rolled her eyes. Rose grinned.

"I'll take that as a yes." I paused a moment, staring at them intently. "Look. You girls are all sisters. If something is happening to one of you, then it is happening to all of you. From now on, the three of you need to watch out for each other. If I hear again that that is not happening, there will be consequences."

"I asked *you* for help," Poppy said behind me. "Not them."

"You see, she doesn't even want our help," Rose jumped in.

"Well, I'm officially one minute late now," Violet stated. "Thanks, Mom."

"I'll write you all a note," I said turning to the counter. "You can sign in at the office before you go in."

"Well, if I just leave now–" Violet began.

"Enough!" I shouted.

Silence.

I found a piece of paper and began writing.

"Gee, Mom…" Rose muttered.

"Everything is going to change," I said loudly. "Things aren't going to go along like this anymore."

I folded the note and handed it to Violet.

"What's that supposed to mean?" Poppy asked.

"Now's not the time." I went back to the counter to retrieve her lunch bag. I handed it to her. "You girls will never understand this, but each of you are lucky to even be here at all."

"Thanks, Mom," Violet said, grabbing Rose's arm. "Love you!"

"Bye, bye," Rose sang.

Poppy walked by me. "Have a good day, Mom."

I watched them leave. One at a time. No golden ribbons waving through the air. No yellow bananas waiting to be shared. In our garden of flowers, it had been the daisies that had withered and died.

CHAPTER 3

The girls don't know. The girls will never know. I will hide this secret from them till the day I die. The girl in the mirror, the girl at the park, the girl who looked just like them. The girl with a yellow ribbon in her hair. She was made-up. Make-believe. An imaginary friend they'd dreamt up simultaneously. They'd shared my womb together, and they shared each other's dreams too.

No, I'm not crying. Daddy will be back soon. Avert your eyes, children dearest. Those police cars aren't for us. You're still dreaming. You're watching this all on TV. You have a perfect home and you have a perfect mother. Don't talk about the white-and-yellow flowers in the garden. They don't have a name. And now, you don't remember any of this.

It's been seven years, and after that much time has passed, you have to move on. You have to forget it ever happened. Which is why it is especially hard when the call comes in right after the girls are on their way to school, and I have to go to the police station again.

* * *

We don't know if it's Daisy.

So much time has passed that even a mother wouldn't know their own child.

But for her three sisters.

Who'd look exactly like her.

I'm standing in the station foyer, waiting to be seen, and that sick feeling is back in my gut. You can just imagine it. A belated answer to our prayers. Not a kind answer, of course. Not a gentle answer. But an answer that would remind everyone of who they were.

"Mrs. Greene?"

I shifted my gaze to meet with that of a gray-suited, robust gentleman with a thick moustache. He was in his late forties, so a few years older than me.

"I'm Detective Gordon Burke. Thanks for coming in at short notice. If you'll kindly follow me…"

He held the door open.

We walked through the corridor together.

"Where was she found?" I asked, with a slight tremor in my voice.

"We can't disclose too many details just yet," Detective Burke answered. "As you can understand."

"Are you sure it's her?"

"Not until she's identified."

We were already at the morgue where she was being kept. I glanced behind me, startled at how close this area was to the main lobby.

"Are you ready?" Burke asked me.

"After seven years, I think so."

We entered the room.

The body was on a slab in the middle. A woman in a lab coat standing over it.

Green sheet covering all.

"Now, you take as long as you need, Mrs. Greene," Burke said. "Okay?"

I stood opposite the woman. Nodded reluctantly. Gloved hands reached down to the top part of the sheet. It was lifted back.

The child's face was now exposed.

"Ough."

A yelp. A squeal.

A grimace.

Their faces shifted through my mind on a slider.

Violet. Rose. Poppy.

One of my flowers was dead.

CHAPTER 4

I was taken to an empty conference room and left there for twenty minutes to stew in my thoughts. Tea. Coffee. Biscuits. I was told a sandwich would be prepared if I was hungry.

Never had such a senseless offer been made.

Sitting in the chair, my eyes still glued to the table's blank surface, there's a part of me that wants to cry. I imagine a sharp pickaxe, hacking away at lumps of ice around my heart. Any minute now, the dam will break. The entire cavern will be flooded. Men, women and children are running away screaming in all directions.

And here I am.

The ice queen. The heartless mother.

I opened my mouth.

I called Daisy's name…

"Mrs. Greene?"

Detective Burke had finally returned. He was with a slender blonde woman in her mid-thirties. Like Burke, she was wearing a suit.

"This is my colleague, Detective Ashley Irvine. She'll be assisting me with this investigation."

Irvine offered me her hand and I had to get up to shake it. "Hello."

Irvine abruptly took her hand back.

I put my other hand on the table to regain balance.

"Detective Irvine is new to this office, so we may be going over some old ground, if that's okay with you," Burke explained, getting his papers situated.

Irvine produced a laptop notebook from the carry bag across her shoulder and set it up in front of them, with the screen facing away from me.

I sat back down and put my hands in my lap.

"Shall we get started then?" Detective Burke asked.

I was confused as to whether he was addressing me or Irvine.

Of course, the question was rhetorical.

"Now, Mrs. Greene, given that you've positively identified your daughter as the deceased, we are going to have to go back and unearth the fundamentals of your family, and your daughter's prior abduction, which currently remains unsolved…"

"That's fine," I said softly. "But I can't tell you anything that you don't already know."

My eyes shifted to Detective Irvine. Her resting face was not pleasant.

"I haven't seen Daisy in seven years."

Detective Burke reached into his folder and produced a thin, plastic evidence bag. He pushed it across the table towards me.

It contained a shiny yellow ribbon.

"Yes," I said. "Yes, this was hers."

Burke made a note.

I looked to them, searching for further explanation. "Was she wearing this still?"

"She was," Detective Irvine answered. "You're sure it's the same one she had when she was taken?"

I picked up the plastic evidence bag and studied it. "Yes. I'm certain."

"Good," Detective Burke said.

Irvine put her hand out, wanting the ribbon.

"Don't I get to keep it?" I asked.

"We're still running some tests," Burke replied.

I reluctantly handed it over.

"Just so we're clear," Irvine said, "you say you never saw your daughter since she was taken?"

"That's right."

"What about your other daughters?"

I leaned forward. "What about them?"

"Are you sure they haven't seen Daisy since that day?"

Now it was my turn to stare.

I understood they were just doing their jobs, but I couldn't stand being asked these outrageous questions.

"If they had, I'm sure they'd have mentioned it," I said, maintaining composure.

"Are you sure about that?" Irvine quickly countered.

I flinched. "What did I say?"

Burke took a breath. "We have reason to believe *one* of your daughters was in contact with Daisy in the weeks leading up to her death."

No.

Never.

It can't be.

"What is this?" I shouted. "What are you getting at?"

They didn't answer.

I lowered my voice. "Okay." I sighed. "Which of my daughters do you think was in contact with her?"

Burke and Irvine shared a glance. "We don't know," Irvine said.

CHAPTER 5

Without so much as a word of explanation, Detective Burke rose from his chair and exited the room. I immediately turned my attention to Irvine, who seemed unaffected by the man's departure. Her fingers were at the keys of her notebook, punching away.

"Alright," I said stiffly. "Where's he gone then?"

Irvine didn't answer.

Tap, tap, tap.

On the keypad.

"Look!" I shouted, throwing my fist into the table. "You can't play games with me! I'm in serious distress here!"

Her eyes lifted. "How long did you say it was since you'd last seen your daughter?"

"Seven years."

"Hmm." She leaned back in her chair. "We'll see."

She doesn't believe me. Not a word I'm saying.

I can't understand her lack of compassion. From one mother to another. Well, I see now there's no ring on her finger. I suppose it's possible she has no children. But even though. She still has a duty of care to–

The handle turned, interrupting my thoughts.

"Detective Burke?" I asked hopefully.

He reentered the room, standing at the furthest edge of the door so that a young man in uniform could move past him to face me directly.

He was tall. He was blond. His face was troubled, inquisitive, and sincere.

"No," he said after a moment. "It's not her."

"What?" I spat out.

Burke closed the door. "Take a seat, Jeremy."

The young man moved by Irvine and positioned himself on the opposite side of the table, next to me. He sat down and Burke returned to his chair.

"Do you want to explain what's going on here?" I demanded.

"Jeremy?" Burke prompted.

Jeremy nodded. "Ma'am, I was one of the first responders to the call we received this morning. Upon arriving at the scene with my partner, I was forced to check the deceased for any sign of life. It was at that point I realized, she and I, had previously met."

"Three weeks ago, on the third of this month," Irvine continued, "two young girls were caught shoplifting at the Walmart in Lyndon Village. Incidentally, that's half a block away from where we found Daisy."

"I was on patrol that night," Jeremy explained. "Regrettably, although I was wearing a bodycam, it appears it was not recording at the time in question."

"We do have video of the girls in the squad car though," Burke stated.

"Where is this going?" I asked. "Who were these girls and what do they have to do with–"

"The Walmart manager was prepared to let the girls go with a warning and didn't want to press charges given their young age. While it isn't exactly procedure, I was there mostly to give them a bit of a scare," Jeremy said. "And of course, a parent had to be notified. I spoke with their mother over the phone. She identified herself to me as Sarah Greene."

My jaw dropped.

"The request was made that she come to pick up her daughters, but she said she was coming back from the city on the train, and asked if I could drive the girls to the station to meet her. I agreed."

"I don't understand," I blurted out. "Who are these girls? Why did the woman give my name? I mean, it wasn't me. I don't know anything about this!"

Jeremy nodded. "They said their names were Lily and Daisy. One of them was wearing a necklace with pink beads, and the other was wearing a yellow ribbon. Otherwise, the girls were wearing the exact same clothes."

I shook my head. "I don't know these people. My girls have never been to Lyndon Village. It's… gotta be a misunderstanding."

"I met their mother, Mrs. Greene, at the station as planned. She hugged both the girls and they stood beside her. We had a few words together, and then I watched them walk away. Although this was a few weeks ago, I have no doubt that the girl we found this morning, the girl I'm told you've identified, was one of the two I picked up that night."

It was a lot to process. Too much at once. My mind kept going in circles, searching for the place where things had been mixed up.

"Well, you know it's not me then. I wasn't there at the station."

Jeremy nodded. "The woman I saw was… older than you. And she had much longer hair."

"So that's her then," I said. "That's who took Daisy. That Goddamn woman in the park. Please find her. You must…"

"And what of the second girl?" Detective Burke asked.

I shook my head.

"Lily," Irvine chimed in.

"How should I know?" I snapped.

"Well, unless there's a fifth daughter somewhere you're not telling us about–" Burke began.

"The girls were identical, Mrs. Greene," Jeremy said. "If it weren't for that necklace, or that ribbon, you'd never tell them apart."

I swallowed. "What time at night was this?"

"It was after ten thirty. Going on eleven."

"No," I whispered. "No!"

The three of them looked at me.

"My girls were at home asleep!" I yelled. "They were safe and snug in their beds!"

CHAPTER 6

I know what you're thinking. This woman's *naïve*. Her love for her children is blinding her to what they might be capable of. Call that my test then. Call that my journey out into the road. It's such a difficult obstacle for a mother to overcome. Not Violet. Not Rose. Not Poppy. Surely not.

Needless to say, I don't stand by my overly emotional outburst. It's not a clear deduction. Every child on this planet lies to their parents at some point. Maybe it's something little, maybe it's something big. I don't hold it against them. During the course of my tumultuous parenting experience, I have lied to my children more times than I can count.

White lies. Black lies.

Gray lies.

My girls are the colors in this garden, and I am the sky and the shade. I am the passing from day to night – I am the moon watching over them. It's a make-believe world that I have created for us to live in. Outside of our garden, we go back to the earth. Where people do horrible things. And there is nothing the gods won't allow to happen.

Nothing.

So then. It's on the screen from Detective Irvine's notebook. HD quality. Refined textures. Sublime lighting. Daisy is captured sitting in the back of Officer Jeremy's squad car. Next to her, an identical sister. Who wore a pink necklace. And called herself Lily.

"Is there any doubt," Detective Burke asked, "that Lily is one of your daughters?"

I watched Lily lean over to Daisy and whisper something in her ear.

I watched them smile.

I watched them giggle.

And it's like I have to stop myself falling off a cliff. I have to anchor myself down.

My mind, my heart. They want to fly through space and time.

I blinked the feelings away. And took hold of a lurking resolve.

"No," I exhaled. "There is no doubt."

Irvine shut the notebook.

"Thank you, Jeremy," Burke said, shaking the young man's hand at the door. "If there's anything else we need, we'll let you know."

Jeremy glanced back at me before leaving. "I'm sorry, Mrs. Greene."

I let out a sigh.

Burke closed the door.

"What does it mean?" I asked. "That Daisy found my girls? That my girls found Daisy? Is it just one of them? Do all three know? Why didn't they tell me?"

Burke took his chair again. He leaned across the table. "There are a lot of unanswered questions at this point, we can be sure. What's most important though, is finding out which of your daughters was with Daisy that night."

"Where are your daughters now?" Irvine asked.

"At school." I paused a moment. "I don't want you rushing this. In case they don't all know… I have to be the one to tell them."

"Why would any of them know that Daisy was dead?" Irvine fired back. "Are you saying you believe one of your daughters was involved in her murder?"

I let out a gasp.

I hadn't meant to say that at all.

"You never told them, did you?" Burke asked, reading my face. "They're not even supposed to know about her existence."

I shook my head. "They were all so young. It was easier just to make them believe Daisy wasn't real."

"And did you convince them of that?" Irvine asked. "Did they really believe you? Or did they just pretend?"

Anchor down.

"I guess, if I'm going to be honest," I said, "I have no idea what they believed to be true."

CHAPTER 7

It's a bit after midday when I accompany the police back to the house. Detective Burke has reassured me that the officers will be careful. They know this isn't a drug raid. They're just looking for that necklace. Once it's found, they can stop what they're doing. There'll be no need to read the children's journals. Or look underneath their beds.

Violet's room was first.

Light lavender walls, with mauve carpet. Thick blue-violet curtains by the window at the end. Her bedspreads were wisteria. Her pillows magenta. Everything was perfectly organized. Nothing was out of place.

As the men investigated, I saw them take care when replacing the items they picked up. But of course no matter how hard they tried, things were never quite the same once they'd interfered with them.

"Diary!" one of the officers exclaimed.

It was hardly a great discovery. Top drawer, by the bed. Violet recorded her thoughts every night with a purple-inked pen.

The diary was handed to Detective Irvine who placed it in a sealed plastic bag.

As Daisy's ribbon had been.

"Why are you looking at me that way?" Irvine demanded. "Do you wish to object, Mrs. Greene?"

"No, I… I just wish you didn't look so pleased."

Irvine chuckled. "Maybe you're better off waiting in the kitchen. I'm sure some of our officers could use a strong cup."

One of the officers ripped open Violet's wardrobe and began leafing through her garments.

"It's real hard work you're doing," I muttered.

Irvine snapped her fingers. "Two of you, now. Next room."

She walked by me and proceeded through the hallway.

I looked hesitantly after her, two officers passing as instructed.

There were two more still present in Violet's room.

One of them had his hands in her underwear drawer.

"Hey, hey, hey," I shrieked. "What are you doing?"

He glanced back over his shoulder. "I take mine white with two sugars," he said.

"Can't wait till we get to your room," someone else said from the hallway.

"What?" I shouted, turning around.

I rushed out to see the man in question opening Poppy's blue door at the end.

My own door stood closed adjacent.

Irvine poked her head out of Rose's doorway. "We have a necklace!"

My face fell. "Really?"

Detective Burke brushed by me. "Let me see it."

Irvine turned back into the room, before producing another evidence bag.

Burke pried it away from her.

"Is that it?" I demanded.

It can't be.

Rose…

"Stand back," Burke said.

I covered my mouth in shock as he went by me again, Irvine following him, another officer following her.

I turned to join the pack, but a burst of slicing laughter caught my ears from the far end.

I looked back and saw my bedroom door was open.

"What are you doing?" I cried. "Who said you could go in there?"

"Mrs. Greene," Detective Burke called from the opposite end. "You're going to want to see this."

Shuddering. Disorientated. Dizzy.

My hands found the sides of the hallway and I eventually emerged into the kitchen where Burke was holding the sealed necklace up to the light from the window.

I didn't even need to get close to see it.

"That's not the same necklace!" I thundered. "That necklace is red, not pink!"

Burke ignored me and handed it back to Irvine.

"They're the same type of beads though."

"Compared to what? The patrol car footage?"

The man approached me. He suddenly had a very serious look on his face. "I think we're going to have to get your girls out early today."

"Oh please, is that–"

"Burke!" one of the men hollered from down the hall. "Got something!"

Burke nodded and walked by me back to the hall.

I caught Irvine smirking before catching up with him.

I followed hastily.

One of the officers was standing outside Poppy's room, holding something.

"Hey, I got something as well," a second officer said exiting Rose's room.

The detectives stopped in front of him.

Before they could take a look, a third officer came out of Violet's room, right by me.

"Is it a photo?" he asked.

"Yeah," the middle officer said.

"A photo here too," the end officer called.

I looked down at the nearest officer's hands.

I saw the picture clasped beneath them.

"Give it here!" I screeched.

I snatched it from him and ran out into the kitchen and then through the lounge. I would have stopped there, but footsteps were coming after me.

"Stop, Mrs. Greene!"

"That is evidence you're holding!"

"Go away!" I yelled back.

I pulled open the front door and stumbled down the driveway.

Then, before they had a chance to catch up, I held the picture out in front of me.

"Oh no!" I gasped.

CHAPTER 8

I think the saddest thing I've ever realized, is that our happiest memories bring the most pain. In my mind, I can go back to the moment I let my child go. The look of fear on her face as I told her to get into the woman's car. She knew. She was only four years old, but she knew what was going to happen to her. While her sisters were still running and laughing through the playground, Daisy was getting into the car of a stranger. And she would never be in my arms again.

I think of those moments, but it isn't sadness I feel. It is more like I'm staring into an emotionless void. A dark memory, where everyone is at their worst. But the sun rises again. It spreads its warmth across the flowers. There is redemption to this story. I think of the pain, and I can take it.

There is one photo I have of the girls at that age.

I had it blown up, placed under glass, and mounted in the living room. Barely a few months before their father left.

He was around on the day that photo was taken, although he wasn't in the picture. It was just my three girls.

Violet.

Rose.

Poppy.

All three were standing side by side in their little summer dresses. Smiling for the camera. Eyes sparkling.

That's all there was.

Sunshine, and warm winds. A fairytale in the background.

One, two, three.

I kept the picture in the living room so that the girls would see it every day. It was a special occasion, and I'm sure they remembered it. We all drove up to their father's recently inherited estate in the country, where his cousin's wedding was being held. Weeks later, something terrible happened.

So, this is what we remember.

From time to time, over the years, the girls have asked me about that day. I talk about the wedding cake. How big the house was. How beautiful the bride's dress.

I don't say much about the people though.

I don't say much about one person in particular, who never should have been there.

And she wasn't. That's the whole point. That's why I had that photo framed and on display.

But as I realize now, holding the picture the police found in all three rooms – my work has been undone.

Someone has been speaking to my girls.

They are saying things that never should be said.

In my hands, it's the same photo of the girls that day.

Violet. Rose. Poppy.

And Daisy.

In the original picture, she's standing at the end.

CHAPTER 9

Every child is guilty. Every child knows the truth. I am the one who has been in the dark. Standing in the kitchen, glass of wine in hand. Crying on the phone. The empty hallway around the corner was full of little eyes watching and little ears listening. I go to bed. I think I am strong. I think I am the heroine of this dream.

But now I know the truth. I can feel their presence in the room after I have gone to sleep. The three of them, all in it together. As silent and motionless as flowers in a garden.

The children have waited. The children have been patient. Day after day they could have revealed what they knew. But now the door has opened, and there's no way back. I don't know the full extent of anything. I don't know what's happened. I don't know what they're capable of.

Sitting in the back of Detective Burke's car on the way to the school, I'm trying to find a word for what I am. Is this paralysis? Is it a mental breakdown? Is it shock? Surprise? Or are these just the hurt feelings of a mother who has been betrayed?

All of it is in vain. Their deception is a result of my own doing. I have lied to them for all these years. I have denied their sister's existence. I tried to put them in a perfect, made-up world, while keeping both my feet back in the real one. I tried to separate them. How foolish of me. My girls are eleven now. And for some time, it seems, they have been fast on their way to growing the hell up.

"If you want my full cooperation," I said to the detectives as we pulled into the schoolgrounds, "then you have to handle this my way. On my terms."

Irvine made eye contact in the rearview mirror. "What did you have in mind?"

CHAPTER 10

Violet is first. Rose is second. Poppy is third.

That's the way we've been playing it. That's the way we're going to keep on playing it. Together the girls have strength, but isolated their defenses soften.

I always knew Violet was the smartest of the three. I'm not so sure I would call her the ringleader – that would be more Rose, pushing her way to the front of the pack. But Violet was definitely the brains. She was the most academically gifted. As a woman, she'd be the one to take on a proper career; success was important to her.

Of course, all these observations are past assumptions. Knowing what the children knew, I have to look at each of my daughters in a new light.

I am their mother and I love them, but I can't be swayed easily.

Their homeroom teacher, Ms. Bright, is a young, cheerful lady who – once cornered by the detectives – immediately broke down.

The sight of this was somewhat alarming. I'd always seen Ms. Bright as a fiery go-getter, who would have taken a bullet for her students if it should ever have come to that.

She was the last obstacle between the police and my girls.

But as it turned out, the authorities of the day just had to say the word… and she stepped out of the way.

Afterwards, Ms. Bright was walking with Violet slowly down the corridor. Her sisters were back in the same classroom, blissfully unaware of what Violet was about to encounter.

Or that they'd be next.

"Mom?" Violet exclaimed while we were still several feet apart. "What are you doing here?"

I couldn't answer that.

Her head then turned upward to Ms. Bright… and my sadness thickened.

"I'll leave you to it then," Ms. Bright said calmly, and then turned around and walked away at the same slow pace.

I stared down at Violet.

She was afraid.

"Mom?!" she cried. "Why are you looking at me like that?"

"I was wrong not to tell you the truth," I began. "I am sorry I kept it hidden from you."

Her eyebrows raised. "What?"

"The lies stop today!" I shouted.

Violet's whole body shook at my outburst.

And, of course, there's that maternal instinct to grab hold of her and comfort the tears away, but I can't do that now.

I've got to anchor down.

I reached out and grabbed her hand roughly.

We started walking quickly down the corridor.

"Mom!" Violet pleaded. "What is going on? Tell me!"

"How long have you known about Daisy? Don't even think about pretending you don't."

"Whoa, Mom, I don't–"

"It's over, Violet. It's done. The police were at the house today–"

"The police?!"

"We found the photos in your rooms."

"What photos?!"

I shuddered in disgust.

They were still playing.

We… *we* were still playing.

I stopped abruptly and grabbed her shoulders. "It's *over*. It's *done*. She's dead, Violet! Don't you understand? Your sister is dead!"

And now, here, came the tears, the tears I didn't want. I'd say I wasn't as strong as I thought I was, but in all honesty, I never held such a high opinion of myself. My hands continued to press into my child's shoulders, and she cowered at the look of horror in my face.

I searched for the recognition in her eyes, but there was none.

I searched for sympathy. None.

I searched for sadness and understanding.

I searched for a will to heal this bond.

"I don't know what you're talking about!" Violet shrieked.

And we're still playing.

CHAPTER 11

I was not going to sit next to Violet. Detective Burke, in the midst of a brain fade, pulled out the chair next to her in expectation that I would take it. But that's not how it was going to be.

I walked in the opposite direction. Past Irvine seated to the left of Violet. Around to the other side. When I stopped at a chair, I was facing Violet directly.

Head-on.

Detective Burke, now humbled, returned to the sliding door leading back to the corridor. He half-opened it and poked his head out. Detective Irvine had finished with whatever notes she was taking in front of her and leaned back in her chair. I could see her mind was busy.

Burke shut the door again. "I am very sorry to have to pull you from class today, but unfortunately tragedy has struck. Seven years ago, your sister Daisy was taken by a stranger. A woman." He was now walking behind her. "Your mother tried to cover up the disappearance for you. She wanted you and your sisters to forget. She wanted you to be spared the pain. Of course, your mother never gave up hope of finding Daisy again. And there have been many people inside our department who have committed countless hours over the years to the investigation. What happened to Daisy – what happened to your family, it mattered to a lot of people." He took his chair across to Violet's right and my left. "If you haven't already been told, I'll give your mother a chance to break the news to you."

He looked away from her and shifted his gaze downward.

Violet was staring directly into my eyes. Her lips were turned inward. Her cheeks had darkened.

I breathed in deeply. "It is hard to restrain myself. I can't stand the lying. But it's my own fault you and your sisters are this way. I tried to fool you, but in the end, I only ever wound up fooling myself."

Violet lifted her left arm. She put her hand on the table. "How am I supposed to feel, when I tell you the truth, Mom, and you don't listen?"

I swallowed, eyes darting between the detectives. "Has someone got that photo here?"

Burke straightened himself up but didn't answer.

Irvine's posture had frozen. "Will a description of the photo not suffice?"

"A picture tells a thousand words," I said dully.

There was a brief pause.

I saw Burke nod in my peripherals.

Irvine exhaled. She went through her folders and produced the photo for me in a thin plastic envelope. The word 'Evidence' was printed on it.

"We also had a read of your diary, Violet," Irvine added while I delicately held the sealed photo.

"You did?!" Violet exclaimed.

A moment of silence.

"It was blank," Detective Burke said gruffly.

I turned the photo away from myself and pushed it through the center of the table until it was directly in front of Violet.

I watched her squint at its appearance. Mild confusion straining its way to the upper part of her face.

And then that voice comes in.

The nasty voice. The cold voice.

The unloving voice.

It says, *Is she acting right now?*

"Who's she?" Violet asked suddenly, cutting through the silence.

Her finger was outstretched, pointing at Daisy in the picture.

She did it so matter-of-factly, so deliberately. So sharply.

It actually scared me.

"That's your sister, Daisy," I gushed uncontrollably.

Violet's face screwed up. "What the *hell* is going on?"

I saw her look from me to each of the detectives.

"What did she tell you?" Violet demanded. "There is no other sister. That photo's a fake. Just have a look in our living room for the real one–"

"They found that photo in your room," I hissed. "They found it in all of your rooms! You've known this whole time! Daisy… Daisy… You were with Daisy and you didn't tell me!"

Violet jumped from her chair and backed away into the wall. "You've gone crazy. My mother needs professional help!"

Detective Irvine got up and went to Violet's side. "Why don't we rewind things a bit? I can see you clearly have no idea what's going on."

"That's what I've been trying to tell you," Violet said quickly.

Irvine turned to me. "If we can lower our voices, that would probably help as well."

I nodded. "My apologies."

Violet seemed reluctant to return to her chair. "Mom, I don't know what that photo is. I swear to God. I've never seen that other girl before. Why don't you believe me?"

I shook my head. "Where… where did they find the photo in Violet's room exactly?"

Irvine went to her notes. "I think," she said, shifting through, "it was at the top of the cupboard."

"Where all my shoes are?" Violet asked.

"Mmm." Irvine nodded. "In one of the shoeboxes."

"I haven't – I haven't been through that stuff in ages," Violet declared. "I didn't put it there. I've never seen it before. Not with… the other girl there."

"Alright," Detective Burke said. "If that's what you're telling us, Violet, then we believe you."

I shot a glance at Irvine.

"Only, you have to realize, Violet," Burke continued, "if you aren't being truthful… if you're too scared you might be in trouble… you shouldn't be. We're just trying to help."

"Violet knows that, don't you, Violet?" Irvine said. "You're a smart girl, aren't you, honey?"

Violet nodded slowly. Then she turned to me. "Mom… Mom, I think I remember her."

"What?" I gasped.

"When we were little…" She looked at the photograph. "Like we were little then. I thought… she was my imaginary friend…"

I exhaled, covered my mouth.

Violet started to cry. "You said I couldn't see her anymore, because I'd grown up. You said I didn't need her. You said she went to see another little girl who didn't have any brothers or sisters to play with. So, what happened, Mom? Was she a real person?"

"Yes," I answered. "She was real."

"Where did she go?"

"She was taken from us. By a stranger."

"And what about now?"

I turned away from her.

"Mom! Where is she now? What happened to her?"

"Someone hurt her," I whispered. "And now she's gone for good…"

CHAPTER 12

Snap. Snap your fingers. Middle and Thumb. Just let them go bang. And the room is still the same. Burke on my left. Irvine on my right. The tears are gone. The emotion is drained. The black void encompasses all.

Violet is no longer in the chair opposite me. Ms. Bright took her off to the library or something. I know she can't go back to class. She can't give a message to the third sister. She can't tell her to get ready. She can't tell her to prepare. Although by now, after seeing the other two go, she's probably starting to work things out.

"Well?" I prompted. "What have you got to say for yourself?"

The detectives decided to leave the photo on the table where Violet left it. They wanted to see what the reaction would be. If we would get the same show as Violet gave.

Or if it would be something different.

Rose kept both arms by the sides and rocked forward in the chair a little. She still looked like she was smiling, even though her lips were angled down.

"I could tell you something funny about that picture," Rose said. "But you wouldn't believe me."

"Do you know where the police found this photograph?" I asked accusingly.

Rose looked at the detectives. "Is that who they are?"

"I'm Detective Gordon Burke. This is my partner, Detective Ashley Irvine. We're conducting a very important investigation, and it's crucial you're straight with us. Do you understand, Rose?"

Rose took a breath and leaned back in her chair.

She reflected a moment then asked, "What's the investigation for?"

"We'll get to that," Detective Irvine answered. "What would be great now is if you could answer our questions. Starting with your mother's."

Rose shrugged. Turned to me. "Fire away, Mommy."

Here comes the voice. *She's treating this as a joke. Is that because she has no idea what's going on? Or does she know everything and she's just gloating?*

"You know this photograph?" I asked.

"Uh-huh." She nodded.

"So, where did we find it?"

"Well, I'm not a mind reader, am I?" Rose replied. "You tell me."

"Your room."

"Mine?"

"And Violet's. And Poppy's." Before she could talk back, I threw my fists at the table. "Three of these photographs, in each of your bedrooms. Don't tell me you didn't know it was there. You don't even look shocked to see…"

My lips trembled.

Anger. Confusion.

I don't know what she knows.

I don't know who she is.

"To see…?" Rose finished. "What? Who?"

She batted her eyelids.

"*Daisy?*" she asked.

My whole body shuddered.

I felt a wave of terror go through me. "You *know*?"

"About what? About her?" Rose glanced at the picture. "Of course I do. How could I not know?"

"Where'd you get this picture? Who gave it to you?"

"They didn't. No one – I mean – it's not mine."

"Oh, cut the–"

"Alright, alright," Detective Burke interrupted. "Let's not lose our tempers again."

"Again?" Rose said. "Oh, you mean with Violet?"

"Was it Violet?" I asked. "Did Violet give you this picture?"

"No, I've never…" Rose stopped herself. "You know, I probably shouldn't say, but yes, I have seen that photo before. It was at Dad's one time. It was in an open drawer. He thought he shut it before I could see, but I saw. It just confirmed what I knew anyway."

"Which was what?" Detective Irvine asked.

"That we had another sister, of course," Rose said. "Daisy. I mean, it's not like we ever forgot about her."

"Well, at least you admit it then," I murmured. "You didn't believe me when I said she was made up."

"Violet believed you. Violet wasn't interested in the truth. I tried telling her, and Poppy too, but they thought I was being stupid."

I stood from my chair. "Rose, we're not doing this. You're not going to sit there and pretend you didn't have that photo in your room." I put my hand out to Irvine. "I'm sorry, okay. I just… Was it your father who gave you the picture?"

"No," Rose said.

"Well, we know one of you was with Daisy the other night. You're saying it wasn't you?"

"Oh my God," Rose exclaimed. "Are you saying you found Daisy? That's awesome!"

"No, that's not what I'm saying–"

"She can stay in my room if she wants. I'll move my dollhouse out of the way, and we can–"

"Stop it," I said furiously. "Just stop!"

I covered my eyes and went into the corner.

"Mom?" Rose called. "What's wrong?"

"We need to show her the necklace," Detective Burke said quietly. "Do you have it there?"

"Somewhere," Irvine replied.

"Where's Daisy?" Rose asked. "Has something happened to her?"

I can't do it. Not all over again. Not a second time.

Someone is doing this to me. Someone is telling lies.

One of them was with Daisy in the back of that car…

I turned around. Locked eyes with my daughter.

"You said something was funny about that picture," I recalled. "But you've never seen it before. Apart from your father's desk."

Rose went still. She seemed uncomfortable.

I walked behind Irvine to approach Rose from the side.

I stood over her. "Please, tell me, Rose. What was so funny?"

She looked up to me. A cold, somber, serious expression. Then she burst out laughing.

"You little–" I growled.

"You put it on the wall in the living room!" Rose thundered. "I've seen that photo so many times I can't remember! And it's so funny because you did it to make us forget about her–"

Yes. Yes. Yes. What are you trying to say???

"But you cut out the wrong one! You cut out *me*!"

Rose scooped the photo off the table.

"That's *me*," Rose said pointing to the girl with the yellow ribbon in her hair.

Her finger then switched to the second girl, with the red ribbon in her hair. "That's *Daisy*."

"What do you mean that's you?" I yelled. "Are you saying you and Daisy swapped ribbons that day?"

"Oh, Mom," Rose said with sorrowful joy. "We do it all the time…"

CHAPTER 13

Violet wears a headband. Rose has a flower above her ear. Poppy has a feather clip above her eye. That's today. Or at least how we began the morning. You can imagine what time passing does to the objects and colors. They're shifting in and out of focus. Purple headbands turn red. Red flowers turn blue. Blue feathers turn purple. The girls are stationary while the colors change. I'm sitting in the chair opposite. Head-on. I'm trying to pay close attention. I'm trying to see how the red ball moves…

Third time lucky perhaps. Poppy's face is awash with anxiety. Her body has gone inward. She is making herself small.

Detective Irvine leads the questioning this time. "Will you take a look at the photo there, darling?"

Poppy half-looked at it.

"You can pick it up if you like."

Poppy chewed her lip.

"Can you tell me what you see in the photograph, perhaps?"

Poppy glanced at me. I kept my composure.

She turned to Irvine. "It's me and my sisters."

"Do you notice anything strange about the picture?"

Poppy looked at the photo again, sideways. "No."

"No? Are you sure?"

She nodded.

Irvine forced a smile. "Why don't you tell me each of their names? As the appear in the photo, left to right?"

Poppy inhaled. She put two fingers to the photo and shifted it closer to her. "Violet… Rose… Me…" She trailed off.

"How about the last one at the end?" Irvine prompted.

Poppy blinked a few times. "I'm not supposed to talk about her."

My jaw fell.

Poppy looked at me weirdly.

"Who said you're not supposed to talk about her?" Detective Irvine asked.

"No one."

"Was it your mother?" Irvine pressed.

No response.

"Your father? Did he tell you not to talk about her?"

No response.

"Was it her? Was it… Was it Daisy? Did she come visit you?"

Poppy's eyes lifted. There was a look of confusion.

"May I?" I asked Irvine.

Irvine hesitated. "Alright."

I stood up and put my hands to the photograph. "You know what Rose just told us? Rose said that *she's* the girl at the end. She's wearing the yellow ribbon. Did you know about this?"

Poppy squinted. She took the photo away from me to study it carefully.

Then she shook her head. "No."

"No?"

She handed it back. "Rose is lying."

"How are you so sure?" I asked.

"I can… I can just tell," Poppy replied. "Can't you?"

I looked at the photo again, and my heart sank.

I honestly couldn't.

"Please, Poppy," Detective Irvine said, shifting closer. "You're a bright and intelligent girl. The other two underestimate you, don't they?"

Poppy appeared to warm to the statement. "Perhaps."

"We need to know everything you can tell us about this photograph. Particularly, who told you not to discuss it."

"Alright," Poppy said. She turned to me. "You can sit down, Mom."

I dropped the photo and fell into my chair.

"It was last summer, when we were on holidays, when something woke me up in the middle of the night," Poppy said. "I got really scared because the curtains were closed, and I kept hearing this tapping on the window. There was a person out there. I was about to run to your room, but then I heard them call my name. And I knew it was one of the other two. I thought maybe they were locked out or something. I pulled back the curtain, and that's when I first saw her…"

Poppy paused to take a breath. She put her arms on the table and pulled her chair in.

"I was so confused. I thought it must have been one of the other two playing a trick on me. It was hard to see. She said she was my secret sister, and that I should come out with her to play. But I didn't want to. I didn't go. Then I watched her go and knock on Rose's window."

"Did she talk to Rose?" I asked. "Did Rose go out with her?"

Poppy shook her head. "I don't think Rose answered. But she went over to Violet's window and talked to her for a bit."

"What were they saying?"

"I don't know. Same as what she said to me. After a bit, Violet went out the front door and I watched them walk down the street together."

"Violet," I whispered. "I can't believe this. Why is she lying?"

"It was a few days later," Poppy explained, "I asked Violet about it. I wanted to know about the girl, but Violet said if I ever brought it up again, she'd hurt me. I think she meant it."

I exhaled. Turned to Irvine. "Are we bringing Violet back in here then?"

"No!" Poppy cried. "Don't tell her I told you."

"Uh, Poppy," Detective Burke said, catching the girl's attention. "Was that the only time you saw Daisy? Did she come to the house again?"

Poppy's eyes fluttered. "Who's Daisy?"

Silence.

"Your other sister," Irvine answered. "She wore the yellow ribbon in her hair."

Poppy shook her head. "In that photo you showed me, yes. But when she came to the window, she wasn't wearing a ribbon."

"What was she wearing?"

"Uh." Poppy thought for a moment. "She had a pink necklace with beads. She said her name was Lily…"

CHAPTER 14

Say hello to Ms. Bright. Then say goodbye. Back to the library. Back to class. The girls will open their books to listen and learn, while the rest of us are left sitting in this room trying to make sense of what just happened.

"I can't believe this," I muttered. "Why are they lying? What have they got to hide?"

"Why is *who* lying?" Detective Burke asked.

"Exactly," I said. "How can I trust any of them?"

"Poppy was rather convincing," Irvine remarked. "And I wouldn't put a line through anything Rose said either."

"So, it's Violet then," I said. "Violet's the liar."

"That deduction is, at this time, the most consistent with the facts," Irvine confirmed.

"Violet who stood there and cried real tears. She… she begged me to believe her."

"So, you think Poppy was lying?" Burke queried.

"Maybe," I said. "I don't know."

"Well, we don't have to worry about that right now," Detective Burke said. "We have other lines of inquiry to follow up. It's probably best we let things rest for a few days. Perhaps whoever was with Daisy that night, will find the courage to come forward between now and then."

"It was curious though," Irvine reflected, "how Poppy said Lily was the one at her window. Since we've already seen Daisy and Lily together, can we assume that Lily is one of Violet or Rose? But then Poppy said Lily went to Violet's room and spoke with her. But Rose didn't answer. So, was Rose pretending to be Lily? And that's not even Daisy she's pretending to be. Um… I just…"

Detective Burke nodded and closed the file in front of him. "We'll come back to that." He stood from his chair and waited until each of us were on our feet before heading back to the door.

We moved through the corridor in silence.

Burke and Irvine handed me their business cards once we were at the office.

"If there are any more developments, you can contact either of us," Burke assured me. "Now, can we offer you a ride home or–"

"No, that's alright," I said. "I'll phone a friend or something."

"Very well." Burke stepped outside. "Take care, Mrs. Greene."

Irvine lingered a little on her way behind him. "Children lie. It's in their nature. Go easy on your girls. They've had a rough ride."

I rolled my eyes. "I'll remember that, shall I?"

The door swung shut after her.

I turned to the nearest armchair and plonked myself down.

For a minute or so, it was just me and my thoughts.

"Would you like some tea, dear?" the receptionist asked from the office window.

I looked up, unaware she'd been watching me.

"Yes, thank you." I smiled. "That sounds lovely."

CHAPTER 15

The war has begun. It's me versus my girls. At the moment, they're beating me. Because I didn't know this thing had started.

My goal is happiness. My objective is a peaceful family. I want all three of them to grow up into wonderful ladies who live beautifully enriched lives. I want the best for them, at all costs. But before any of that can happen, I must grieve the death of my fourth child. I must heal this wound. I must cry and cry and cry until there are no more tears left but those of gratitude. Because I still have three more girls, whom I individually adore.

But I don't get to heal. I don't get to put Daisy's shadow behind me. Not until I know exactly what happened to her. Not until I untangle the web of deceit those girls sowed back there.

It hurts.

It hurts to suspect them.

Because I don't know if it is one of them who is lying. Or if it is two. Or if it is all three.

In actual truth, I don't know if there is some miraculous undercurrent passing by that enables a reality where all three are telling the truth whilst simultaneously contradicting one another.

They are children after all. Mistakes will be made.

What is not there, will be seen.

What is silent, will be heard.

Imagination is a funny thing. Right now, I have to imagine how I'm going to unravel this illusion. I must dispel all misconceptions. I must obliterate all lies. My girls are clever, yes. They may or may not be working together. But I am their mother. It is my house they live in. I was the one who painted the colors in their rooms. I was the one who bought their feathers, and flowers, and ribbons.

I gave them their names.

And once upon a time, one afternoon, while they were playing in a park, I decided which of the four would live.

And which one would die.

CHAPTER 16

The smell of bleach, and ice-cold air-conditioning set the mood as I walked through the downstair lobby of the corporate office building where my ex-husband works. The receptionist is a heavily made-up, jet-black dyed brunette in her twenties named Jessica. We have shared words on a number of occasions, but this is the first time I'm seeing her face to face.

She looked up from her computer screen and didn't even have the courtesy to issue a greeting. I wondered if it might be company policy. Or if the air of self-importance was internally manufactured.

"Nicholas Greene," I said tonelessly.

"Your name?" she replied.

"Sarah Greene."

Her cheeks immediately paled.

She pulled her chair forward and straightened her posture. "Sarah. Hi. Nice to finally meet you in… person."

Now it is my opportunity to not issue a response.

She adjusted herself again. "Uh. Does Mr. Greene know you're coming?"

"No."

"Have you tried reaching him on the phone?"

"He's not picking up."

"Alright. I see. I'll just try and get a hold of him then for you. One moment, please."

She maneuvered her chair to the side and picked up the telephone.

I turned away briefly, looked up to see how high the ceiling went.

All those offices upstairs. All those shut blinds and closed doors.

It brought back some memories.

"I see. Thank you."

I turned back to the desk.

"I'm sorry," Jessica said, "it seems Mr. Greene has gone to lunch."

"Has he?"

She nodded.

"You wouldn't know where, by any chance, would you?"

CHAPTER 17

I'm not dressed well enough for a restaurant this fancy. Faded jeans and a loose sweater. It was good enough for where I was supposed to be. At the police station, sitting with Detectives Burke and Irvine. I didn't hear Daisy complain either.

My special day. Seven years of waiting to finally see her again. And yet, it would seem it was less of an occasion than a weekday lunch.

"Ma'am," someone is calling behind me. "Ma'am, you can't come in here like that. Ma'am!"

It's too late. I've already spotted him.

Black jacket and collared shirt, striking silver tie. There are six of them at the table – all men, all suited-up and drinking white wine.

"Sarah," Nicholas exclaimed. "What on Earth are you doing here?"

"Looking for you."

"Ma'am," the restaurant host said closing in. "Would you please kindly step away from the table?"

"You're coming too," I ordered Nicholas.

He smiled apologetically and rose from his seat. "Family matters. I shall return shortly."

The host tried grabbing my arm, which I abruptly shook off. "I'm leaving!"

I stormed out back through the entrance and with a few more feet I was in the parking lot.

The office building where Nicholas worked was just up the street and could be seen easily from here, towering in the sky.

"What the hell was that?" he yelled.

I turned around as Nicholas approached me.

"Rule number one is do not disturb me at work. I don't know what you're thinking coming in here–"

I slapped him.

He took a step back, his face swelling with anger.

But I was no longer afraid.

"I'll take it then that the police have yet to speak with you."

"Police?" he stammered.

"I was at the station all morning," I replied. "And then we all went to the girls' school."

"Slow down," he said.

He rubbed the mark on his cheek, whilst fixing his tie with the other hand.

"You can forget about your lunch," I told him. "Something's happened."

"Yes – something's happen," he muttered. "Are you going to tell me what?"

I crossed my arms. "That depends. Are you going to listen?"

CHAPTER 18

Nicholas will now learn the truth of what has happened to his child. I will take him through every moment. I will show him every detail. But it will be on my terms. I'll make sure the weight of this sinks in.

His hands are on the wheel. I'm in the passenger seat. It's an expensive car. A new car. It smells like his office. Nicholas has done very well for himself. But then, his family always had.

"Are you going to tell me where we're going?" he asked.

"Take the next right," I replied.

It wasn't the best marriage. I guess that goes without saying. Nicholas wanted me to be a submissive and hypersexual wife. I wanted him to be a gentle husband. Perhaps in the beginning, I was a little more submissive, and a little more sexual.

But he was never gentle.

"You can slow down. Park at the side here."

The wheels glided in.

He turned to me while we were at a standstill.

I reached over and pulled the keys out.

"Are you done playing games?" he said, snatching the keys from me.

"I made them drive here," I muttered. "Before we went to the school. I wanted to know where they found her."

"Found who?"

I pushed open the car door. Walked into the middle of the road.

Traffic was coming right for me. My eyes were closed to it. All I could see was Daisy.

I heard the brakes, from far away. The sound of the horn. Thankfully, before I was in any real danger, I felt Nicholas's presence behind me, ushering me to safety. And then, we saw the police tape.

"Found *who*?" Nicholas repeated.

I could see it in his eyes though, he knew who it was. There was only one of us missing after all.

I nodded to the alley.

His arms left me. I watched him walk to the edge of the tape.

"She's not there now," I whispered. "But this morning she was found behind that dumpster."

Nicholas put his leg over the tape.

He moved towards it. I followed.

There was another barricade near the dumpster. The tape was barely as high as our ankles. But we could see. We could see the space where she'd lain.

"No," I heard him gasp.

He collapsed to his knees and bent over the tape.

He put his hand to the bloodstained surface.

It was dry.

"No!" he shouted.

A shiver ran through my body.

"I'm sorry," Nicholas moaned. "I'm so sorry…"

I was sorry too.

CHAPTER 19

I go back home, get the car, then drive to the school and get all three of my girls out an hour before home time. They're not happy. They can see I'm not being normal. They're afraid for what's about to happen.

And they should be.

I drive the four of us up to Nicholas's house, just outside the city. We go up the pebbled driveway. We walk up to the front door. The whole time, they're asking constant questions. But I won't answer any of them. I can barely bring myself to speak to any of them again. Not until we know the truth. Not until we know where the woman is who took our daughter.

Nicholas is waiting in the living room for us. I instruct the girls to sit down on the sofa together. He's already set up his camera phone on a stand, so everything that happens in this room will be recorded.

"Girls," Nicholas began with a crack in his voice. "If the police didn't make it clear this morning, your sister Daisy has been murdered. Someone brought her out to a cold alley last night, and made her crouch down by the bins. They took a sharp knife. And they stabbed her until she fell over."

I can see it as he says the words.

I can hear her cry for help, and there's nothing I can do.

"They left her there, in that alley," Nicholas continued. "Lying on her back. Bleeding out. Bleeding to death. We don't know who killed her yet, but whoever it was they were consumed by pure evil."

He paused to refill his Scotch glass.

Threw back another one straight.

"Now, over the past seven years, we believe Daisy was still living with the woman who kidnapped her. What the police have told us, and what your mother has seen for herself, was one of you sitting in the back of a police car with Daisy a few weeks ago. You went with the officer to the train station, where he left you in the company of a woman who claimed to be your mother. Whatever stories you have told up to this point, whatever games you've been playing, they end now."

He paused for effect.

I studied the girls to see how each was reacting.

Violet was sitting up straight and alert.

Rose was looking down, eyes on the floor.

Poppy was looking at me.

"I am your father," Nicholas boomed at them. "Never mind the police. Never mind your mother. You are not going to sit there and lie to me. None of us are going to leave this room, until we find out which of you was in the back of that car."

Poppy shifted her gaze over Rose's head, towards Violet.

Violet caught her looking and jumped. "What?"

"Tell them," Poppy said. "Tell them about Lily."

"What Lily?" Violet snapped. "Who's that?"

"Well, tell them about how you were sneaking out."

"I most certainly did *not* sneak out," Violet shouted. "How *dare* you accuse me. You little, weirdo liar!"

"Girls!" Nicholas shouted. "Enough!"

Rose got up and walked away from the sofa towards me.

"Hey," I said. "Where are you going?"

"Well, it's clearly one of them, isn't it?" she said. "I'm not sitting there while they're being shouted at."

"Hey!" Nicholas cried again. "I'm not done with you."

Rose sat down on the floor beside me.

Violet got up. "This is *insane*."

"Sit back down," Nicholas snapped, waving his finger at her.

Violet recoiled in anger. She held her ground.

"Did you not hear what I just said?" Nicholas asked.

"What are you going to do?" Violet countered. "Hit me?"

Nicholas stared at her. "Hit you?"

"I'll press charges. Believe me."

Nicholas was stunned. His mouth opened, but no words came.

"No one's pressing charges," I said firmly. "And no one's hitting anyone either." I went over to the mantle and poured Nicholas another Scotch. I handed it to him and took my place opposite Violet.

"You look me in the eyes, and you tell me you don't know what Poppy's talking about."

Violet glared at me. Her eyes did not blink.

"She's full of it," Violet said.

I turned to Poppy. "Well?"

Poppy adjusted herself. "If I was lying, I would just tell you."

"No, you wouldn't," Rose called.

Nicholas and I turned as Rose got up off the floor and approached confidently. "Clearly, it's Poppy who is lying," she said. "Not Violet."

"Thank you," Violet said softly.

Nicholas handed me his glass back, now empty, and approached Poppy on the sofa. He crouched beside her. He reached out and took her hand into his. "Tell the truth," he said. "Please, Poppy. Do it for me. I know you want to."

All eyes moved to the girl with blue feathers.

Poppy looked to each of us. There was a sadness in her eyes, but it seemed restrained. Sedated.

"I don't care whether you believe me or not," Poppy said. "I'm sorry about what happened to Daisy. But I didn't have anything to do with it."

"No one's accusing you," Nicholas said. "We're not… we're not accusing anybody."

"Then why are we all here?" Violet demanded. "Don't you think one of us killed her?"

"No!" Nicholas cried. "Of course not! Right, Sarah?"

I looked from him to Poppy on the couch.

Small and huddled together.

I looked to Violet standing tall and proud.

Then to Rose, crouching by my feet.

If I could just burn away my memories of her. If I could just let that yellow ribbon out of my grasp, to carry on the wind–

Ringtone activated.

I turned around to retrieve my handbag from the floor and pulled out my cell.

"Hello?"

"Mrs. Greene?"

"Yes."

"This is Detective Burke. Where are you now?"

"Why? What's happened?"

"I can't say until you get here."

"Alright," I murmured. "Should I bring the girls? Or should I leave them with their father?"

A pause. "You better bring them with you. I'd think about calling your attorney too."

CHAPTER 20

It's over now.

It's over for one of my girls.

I feel it. I know it. New evidence has come to light. The police have worked out which of my children was with Daisy in the car that night. This could be the last time all four of us are together. Or should I say five of us?

Nicholas has no idea. He makes the call to have his company lawyer meet us at the station. But he hasn't grasped the significance of what's happened. Maybe he's not good at reading faces. Or maybe I'm good at hiding mine.

The car ride is painful; Nicholas in the driver's seat, me in the passenger, our three girls in the back. We could just keep driving. We could start again. We could become different people. Nicholas will change for me, and I will change for him.

Our girls are perfect. Our girls are special.

I think about them growing up. First as teenagers going to high school. Then young women in college.

I think about where they'll be when they're my age. How Nicholas and I will visit them and their families on the holidays.

We won't talk about her. We won't talk about the one who got away.

Daisy didn't die in some cold alley. Daisy wasn't stabbed to death.

She was an imaginary child, the five of us made up.

And now it's done. The yellow ribbon is floating away.

The past is behind us. All that matters is their happiness.

At any cost.

***

Click.

The door to the interview room is unlocked and opened.

Four chairs. Small table.

It's just me and the detectives at the moment. Nicholas is still in the lobby with the girls, waiting for the lawyer. I'm the one who's going to find out what the police have first. Who they're looking at, in particular.

And there is an answer here.

There is a true path through our garden of lies.

I'm not sure who I suspect.

Only, whoever the liar is, they're very clever.

"…the time is 4.05 p.m.," Detective Burke is saying. "You understand, Mrs. Greene, you don't have to answer any of our questions, and you have the right to have an attorney present?"

"He's on his way," I said.

"Would you like to wait until he gets here?"

I shook my head.

"Please, Mrs. Greene. For the tape."

"We don't have to wait," I said. "I just… want to know what's happened."

Detective Irvine shifted a plastic box in front of her and undid the clasps. She pushed open the lid and extracted a large kitchen knife, sealed in an evidence bag.

She placed it on the table in front of her. "Have you ever seen this knife before, Mrs. Greene?"

I noticed it had a pink handle. "No. Is that what they used?"

The detectives stared at me blankly.

"One more time, Mrs. Greene," Detective Burke said. "Have you seen this knife before?"

I shook my head.

"Or another knife like it?" Irvine pressed.

"I swear."

Irvine leaned back in her chair. They were both making me feel uneasy.

"Am I supposed to have seen it?" I asked.

"Well, have you?" Burke replied.

"Not to my knowledge."

"Have you made any purchases of knives recently?" Irvine asked.

"Are you serious?"

Detective Burke let out a sigh. "Can you tell us where you were last night between the hours of eleven and four?"

"I told you already," I snapped. "At home. Asleep. That's… that's where we all were!"

"Are you sure you're not mistaken?" Irvine said.

"Yes."

"You didn't go out last night?"

"No."

"You didn't visit a hardware store at 11.40 p.m.?"

Okay. Time to take a deep breath. This isn't going where I thought it would. They've obviously got something mixed up with–

"Here's a copy of your debit card statement," Detective Burke said, producing a sheet of paper. "You'll note the time and location of the purchase, last night at 11.40 p.m."

I snatched up the paper.

He was right. A charge of $15.49 at a hardware store.

I immediately reached into my handbag to check my card was still in my purse.

It was.

"That's wrong," I said. "It's a mistake. I was at home. Unless… Unless–"

Detective Burke leaned over and whispered something in Irvine's ear.

She nodded and got up from the table. "Be right back."

She left the room.

"What's going on?" I asked.

Burke stared at me. "This is never easy. It's best you just come clean now. You don't want to put your girls through this, do you?"

I pulled the chair forward. "Look. I don't know what's going on here. Are you saying that someone used my card last night, to purchase this knife?"

"I'm saying *you* purchased this knife."

"No. No, if… if someone used my card. Surely the hardware store has surveillance."

Burke nodded. "We have that."

"What?"

"We have the surveillance." He hesitated. "I will show you two stills. And then you're going to tell me what really happened last night."

I straightened up.

He pushed out the first still. An image capture on a sheet of paper.

It was my car in a parking lot.

Time stamped at 11.34 p.m. last night.

"That's impossible," I whispered.

"And this is the purchase," Burke said, shoving another sheet in front of me.

And there she was.

A woman wearing my jeans. My jacket. Carrying my handbag.

Her hair is the same length and color as mine.

It actually looks like me.

"Oh gosh," I whispered. "I'm being framed."

"No," Detective Burke said dismissively. "You're not being framed, Mrs. Greene. You purchased that knife at 11.40 p.m. last night, and within a few hours you murdered your daughter."

I pushed the pictures back at him. "You can't say that that's definitely me! The camera's too far away. The focus isn't clear."

"That's where eyewitnesses come in. Due to the footage, we know you weren't alone in the store."

The door opened.

Detective Irvine reentered.

She made way for my three girls.

"Alright then," Irvine said, closing the door after them. "Just tell him what you told me."

"Mom woke us up at eleven," Violet said.

"She put us in the car," Rose added.

"We drove to the store," Poppy finished.

"No!" I shouted at them.

"Please, Mrs. Greene, you must contain yourself," Detective Burke advised.

Detective Irvine picked up the knife from the table.

I got up out of my chair.

"Have you seen this before, girls?" Irvine asked.

All three of them said, "Yes."

"You little liars," I hissed.

They gave no emotion.

"Alright, that's enough," Burke said.

Irvine led my children away.

Burke stood up. "Why don't we take a break, Mrs. Greene? You have a think about what you want to do."

He lifted another still and placed it on the table before leaving.

I took a moment, watching the door close. The anxiety. The confusion. The terror.

Somehow in all of this, I had lost my way.

I'd lost my family.

I put my hands on the table and looked down. It was a shot of the woman entering the hardware store.

Violet, Rose and Poppy were all walking just in front of her.

Head-on.

PART II

Jessica

CHAPTER 21

One woman falls. Another rises in her place.

How I've waited for this day. It goes further than wants or desires. Further than a wish upon a star. I consider this to be what is owed to me. The universe has shifted, and now I am finally able to crawl up out of the dark. I will be recognized as their mother. I will be recognized as his wife.

Too bad for Sarah. It's just dominoes falling at this point.

She can't do a thing to stop me…

"Can you see the train, Georgie?"

Georgie pressed himself against the window in the passenger seat next to me. "No, not yet."

"Keep watching," I said without looking up from my phone. "It will be here any minute."

"Okay…"

Georgie is eight years old. He is an energetic, happy boy. He has a smile wide enough to melt any mother's heart.

"I think I hear it, Jess."

He's very excited today.

"Hear what?"

"The train."

I chuckled to myself. "Just let me know when you see it."

I am Georgie's biological mother. Not many people know that. I haven't told Nicholas yet. I'm not sure I'm going to. Georgie was conceived when I was sixteen. It was a bit of a chaotic time for me. I've narrowed down who his father is to eight people. Needless to say, there wouldn't be much point in tracking them all down for DNA tests. I suppose it could be done. In the meantime, the official line is that he's my adopted brother. My parents did most of his raising. Of course, he's mine, and I'm a grown woman now. So I'll have my boy at my side as much as I can. Our future looks bright anyway.

Nicholas Greene, my potential husband, is rich rich rich–

"Train! Train! Jess, it's the train!"

"Where? I can't see it," I said playfully as Georgie shook my arm.

"It's right there! Are you blind?"

I laughed and put my phone away. "Alright then. I guess we better get out."

Doors unlocked. Exit vehicle.

Before we crossed the road, I pressed Georgie up against the side of the car and straightened the creases in his shirt. I put my fingers through his strawberry-blond hair and made sure his face was clean.

"Jess! Stop it! Seriously!"

"Now, now, now. We want to make a good impression, don't we?"

"Yeah." His voice quivered a little.

"What is it, Georgie?"

"Nothing." He shrugged. "I'm just nervous."

"You don't need to be nervous," I reassured him. "You're a handsome, handsome boy! They're going to love you."

And they're going to love me too.

CHAPTER 22

The girls were all wearing black. As though there had been a death in the family. I guess in a way, there had been. It's horrible to think about – that poor child cowering in an alley before that psycho hacked her to pieces. Sarah probably went stir-crazy in that little suburban dump the four of them were living in. I know I would.

"Girls!" I called whilst Georgie and I were still crossing the road. They'd just made their way down the steps outside the station's entrance. "Over here!"

Bags. Suitcases. Over shoulders and on wheels.

Everything that belonged to them was literally by their side.

"Come along then, my sweeties!"

Collectively, the girls lacked the certain excitement and rigor I was anticipating. Of course, I was prepared to deal with them however they came. In two days' time, by Sunday night when Nicholas returned home, the girls would be exactly as I wanted them to be.

"Hello, hello, my lovelies," I said once we were at arm's length. "I'm Jessica. This is my little brother, Georgie. No need to be shy now. He doesn't bite."

I gave Georgie a soft push so he was right in front of them.

"Uh, hello," Georgie said awkwardly.

The girl in the middle smiled thinly. "Hi there. I'm Rose." She motioned to her right. "This is Violet." She motioned to her left. "This is Poppy."

"Hello," Violet said politely, looking at me.

Poppy gave a light wave but said nothing.

"I was told you girls usually wear colored accessories to tell you apart," I remarked. "And yet here you are without any. And you're all wearing the same clothes."

"We just told you what our names are," Rose stated, her smile fading.

"And not for the last time, I'm sure," I said breezily. "It should go without saying that your father expects you to be on your best behavior whilst you're staying with us. How we all get along this weekend could actually determine your future. I want us to get to know each other, whilst also having lots of fun together. So, who is happy to be here?"

Eyes darted round.

Violet was the first to break. "I'm happy. I… thank you for agreeing to look after us."

"Oh, it's no trouble at all," I said gleefully.

Then I looked at Rose and Poppy.

"I've got some questions for you," Rose said.

"So you're the difficult one then, are you?" I countered. I shifted to Poppy. "What about you? Are you the silent one?"

"No, ma'am," Poppy replied stiffly.

"Are you happy to be here, then?"

She nodded.

"Say it."

"I'm happy to be here."

Rose chuckled. "Where, at the train station?"

Violet elbowed her. "Shut up."

Rose glared at her sister, before turning back to me.

She smiled with her mouth wide open, baring her teeth.

"Alright," I said. "Car's just across the road there. Luggage goes in the trunk. The three of you in the back. Georgie sits up front with me."

I maneuvered Georgie away from the girls as we turned and walked back across the road together.

"Jess," he whispered.

"What's that, Georgie?"

"You didn't tell me they were twins."

"Yes." I paused. "They're very beautiful, aren't they, Georgie?"

"What?" Georgie blushed.

"We are so lucky, to have these beautiful girls staying with us."

And *they're* lucky, Georgie.

They're lucky to have us.

CHAPTER 23

The train came in at twenty past four. It's a warm afternoon, but in the evening it will be cold. Truth be told, if the train was even slightly within the realm of walking distance from the house, our three girls would be walking. I've almost a mind to pull over to the side of the road, next to these ever-sprawling meadows and farmland. The girls can walk the rest of the way.

Of course, I am a generous person. I am so generous that I won't do that, and I won't even say anything to the girls about it. Not during the ride. Not after. It will be our little secret. The sacrifices I make…

"Inside our home, each of you will be given your own room. The guest wing is located on the second floor. Inside each of the rooms you will see there is a bed with sheets and covers and a pillow. In the room you will also have access to a chair and table, along with a closet and shelf to store your belongings. The wing's power goes out at 9 p.m. sharp every night, so you will be tucked away in your beds before then. Breakfast is then served at 6 a.m. for which if you are but a single minute late, you will not receive any. Therefore, it is recommended you are early to rise, but of course not too early as the rest of the house is off-limits to you during night-time hours. Are you following all this?"

I scanned the children behind me in the rearview mirror.

One was subdued. One seemed frightened. One seemed angry.

I dropped my eyes back to the road.

"Why all the rules?" one of them said.

I swiftly looked back to the mirror, but there was no indication as to which child had spoken.

"We at the Chantley House strive for the utmost perfection and diligence when it comes to conducting ourselves in day-to-day life. During your stay with us, you will be hard-working and disciplined. You will show respect to me, your father and the servants at Chantley as you are both extremely humbled and grateful for our charity towards you."

I paused, watching their little faces in the mirror. It would take a few seconds before what I was saying really kicked in.

"Of course, if you do not abide by the rules… there will be… serious consequences…"

I let the car slow as we approached the house.

Its exterior. Its shadow. Chantley's structure left one with a foreboding feeling. A sense that there were hidden places inside its grounds – whether that be within the building itself, across its lands, or somewhere underneath.

Iron gates waited for us ahead.

"How long have you lived here?" one of the girls dared to ask.

"Since I began having sexual relations with your father," I answered. Then I leaned over the seat to face them directly. "During the week, Georgie and I would stay in the city with your father. It was only when you girls came to visit on the weekends that he sent us away here."

"Why?" one of the girls asked.

"Well, I…" I bit my lip. "I guess we weren't deemed worthy enough to meet you. But thanks to Sarah, circumstances have changed. Nicholas has given me leave from my job in his office. If things work out between us, I could be looking after you full-time."

"And what if things don't work out?"

My mouth dropped a little. The question was incomprehensible.

"I am without doubt that, if it comes to it, your father will pick me over you."

"Is that right, Jessica?" one of them said.

I inhaled deeply and turned away. "He abandoned you once. He'd do it again."

I clicked the button to the gates, and after they parted, we drove in.

CHAPTER 24

Safe to say, it had not been the best introduction to the children I could have hoped for. Once parked and outside the car, I saw the girls whispering amongst themselves as they collected their bags from the trunk. Words were spoken that I was not supposed to hear. Already, I had put a wedge between them and me. Perhaps I was being too hard on them. Perhaps it would be easier to sit in the living room watching TV till midnight, filling our bellies with popcorn and ice cream. I could picture them all around me. Leaning across me for the soda. Banging into my head whilst getting the remote.

Jumping on sofas. Dancing in the corner. Spilling mess all over the rug.

The girls would say how much they loved me, in between sneaking the boys into their bedrooms and staying up all night. First on cigarettes, later on meth.

You know, when I was a girl growing up, I loved my parents because they let me do anything I felt like.

Now that I'm an adult, I hate their guts for it. At least they didn't screw up Georgie. For that I'm thankful. Of course, Georgie's an exceptional boy who would make the most out of any situation. But these three girls… I know they're just looking for trouble.

"Good afternoon, girls," our manservant Leon called coming down the steps at the front of the house. "Shall I help you with those…?"

One of the girls was attempting to burden Leon with her luggage.

"She can carry that just fine," I said icily.

Leon looked at me and expressed his surprise. "Are you sure, Miss Hart? I would be happy–"

"Just show the children to their rooms." I then addressed the girls directly. "You may make use of what's available in your rooms. There is a lavatory and washroom at the end of the hall. You may use the rest of the time before 6 p.m. to unpack your things. But at six, I expect to see you downstairs for dinner."

I waited for them to pass me one by one.

Once the last one was inside, Georgie and I made our way through after them.

We remained at the entrance briefly, watching the girls climb up the stairs.

Soon enough, they were out of sight.

"Alright then, Georgie. Let's see how the kitchen is getting on."

Georgie obediently followed at my side.

We crossed through the spacious resting area below the stairs and moved swiftly into the hallway. We followed it down to the end where the door was open, and our chef Brian and his apprentice Natalia were preparing dinner.

"Ah, Miss Hart, you're back," Brian exclaimed. "The girls have arrived then?"

"They have," I confirmed.

"And would you like something special to celebrate their welcome to Chantley?"

I forced a smile and motioned for Georgie to take a stool at the bench.

"Do you have this week's menu there, Brian?" I asked.

"Oh. Oh sure, Miss Hart."

He went to the back bench to search for it, whilst Natalia finished whatever she was doing, then approached. "Hello, Miss Hart!" She beamed. "I've just finished baking some lemonade scones for the girls. They're still hot but you can, or *I can* take them up if you approve."

I nodded slowly. "Where are they?"

She turned back to her bench and unveiled the covering of the scones. They appeared to have just come out of the oven, and Natalia was putting on the last finishing touches of cream and raspberries.

"Why don't we see what Georgie thinks of them first?" I suggested.

"Oh yes, of course," Natalia said hurriedly. "Master Georgie? Would you like to try a scone?"

In the meantime, Brian had managed to retrieve the menu.

I put my hand out, requesting it.

He handed it to me, and I opened it to Friday's page. "Cream of asparagus soup, with cinnamon figs in Greek yogurt."

"Ah yes, of course," Brian said, blathering. "I just thought perhaps since–"

"Hold that thought."

I turned to Georgie who had been handed a scone on a napkin.

"Where's his plate?"

"Uh, uh, oh, sorry," Natalia gushed. She went around to the cupboard and fetched a plate for Georgie who repositioned his scone.

I turned to Brian. "I expect the kitchen to be the cleanest room in the house. We don't need crumbs falling about everywhere in here."

"Of course not," Brian said. "My apologies, Miss Hart."

I scoffed at the pair of them and turned to Georgie.

He was waiting for my permission.

"Yes, little brother," I said. "Eat, eat."

He bit into the scone. As expected, crumbs fell from it but were safely caught by the plate.

"Well?"

Georgie gave a big smile. "Yummy." He then turned to Natalia. "Thank you."

"Oh, you're welcome, Master Georgie."

He went to take a second bite.

But then he saw my face.

"Thank you, Jess," Georgie said sheepishly.

I nodded. "Enjoy."

CHAPTER 25

Five fifteen. Dinner was in forty-five minutes. I would soon have to shower and change.

Leon stopped by the kitchen to report that the girls had picked out their rooms and were in the process of settling in. His eyes went by the scones several times during his report, as did Natalia's who had presumably forgotten about all the work she should be doing. I sent Georgie away to occupy himself, at which point I looked out the back window and noticed the dogs running across the grass. "Have they been fed yet?"

"Pardon me," Brian said turning from the stove.

"Danny and Donnie. It's after 5 p.m."

"I guess we're behind today," he confessed. "Shall I–"

"No, I've got it under control. Just make sure the soup's ready by six."

"Yes, ma'am."

I grabbed the tray of scones from the bench and brushed past Natalia on the way to the back door.

Once outside, I set the tray down by the wall near the water bowls, and turned back to the yard.

"Danny! Donnie! Dinner time!"

Danny and Donnie were two golden Labradors who had been at Chantley for some years. Nicholas described them as his pride and joy and would often take them for walks on his rare visits here.

The dogs bounded forward to greet me, and I had each one sit so I could remove their scarves before they ate.

"Okay," I commanded, and the dogs dived on the tray together.

I turned to the back door clutching the rags. "Natalia?"

"Yes?" Natalia replied.

"Come out here, please."

Natalia briskly made her way outside.

"Can you please put these scarves through a ten-minute cycle?" I asked. "And then another five minutes through the dryer."

"Yes, of course," she said accepting the scarves.

She turned to leave but then saw what the dogs were eating. "Are those my scones?" she stammered. She took a few steps towards the dogs and then stopped. She turned back to me. "I don't understand!"

I raised my eyebrows. "Are you trying to embarrass me?"

"Wh-what?"

"In front of the girls. Are you trying to embarrass, or upstage me? So when Nicholas returns on Sunday the little darlings can go and tell him what a wonderful cook you are?"

"Ma'am, that wasn't my intention at all–"

"You know I'm just trying to think about the last time you made lemonade scones for my little brother. It's funny. You'd almost call it favoritism."

"But Georgie ate one of the scones!"

I smiled and closed the gap between us.

"But they weren't for him, were they?" I pressed my index finger sharply into her forehead.

"Ouch!" Natalia cowered.

"If I want you to make scones or cake or biscuits for the girls, I'll ask you, okay? In the meantime, just help Brian and get those scarves back to me in fifteen minutes."

"Uh – yes. Yes, ma'am…"

Just as she was leaving, I noticed what colors the scarves were.

"Natalia?"

She turned by the door.

"Do you know if they have any other scarves?"

"Maybe. Around the yard. They're always biting them and tearing them off."

"I know it's getting late," I said, "but if you could perhaps go and have a look for any before you put those in the wash, I'd be grateful."

Natalia sighed. "As you wish."

CHAPTER 26

White is almost purple. Black is almost blue.

Red is exactly red.

I had Leon remove a vase from the table by the stairs. I had Natalia place the three scarves where the vase had been.

Three minutes to six.

Georgie came down first, punctual as ever. He'd put on an adorable little sweater and was wearing his comfy slippers. "It's cold in my room," he remarked on his way down the stairs.

"The heating's on a timer, remember?"

"I know," he said, sulking.

Once he'd finished his descent, I put my arm around him, and took him to the side. "You have it good, Georgie. Do you know why?"

"Why?"

"Because our three guests don't have any heat in their rooms, at all."

"What? Why not?"

"Because" – I chuckled – "when the power disables in their wing at 9 p.m., that's when the heating goes out to the rest of the house."

"But won't they be cold?"

My smile faded. "They're probably used to it anyway. I doubt their mother could afford central heating."

"Why don't you–"

"Run along, Georgie," I ushered him. "Go have a seat at the table. We'll work it out later."

"Okay."

I waited till he left my sight, then turned back to the staircase.

I checked my watch. A single minute remained, and no sign of the girls.

"Unbelievable," I whispered.

They must not have taken what I'd said to them all that seriously. Either that, or they had no interest in dinner. Also, no interest in pleasing me.

How utterly atrocious…

They suddenly appeared all at once.

One peering down from the landing rail. One in the center of the top step. One hovering somewhere in between.

"Girls!" I cried. "You're late!"

Slowly, the girl on the top step began to descend. Her sisters followed her.

They hadn't changed what they were wearing.

All uniform. All black.

There wasn't any point of physical distinction that I could make.

But that was about to change.

"Stop," I commanded, once the first reached the bottom.

She kept on walking.

I blocked her path. "Are you hard of hearing?"

Her sisters joined her at the sides.

"Oh," I said. "You're the difficult one, aren't you?"

She blinked a few times. The glint in her eyes said she was unimpressed.

"Alright, perhaps I haven't been clear," I fired off. "While you're under this roof, you will obey me. If you fail to do so, then I'll drive you back to the station, and you can catch the night train to see your father, where you can explain to him your absolutely disgraceful disobedience."

I stared at them.

"So? What's it going to be?" I pulled my keys from my pocket. "We're going back in the car, are we?"

"You're really not good with kids, are you?" one of the side girls remarked.

I held back another violent outburst. "Tell me your names again."

"Poppy."

"Violet."

The girl in the middle didn't say anything.

I had to use my memory. "You're Rose then, aren't you? The difficult one."

Rose shrugged.

"Alright. All three of you need to turn around. There is something for you on the table."

One by one, the girls turned.

Violet approached the table. "What?"

"The scarves."

Poppy approached from the other side, turned to me.

"Go on. Take them."

"What for?" Poppy asked.

"It's how I'm going to be able to tell you apart."

A pause. "Oh. Oh no," Violet said.

Rose rushed over to the table.

"We have other things we wear to identify us–" Violet began.

"Oh yes, I know," I interrupted. "Your father assured me you'd be wearing them. But here you are, and you're not."

"I can go and get my–" Violet tried again.

"*It's too late for that!*" I screeched.

Violet froze.

Poppy shook.

Rose whirled round to face me.

I heard Leon come in from the hall. "Is everything alright, Miss?"

"Yes, thank you," I answered. I forced a grin towards the children. "You take those scarves and you put them on. *Now.*"

Violet reluctantly picked up a scarf. She handed it to Poppy, then went to give a second scarf to Rose, but she refused it.

"It's the wrong color," Rose said defiantly.

"Give her the red one," I stated.

Violet switched the remaining scarf with the one she'd been offering.

"Ugh!" Rose said once it hit her hands. "It smells funny!"

"Mine's wet!" Poppy complained, holding her black scarf.

"Mine's wet *and* smells funny," Violet said tonelessly.

"I don't care," I said. "Here's what's going to happen. All three of you are going to wear your scarves around your neck as of this moment, for exactly one week. After the week has passed, you may return to wearing whatever it is you've brought with you. However, if you ever take it off, I will force you to wear something else around your neck that you will find even less pleasant."

I crossed my arms. The girls had a choice to make. Submit or rebel. I took a few steps back and turned away from them. I heard them discuss the matter quietly amongst themselves.

"Uh. Jessica?"

I turned back. Violet, with the white scarf, was speaking.

"We request that the scarves be washed properly first. And then we agree to wear them tomorrow."

I licked the insides of my mouth carefully. "So. You want a favor from me then?"

Hesitation.

Staredown.

Violet nodded. "Yes."

I looked at Poppy. "Well?"

"Yes," Poppy said.

I then smiled, and showed all my teeth.

I looked at Rose.

Rose was squirming with rage.

"Yes," she said.

CHAPTER 27

The dining room table was big enough to seat five people on each side, opposite one another. The girls sat on the same side, facing the hall to the kitchen. Georgie and I sat on the opposite side, but as far away from them as possible. When I looked up from my place at the table, there was no one sitting across from me. And when the girls looked up, there was no one opposite them. Our connection was detached, slanted on a diagonal angle.

Five minutes into the meal, one of the girls spoke up. "We don't like this."

I stared at them through the corner of my eye. Not one of them had picked up their spoon to try the asparagus soup. "Then don't eat it."

Another minute went by.

"We want what he's eating," said one of them.

Georgie froze, his spoon halfway between his mouth and the bowl.

I dropped my spoon and picked up an unused butter knife to brandish at them. "From all the way over there, you don't know what he's eating."

"We can smell it," the girl at the far end stated.

Georgie put his spoon in the bowl and pushed it away from him. "Can I go to bed now?"

I glared at the girls and turned back to my son. "Are they making you uncomfortable, Georgie?"

Georgie winced.

"Alright," I whispered to him. "I'll have the kitchen send up some dessert for you soon."

"Thanks, Jess." He backed his chair out and hurried along out of the room.

I waited till he was gone before facing the girls again. "I hope you're proud of yourselves."

"We're not proud," the middle girl snapped. "We're hungry."

"So, eat your dinner and be quiet."

"May I have some bread?" the girl closest to me asked.

"No, you may not!"

I laughed to myself. At the extremeness of my anger. It was too exaggerated, over the top. I was being unreasonable with them.

I almost had to catch myself, ask what I was doing. What was I trying to accomplish?

When Nicholas returned on Sunday, the girls would surely tell him of my disagreeableness. They would work their charms to have me removed from his and their life.

And that's when I realized it.

I didn't *want* to be their mother.

"Here you are, girls," Natalia said, inexplicably charging into the dining room with a serving tray. "It's rosemary lamb stew, just like Master Georgie was having." She took their soup bowls away and replaced them with new ones.

"Ooh boy," one of the girls cried gleefully.

"Thank you!"

"I'll fetch some bread for you too then."

I stared at her, but she ignored me.

Out of the dining room she went, as quickly as she'd entered.

I backed out a few inches from the table but remained seated.

I noticed only two of the girls were eating. The girl eating in the middle was wolfing it down. The girl closest to me was taking the time to blow on her stew and swallow it slowly. But the girl at the edge of the table wasn't touching her new plate.

"There you are then," Natalia said re-entering with the bread. She laid it down in front of the girls, along with a tub of butter.

The two eaters got stuck into the bread as well, but again the girl at the end refused to.

"Miss Hart?" Natalia said, then facing me. "May I see you in the kitchen for a moment?"

I stood from my chair. I walked slowly along the table, passing the girls as I did so. I didn't know what to say. I didn't know if I was about to lash out. Natalia just kept beckoning me, and I turned away from them. I followed her through the hall and into the kitchen as requested. I felt so angry I was almost numb. But then I didn't know where to begin to…

Leon and Brian were standing there, also waiting. Natalia moved in behind them.

"What the hell do you think you're doing?" I hissed. "Did you forget who's in charge here?"

"No, ma'am," Brian replied.

"But maybe *you* did," Leon suggested.

Natalia came out from the other side, and reapproached. She offered me a cell phone. I snatched it from her and put it to my ear.

"Who is this?" I asked foolishly.

CHAPTER 28

Picture him by a skyrise window. Picture his reflection in the glass. Picture his gray suit and silver tie. He's on his way out. He's got something important lined up in the next hour. You'd think he'd be far too busy to worry about what's going on here. I can only imagine the horrible things the servants have been saying.

"It's Nicholas," he said swiftly. "Who were you expecting?"

"Oh no one, I just–"

"What's going on there?"

I hesitated. I put my back to the servants and exited the kitchen. "We picked the girls up," I said. "Right on schedule. We… we were just having some dinner…"

"And how are you getting on with them?"

"Fine. It's… it's all fine."

"So, when I talk with the girls, that's what they're going to tell me?"

I slowed down. "Yeah. Yeah… I'm working up to telling you about what's going on…"

"I'm listening."

"Well, the girls are being difficult. Rose, in particular. Violet mostly tries to be polite, and Poppy's the quiet one. Although it's a wonder I'm keeping up because they're all wearing the same clothes, and I can't tell them apart."

"Tell me about the scarves."

"The scarves? You… you mean the–"

"You know what scarves I mean."

I shuddered, then re-entered the dining room.

"I just thought they could wear them so I could see who's who."

The girls' eyes followed me as I walked by them.

"The scarves that are normally worn by the dogs?"

"Correct."

"You don't see anything wrong with that?"

"I was trying to punish them for refusing to put on their colors."

A pause on his end.

I left the dining area and proceeded through the main entrance.

"I'm going to ask you a question, Jessica. And I want you to consider your answer."

"Alright."

"If I were to give George one of those scarves to wear as punishment, and you came home and found him wearing it, what would you say to me?"

"Well. That's different."

"In what way?"

"Georgie is my brother. Not my… child."

"Are you trying to say you wouldn't mind because he's your brother?"

I exhaled. "I don't know what I'm trying to say."

"How about I put it like this, Jessica? My girl are not dogs."

"No."

"We don't treat them like dogs."

"No."

"And yet, apparently, I'm also told that you fed my actual dogs a tray of scones that Natalia had baked for my girls?"

"Why are you picking a fight with me?"

"I'm not picking a fight. Or if I am, it may well be with good cause."

"I just don't understand why you're so bothered about some scarves and some scones."

"So, you're playing dumb with me then, are you?"

"Stop yelling at me."

"My voice isn't even raised."

"It's your tone."

"Alright, Jess. This is what's going to happen. For the rest of the weekend, the girls will put their meal choices in with the kitchen before anything is prepared. You will not make any more comments about how they dress or their appearance. If you aren't sure who is who, you may ask them politely. As many times as is needed."

"Okay," I whispered.

"I'm going to ask you to put them on the phone now. And I will be keeping regular updates with them until I arrive. If I hear anything more about mistreatment or punishments – from either them or the kitchen staff – then things will be over between us. Do you understand what I'm saying?"

My jaw dropped. I couldn't breathe. I couldn't move.

"Jessica? Are you still there?"

"I… I don't know what to say…"

"You'll say you understand, and then pass the phone on to the girls. Or else–"

"I just never realized how little you value me."

"No, Jess. No. *You* didn't realize how much I value my girls. It goes without saying, you are going to have to work very hard to regain my trust again. Consider this your first and final warning."

"Alright. I'll… make more of an effort now."

"Good."

"I love you, Nicholas."

A pause. "And I love you."

Good.

That's all that matters.

CHAPTER 29

Three perfect, little angels.

Three daddy's girls.

They are the same. They are untouchable. They are protected.

Or are they?

I watched the girls speaking with their father over the phone, one at a time, and then all together.

And here I am. Standing awkwardly in the corner.

He thinks he can protect them. He thinks he's running this house when he's not even here. Murder is on my mind. Murder is on my brain. These are sick thoughts I'm entertaining. You hear about people having a victim mentality, or a victim complex. Well, from where I'm standing, the whole world is in direct opposition to me, so I guess I've got a villain complex. I am the bad guy, or bad woman, in this situation. The killer is me. I haven't killed anyone yet, but oh goodness, how I'd like to.

Just look at them. They think they can get away with this. They think they can refuse to do what I say and I'm just going to go along with it because I'm under his thumb. Well, I'm not. I'm not afraid of what he's threatening. Of course, I need to be perceived to be afraid. I can't show anything of what I'm thinking or feeling. In fact, I must be very careful of that. Now that I have decided to do something evil, I'm going to need to go the extra mile to make sure I'm not caught.

The phone call is coming to a close. The girls are going to expect me to address them. I have to be wary not only of them, but of the servants as well.

And that's not all.

In certain parts of this house there is constant video surveillance. So, if I am to act on these impulses, with all the danger associated, I am going to need to be very clever.

Very clever, indeed.

CHAPTER 30

I am comfortable in Chantley House. The building, its structure, and grounds are acceptable to me. This is my home. My name may not be on the deed, I may not have access to Nicholas Greene's bank account, but good things come to those who wait.

Of course, I am impatient. But I cannot afford to be so impatient as to do something stupid. After apologizing to the girls and the kitchen staff, I had Brian prepare some dessert for the girls and insisted that I be the one to take it up to them. Natalia wasn't happy about that, and I could see that she wasn't buying my sudden turn of generosity, but still she was the chef's assistant, and I was Lady of the House.

Now, as tempting as it might be to poison these dessert bowls, and sleep soundly while the girls die overnight, there's no way in hell I'd ever get away with that.

For now, I must bide my time.

"Girls! Ice cream and cake! It's here… for you…"

I stood in the center of the wing's hallway, waiting for their bedroom doors to open.

One by one they came out. Their wary eyes watching me, suspicious.

"I didn't make it, don't worry," I said half-joking.

Their little hands took the bowls away.

"Are you *sure* this is okay?" one of them asked me.

"Yes," I muttered. "Of course, it is."

"As long as you're sure."

The other two seemed less interested in interacting with me. I turned from the wing with the empty tray, as the girls closed their doors… And I realized I had to go further. I had to apologize.

"Girls?" I called. "Can you come out… please?"

I waited in silence.

And one by one, their little faces emerged from the shadows.

"I need to tell you, that I am…"

Gosh, this isn't easy… even when I'm lying.

"…I'm sorry. I am really, truly, sorry about earlier. I hope you can forgive me."

They looked amongst themselves. "We're sorry too," one of them said meekly.

"Oh good!" I squealed. That went better than I hoped. "Just let me know if you need anything…"

As they began to disappear, I turned away. Then I felt a tug at my waist. "For Georgie." The girl was offering me her dessert bowl.

"Why don't–"

"I'm not hungry," she said.

* * *

One bowl left on the tray. I exited the guest wing and walked across the landing towards Georgie's room on the opposite side. I found him with the light off, already tucked away in bed.

"What are you doing, Georgie?" I asked, striding in. "Surely you're not asleep, are you?"

Georgie sat up, rubbing his eyes. "I'm just waiting for the heat to come."

I nodded and sat down at the end of his bed. I took the bowl off the tray and handed it to him.

"Thank you, Jess."

I watched him eat it, slowly.

"Georgie?"

"Yes?"

"You know I love you, right?"

"Uh-huh."

I paused. "You saw me earlier, didn't you? You saw me being mean to the girls?"

He stopped eating. "You don't like them."

"Well. I don't like them. Not like you, Georgie."

"What is it about them you don't like?"

I considered. "Well, the way I see things, you and I are family. Nicholas *might* become part of our family, but he's not our blood. And they're not our blood, either."

"But how is that their fault?"

"You know, I… I wanted to like them, you know. I wanted to love them. I mean, I'm going to try to; I have to try. That's what I've told Nicholas. I'm going to try…"

"Are you?"

I gave a small smile.

"Eat your ice cream."

I stood from the bed and went to the door.

"Jess?"

"Yes, Georgie?" I turned.

"Are you going to play the piano tonight?"

I sighed and leaned against the door frame. "It's been a few weeks, hasn't it?"

"I just like it when you play, and I can fall asleep listening to it."

"Oh Georgie, that's so sweet. I'm… I've got a few things to do first. But I might play it later. So if you're awake, I guess you'll hear it."

Georgie smiled. "Goodnight, Jess."

Goodnight.

My handsome, precious child.

Goodnight and sweet dreams.

CHAPTER 31

Nine o'clock. The kitchen is empty. The lights are out downstairs. The servants have gone home. It's just me, Georgie, and the girls.

I'd gone up to the third floor where the master bedroom is, and the lounge with the piano. As I was turning on the lava lamp by the window, I saw the cooks making their way to their cars. Natalia tried to double-back towards the house, but Brian stopped her. He put his arm around her and said something for reassurance.

Eventually they both left.

I watched their cars exit through the gates, and as soon as they were gone, I was sure their minds had left this place also.

There was a stillness in the air. A sensation of loneliness, without being alone.

The central heating poured in with a quiet rumble.

I turned my attention to the grand piano.

Of the many items of elegance on display in this house, this was the one I truly owned.

The piano actually belonged to my aunt before she passed when I was six years old, and my parents acquired it after her death. It wasn't long before I was taking lessons and filling the whole house with the sound of the keys.

Of course, I wasn't especially gifted. I wasn't going to grow up to be a professional pianist, but I started at a young age, and kept going, year after year. It was therapeutic for me; I could express things with the piano that I couldn't otherwise say.

There are pieces for when I'm happy.

Pieces for when I'm sad.

There are pieces that mix emotions and pieces I've written myself.

From a young age, I've learned not to count on other people. It doesn't matter who they are or how much they say they love you. In a blink of an eye, they can disappear. The only thing that never leaves is the music.

Gracefully, I sat down on the stool. Before putting my hands to the fallboard, I reflected upon the evening's events. Thoughts had been imagined. Feelings had been expressed. I would now play, and after I was done, it would be like waking up again. Starting new.

There was every chance all my wicked thoughts towards the children would vanish.

And if that were the case, then perhaps I would see how horribly immature and selfish I was being. I called them angels after all, I called them beautiful, don't forget. In the beginning, I wanted to love them.

Perhaps… maybe… I still could.

CHAPTER 32

Once my fingers are on the keys, and my sweet piano echoes throughout Chantley, I am transported to another world. I am outside, in a forest, somewhere. The children, the servants, the suitors all flock in crowds around the horizon to hear my music. This is communication, a voice tells me. This is magic. I am the Queen of Swords, and my keys are like striking blades through their little hearts. This is the sound of the heavens, the sound of royalty. There's a place where all evil thoughts and deeds have their time in the sun, and the sun melts away the barrier that makes us human. I am bigger than this house. I am bigger than those girls. My life is going to be full of all sorts of miraculous adventures–

"Jessica."

Caught off guard, my fingers slid into the wrong keys and the music came to an abrupt halt.

Standing in the dark doorway was one of the girls.

She approached slowly, wearing a black nightgown.

I searched for a scarf around her neck.

White. Black. Red.

I searched for a ribbon in her hair.

Purple. Red. Blue.

Yellow.

But there was no color to be found.

"Who said you were allowed up here?" I snapped at the child.

Wait a second.

I thought we were trying to be nice.

Remember how–

"I wanted to talk to you," the child replied. "So I followed the sound of the music."

"You're not going to tell me it's keeping you awake, are you?"

"Oh no," the girl said. She stopped a couple of feet away from me. The gold light from the lava lamp shimmered across her face. "I think your music's very beautiful."

I blinked a few times. "What do you want?"

"Like I said, I wanted to talk to you. Away from the others. Is now a good time?"

I sighed. "Go on."

"I want you to know I understand how hard this is on you. Taking in three extra children all at once is a lot to ask for. You wouldn't have to, if our father were more responsible. I want you to know that in spite of everything, what you're doing for us is appreciated."

My balance faltered a little. "Yes. That's what I wanted to hear."

"My sisters and I, we can be rude sometimes. But it has nothing to do with you. All three of us are sad about what's happened to our poor mother. She is innocent, you know."

I shuddered. "I wouldn't be so sure of that."

"In any respect, I wanted to let you know, that we are sorry for talking back to you earlier. I really want us to get along together."

I leaned forward over the edge of the stool, considered her proposition. "Which of you am I speaking to?" I asked.

"There's only three of us now," the girl replied. "Why don't you have a guess?"

I smiled. "Violet? You're the polite one, aren't you?"

No response.

"Well. Poppy then. You're breaking the silence?"

Again, no response.

"Surely. You're not the difficult one."

Another pause with her just standing there, staring back. Looking into my eyes.

"Were you the one who didn't eat the stew Natalia brought out?"

She nodded.

"And then when I was giving out the dessert, you wanted to give yours to Georgie?"

She nodded again.

"So, you're sucking up to me then? You're trying to bring peace?" I asked.

"I know pain when I see it," the girl declared, "and I see it in you, Jessica."

I swallowed. I didn't have a handy comeback for that statement.

"I want you to know, you can count on me," the girl continued. "You and I can be friends."

"And then what of your sisters?"

"We may look the same. But on the inside, we're all completely different. So, what happens between you and each of them, will be its own separate experience."

"I see."

"I would only ask that you give the three of us a chance. You don't have to hide your anger. In many ways, we're more like you than you think."

I stood from the stool. A flurry of images spinning all around me. "I'll take that under consideration."

The girl nodded. "Goodnight, Jessica. Don't forget our little talk."

"Goodnight."

I watched her turn and leave. In the aftermath of this occurrence, I wasn't sure what to make of it. My anger. My hate. It was suddenly seeming a touch one-dimensional.

And I could guess all I wanted. It wouldn't change a thing.

I had no idea which child I had just spoken with.

CHAPTER 33

You wind back the clock. You retrace your steps. You think about what you could have done different.

At this point though, I think the die had already been cast. Before going to bed, I did momentarily walk down the steps to the second floor. I went as far as Georgie's room and saw there was no light coming from underneath. I couldn't hear anything going on in there. He was dead to the world.

Of course, it wasn't Georgie I wanted to check on. I wanted to make sure the girls were in bed, that nothing out of the ordinary was happening.

I don't know what it was that stopped me. I could barely see anything from here to the guest wing. No lights on anywhere. No noise. If they were up, then they'd be together. And if they were together, then they'd be talking. If they were talking, I'd hear them.

But I heard nothing. Chantley was as silent as a grave.

I let out a sigh. Today's problems were done with. Tomorrow would have to look after itself.

I ascended the stairs again and walked along the hallway back to the master bedroom. I closed the door behind me then I took off my clothes and had a quick shower before climbing into bed.

I would've fallen asleep a short time after 10 p.m.

So don't ask me what took place during the hours I was unconscious. Never mind Chantley. Never mind our city. Never mind the world. If you were here and you were awake, you might have seen something. You might have heard something. The shadows were thick, and the silence was forever.

I wish I could say my sleep was peaceful. I wish I could remember my dreams. Where the clues were hiding, I'd never know. You go back over the last few hours, and you analyze what was said, what actions were performed.

You observe each person, like they are pieces on a chessboard.

You look back at it all and you tell me who is white. And who is black.

Please, if you could…

Tell me why I shouldn't be sleeping right now.

Tell me everything I've missed.

CHAPTER 34

It was a short time after 5 a.m. the next morning that I was awoken by the phone on the bedside table, the actual landline to the house. Since not many people had this number, there were only a few possible reasons one might be calling.

"Hello?" I muttered wearily, trying to sit up.

"Good morning, Miss Hart. It's Brian here. I'm sorry to wake you."

"Brian," I groaned. "What's the matter? Are you calling in sick?"

"No, ma'am, I've just arrived at the kitchen. You need to come down immediately."

I wasn't fully awake yet. "Are you locked out? Did you forget your keys?"

"It's best you just come down here."

"Alright. I'm coming."

I put the receiver down and forced the blankets off my legs. I staggered across the carpet to the closet and took hold of the nearest bathrobe, to pull over my pajamas.

Descending the steps to the second floor, I could see there were plenty of lights on downstairs. This was a touch unusual as Brian was the only one supposed to be here to prepare breakfast for 6 a.m. – Leon didn't start until eight and Natalia sometime in the afternoon.

I couldn't hear anything, but it was pretty strange he would wake me. Surely it wouldn't be over something trivial like there being no eggs in the fridge or whatever.

I crossed the landing and continued down the staircase to the ground floor. I walked through the open area into the dining room where I saw Brian hovering at the hallway entrance.

He seemed agitated.

"What's going on?" I demanded.

"I don't want to jump to any conclusions," Brian said. "It's best you see for yourself."

"See what?"

Brian turned and began walking down the hall to the kitchen.

I followed him.

"This is just as I found it, okay?" he said. "I haven't touched a single thing, as soon as I've seen it."

"Alright," I hissed.

We approached the kitchen entrance.

Upon sight, there wasn't anything extraordinary happening that I could see.

Apart from the back door being wide open.

Brian walked into the middle of the room and pointed at the door. "It was wide open when I got here five minutes ago."

"Is that all? Did someone forget to lock it last night?"

Brian shook his head. "No, I locked it on the way out. And I didn't think anything of it at first. I thought maybe you were up early and had gone out for a walk."

"Was the light on?"

"No," Brian replied. "That was me who switched it on."

I stood next to him and crossed my arms. "You know, I bet it's those blasted girls. You saw how they were misbehaving–"

"Ma'am. Ready yourself. There's a knife in the sink."

I stared at him. "What?"

"Go on," he urged me. "Take a look."

I gave a light chuckle and approached the sink.

CHAPTER 35

I would have seen the red falling. *Drip, drip, drip. Pitter. Patter.* The blood is in my peripherals. A line of dots on the ground below me. It started somewhere on the landing upstairs. The trail ended here, in the sink. A dark red glow, nearby slicing silver. We could see our reflections in it. It's telling us a story. A story of what happened last night. After I went to bed. After we were all asleep. After the wind moved through Chantley, and a dark stranger approached the house…

I turned back to Brian. "Are you *sure* you locked up last night?"

"I'm positive," he replied.

"Alright." I paused a moment. "Follow me." I retraced my steps back through the hall and into the dining room, Brian tailing.

"Be on the lookout for anything unusual," I said.

"Sure."

"Hopefully… they're not still here…"

We came to the house's entrance, and I started climbing the staircase.

"Ma'am?"

"Yes?"

"There's blood on the floor."

I stopped around halfway and crouched down to the carpet. There was no mistaking it.

"That's not good," I remarked. "That's not good *at all.*"

My pace quickened. My stress is building. Adrenalin pumps. It's at the landing where the blood can go right or left. Towards the girls, or towards–

"Oh no!" I squealed. "No, no, no!"

"Shall I check on the…?" Brian's voice floats away in the background – his presence drifting out of sight.

Drip, drip, drip.

"No," I gasped, seeing where the blood stopped

I turned the handle. The door fell away.

Pitter. Patter.

"No! No, my baby!!!"

My brother. My son. My boy. My light. The only thing I truly love or care about.

My Georgie.

What have these monsters done to you?

CHAPTER 36

The next part is a blur. I'm somewhere between the bed and the floor, on top of him. Crying my eyes out.

I'm inconsolable. It's complete hysteria. I just keep shaking him, holding him, hugging him, crying into his little ears. Running my fingers through his strawberry-blond hair. Will he wake? Will he respond? *Will he open his eyes for his beloved Jess?*

It isn't hard to see that's not going to happen. The marks are all over him. The blood is everywhere. They stabbed and stabbed until the metal touched bone. His neck. His cheeks. His chest. His arms and shoulders. Puncture wound after puncture wound. A bloodbath. A frenzy.

I'm sick. I'm completely unwell. Georgie's body is cold. He's been dead a long time. This didn't just happen. He's been lying here for hours. Did he call for me while it was happening? Did he get a chance to scream my name? Why couldn't I hear him? Why didn't I wake up? How could I just sleep right through…?

"Miss Hart! Miss Hart, please!"

Brian was behind me somewhere. I could feel him pulling.

"He's gone! Just let him go! There's nothing you can do!"

I was sobbing uncontrollably, trying to speak Georgie's name. I wasn't thinking about the fact that I was in the middle of a crime scene. I'd broken from reality. I couldn't take this. It wasn't happening.

It just wasn't.

"Come on, Miss Hart. Come on… Come on…"

I was being dragged away, out of the room. I collapsed in a heap on the floor, wailing like a wounded deer. I could feel the tears choking the back of my throat.

"I said go downstairs," Brian hissed.

That wasn't to me.

Sideways. Off the ground. I saw the three girls standing in a line.

"You little snakes," I said viciously. "You did this."

"What?" Brian's voice seemed to echo. "No, Miss Hart. There must have been an intruder–"

"It's them! I know it's them!" I shouted.

"Girls! Downstairs, please!"

My hand slid across the carpet in a grasping motion, as they trotted away.

Brian bent down and tried to get me to sit up. "You're in shock, Miss Hart. Take deep breaths. Come on, with me now. In and out and one… Hold it… Release, and two… Hold it… Release, and three…"

One.

Two.

Three.

Violet or Rose or Poppy.

I know it was you.

You can't run away.

You can't hide from me.

As soon as I can think straight, I'm going to kill all three of you.

CHAPTER 37

"Well, she's on the floor at the moment… Yes, she's breathing… No, I said she's not responding… I can't move her. She's just locked down here on the landing… Yes, they're downstairs… They haven't been told… Well, no, I'm not a hundred percent… Yes, I understand, but do you just want me to leave Miss Hart here…? I can try, but she's… Alright…"

Shadows. Distortion.

A hand on my shoulder.

"Miss Hart? I have Mr. Greene on the phone. He wants to talk with you. Miss Hart…?"

Nicholas. What I would give to hear the sound of your voice. You don't know what's happened. You haven't seen it with your own eyes.

To be with me. To be here in this moment. To feel these feelings.

Nicholas.

Your children are the devil.

"Jess?"

His voice now.

His voice pressing against my ear.

"Jess, can you hear me?"

I can hear you, my beloved.

The rest of me is just somewhere else.

"Jess. You need to get up. You need to get off the floor. You need to help Brian take care of my girls."

My lips parted.

A hollow scream chimed within.

"I'm going to be with you as soon as I can. You just have to hold the ship till I'm there. I need you, Jess. I'm counting on you."

"Nicholas…" I whispered.

"Jess?"

"The girls…"

"Yes, the girls–"

"…killed Georgie."

A pause. "No. No, Jess. There was a break-in. Someone broke into the house. You were in the kitchen with Brian, remember?"

"I hate them so much. I was going to kill them anyway. So Georgie and I could have the house to ourselves."

"That's… Look, Jess. Please try and think rationally. I can't have you falling apart on me."

"Whose side are you on?"

"I'm on your side, darling. Don't worry."

"They're not going to get away with this."

"Please, Jess. You need to stay reasonable. My girls wouldn't hurt Georgie. That's absurd."

"They were with Sarah, weren't they? In the alley?"

I heard him swallow.

"Their mother showed them how to do it."

"You're wrong. Okay? There's been a break-in. A burglar. Someone."

I sat up from the floor and took the phone away from Brian. "We don't have to guess with this."

"What do you mean?"

I put my arm out and Brian helped me off the floor.

"Jess?"

"If there was an intruder, we'll have it on the surveillance."

"That's true. But… it's a police matter now."

"They haven't been called yet, have they?"

I staggered across the landing, right by Georgie's room. A hand over my eye. Shielding my gaze.

"As soon as we finish talking, I'll call them."

"Are you going to stay with me then?"

"Well, Jess, they do need to be called–"

"Don't you want to know? Don't you want to be sure your girls didn't do it?"

"I know they didn't."

"No, you don't. You don't know anything."

"What are you doing?"

"You can hear me walking, can you?"

I approached the steps to the third floor.

"Where's Brian? Can you put him on the phone?"

"Oh no. You're not getting out of this." I stopped and turned to find Brian was following me. "Nicholas says to go watch the girls."

"Uh. Alright…" Brian murmured. "What are you doing?"

"I'll be alerting the authorities. Don't worry."

He nodded and turned away.

I started on the steps.

"Jess?"

"I'm still here."

"Please don't."

"Please don't what?"

"Don't look at the surveillance."

"How dare you, Nicholas."

"What?"

"How dare you tell me I can't know what happened to my child?"

"Your child?"

"My brother, who is – was – a child."

"Jess, you don't know what that footage could do to you. You're already in an incredibly emotional state. Whatever is on there… could push you over the edge."

"We're way past that, Nicholas."

CHAPTER 38

He's not here. He's not in this room with me. I left the phone on the floor a few feet away from the office door, without hanging up. I didn't want him in my brain. I didn't want his influence breathing down on me. Nicholas has an agenda to protect his children, at any cost. They are his family after all. Georgie and I are replaceable.

He shouldn't feel too bad though. He's given me a chance to collect myself, and he's given his girls a head start. Without looking at the footage, I know it will be them. I know it in my heart. Georgie is with me now, and his finger is pointed in their direction.

Still. We must be certain.

We must see exactly what happened.

So, I'm in the chair. I'm sitting at the desk in Nicholas's home office. That would be his home away from home. The computer's booting up. There's mere seconds now between myself and the truth.

The CCTV surveillance program is easy to navigate. All twelve cameras record each hour and export the videos into clearly marked folders. Click the date, click the hour, and I can see what the cameras recorded individually, as well as collectively on a split-screen.

Right now, I'm looking at the live feed.

The cold grass sits idle as the sun rises in the distance behind it.

Brian's car is parked out front and the dogs are sleeping by the back door.

Inside, I can see Brian in the kitchen with the girls, making them breakfast.

Toast. Eggs. Cereal. Juice.

They're stretching their arms and leaning against walls.

Carefree.

Back we go.

Back to 5 a.m. I can see Brian's car pulling in through Chantley's gates. The back door is open as he said it was. The kitchen light is switched off. The house is as dead and silent as a ghost.

Georgie is dead at this time.

He's been dead for hours.

But when was he killed exactly?

I remember how cold he was. It could be as early as midnight.

I clicked on that folder and immediately felt sick.

The back door is still wide open.

The dogs are still sleeping.

There's no sign of Brian's car.

Chantley, silent and dead.

I watched the passing footage, with that back door wide open.

That was the moment then.

That was the change I had to see.

As soon as I saw that door shut, I'd know I'd gone back too far.

I'd know there was still a chance.

Georgie was alive.

CHAPTER 39

In the final minutes of the folder marked '8 p.m.', the curtains are drawn downstairs. The lights are switched off. Leon, Brian and Natalia are exiting the kitchen. I see the door close. I see Brian lock it, just as he said he did.

A camera hidden in the ceiling of the second-floor landing captures me walking by towards the stairs to the third floor. Georgie will be in his room and the girls will be in their rooms. I can fill in the spaces where the camera can't see. I was there. I watched the servants leave from the window.

At 10 p.m., about the time I was going to bed, the kitchen door is wide open.

It has already happened.

In fact, it is just 9.03 p.m. when the kitchen door is opened.

Not by a stranger.

Not by an intruder.

One of the girls has left their room and gone downstairs. She has walked through the dining room and entered the kitchen. She's unlocked the door and walked outside.

The servants' cars are still leaving. The gates are still open.

I am still watching at the window.

The moment they shut and they're gone, the girl is seen creeping around from the side of the house, walking head-on, up to the gates.

In this light, it is easy to see her clearly.

At the same time, there is movement on the second floor.

A second girl has left the guest wing and is walking across the landing.

I held my breath as she approached Georgie's room.

She stopped.

Looked over her shoulder.

When she turned back, she made eye contact with the camera. Brief, accidental. Her head goes down and she continues walking past Georgie's room.

I froze in the chair.

Of course.

I would have been playing the piano at this point.

And I was visited by one of the girls unexpectedly–

You wicked little sprite.

I turned my attention back to the first girl at the gates outside. A car had driven up. I don't recognize it.

The girl got into the passenger side of the car.

A few minutes went by. She got out again.

I searched for the second girl. I couldn't see her. So, she still must have been on the third floor, talking with me.

The first girl is back in the house. She leaves the kitchen door open.

Something about her has changed.

Her hair has shifted. It's been pulled apart.

And something else.

She's wearing something round her neck.

"Come on," I whispered. "Which is it?"

Which color?

I couldn't tell from the outside cameras. They didn't get the right angle.

Downstairs the capture was too dark.

Of course, she was on her way up the stairs now.

The camera at the top of the landing would get her.

Purple was Violet.

Blue was Poppy.

Red was Rose.

The girl appeared in the landing camera.

"What is that? Pink?"

She was wearing a pink necklace. I'd never seen it before.

She approached Georgie's room. Went to the door.

I checked for the second girl but there was no sign of her.

Was she still talking to me? I didn't talk to her for that long, did I?

The girl in the pink necklace opened Georgie's door and went inside.

She closed it after her.

Hot tears fell down my cheeks.

9.11 p.m. Georgie's final moments.

I watched as the girl stepped out of Georgie's room, cradling the knife.

She walked downstairs and into the kitchen. She dropped the knife in the sink.

"I'm gonna kill you," I said. "You're dead meat."

And then something strange happened.

Instead of walking back through the dining room, and upstairs, she went outside. She started walking towards the other end of Chantley, where all the trees were.

Eventually, the cameras lost sight of her.

I leaned back in the chair, perplexed. I had already scrolled through the later hours of the night and morning.

They never picked her up again.

"How did she get back in?"

I must have missed her.

I was about to exit the video, before I finally noticed the second girl coming back down from the third floor.

Surely, she hadn't been up there the whole time. What had she been doing?

She walked by Georgie's room again, but suddenly froze by his door.

She turned her head.

Looked directly at the camera.

"What's she doing?"

She knows, she knows, she knows.

"She knows."

I watched helplessly as she turned away and walked back to bed.

CHAPTER 40

Two of them were in on it. One of them committed the murder – presumably given the knife by whoever they met outside. The second one knew it was going to happen. They just had to rub my face in it.

"In many ways, we're more like you than you think." That's what the girl had said.

As I resumed my playing at the piano keys, the girl must have been somewhere on the stairs between the second and third floor. While Georgie was being murdered, his screams drowned out by the music that was supposed to put him to sleep.

Hands shaking, I closed the lid of the laptop.

Three girls. Three daughters.

Three children.

One of them had been in the room with Georgie when he died. The second had listened to his screams.

The third had stayed out of it.

Did it matter to me which was which? If I killed all three in a frenzy, I'd get my revenge. The third child would just be collateral damage. She could blame her sisters.

But of course, it did matter.

I had to know which child it was. I had to look her in the eyes. I had to get her to confess what she'd done. I had to know why. I had to know who helped them at the gates. I had to know why she left the house afterwards, and where she went.

I had to know how she got back in.

There was something going on here, beneath the surface. Something that cameras couldn't see. Something that I was afraid of.

I stormed by Georgie's room, shaking the need to go in and hold him, as the impulse drove at me. I rushed down the staircase to the ground floor, every vein in my body pulsating.

What was I going to do?

How was I going to do it?

How could I defeat them?

In the dining room, Brian was seated at the end of the table, while the girls were finishing up their breakfast.

"Miss Hart," he said stiffly. "The police will be here momentarily. Do you have my phone there?"

"I left it upstairs," I said. "Third floor."

He left his seat, then hesitated.

"It was an intruder," I reassured him. "Just like you said."

He nodded. "Alright. Help yourself to…"

I looked away coldly.

He exited the room.

Once his presence was gone, I moved around to the head of the table. The girls were seated as they had been last night, all in one line together. They were chatting away happily, like nothing had happened. I snatched the knife out of the nearest one's hand and plunged it into the table.

"He was just a little boy. An angel! He was only eight years old – how could you?"

The girls stared at me in silence.

"One of you was in bed while all this was going on. So, which of you is innocent then? Answer me, and we'll see if I believe you."

No response.

"One of you had a conversation with me last night, while I was at the piano. Anyone care to own up to that?"

Nothing.

They wouldn't make eye contact.

"Which one of you is Violet?"

The girl closest to me looked up and nodded.

I turned to the girl next to her. "And you? Are you Rose?"

Rose nodded.

"So Poppy's on the end."

Poppy shifted in her chair.

"This is your last chance. I'm going to ask all three of you, one at a time. What did you do last night?"

A pause.

"Violet?"

"Yes, we spoke upstairs," Violet said.

"Right. What about you, Rose? Were you in bed then?"

Rose rubbed her lower lip. "No, I was upstairs with you."

"Very funny." I turned to Poppy. "Well?"

Poppy looked at her sisters. "I was also upstairs. Talking with you at the piano."

"So that's that then," I said defiantly. "All three of you are liars."

"Two of us," Violet corrected. "Two of us are lying."

"What?"

"Well, you did speak with one of us upstairs, did you not?"

I swallowed. "Yes, but–"

"I know who broke in last night," Poppy said. "I saw them outside from my window."

I stared at her. "Who?"

"It was Lily. Our secret sister."

"Was Lily at the house last night?" Rose asked. "Why didn't she come say hello?"

"Who the hell is this Lily?" I demanded.

"I already told you," Poppy said. "Our secret sister."

"She wears pink," Violet said flatly. "Just like the flower."

Rose grinned.

"Stop playing games," I snarled at them. "There is no Lily. There's just the three of you here and one of you… one of you–"

"We didn't do anything," Violet said.

"It wasn't us," Rose added.

"We were with you, Jess," Poppy said. "We were with you the entire time."

PART III

Ashley

CHAPTER 41

It takes you back. You start to see all the similarities that aren't even there. If we're going to approach this together, then it's important you know some things about me. You need to understand the nature of my emotional attachment to this case.

Of course, I don't know these people – a frantic, traumatized woman; a secretive, brooding father; the faces of well-meaning servants who know both more and less than they think they do. And then, of course, there's the children – a distortion of innocence and violence.

Our eyes are open. Our eyes can see.

The murderer is right in front of us. It's one of three.

Gordon wouldn't understand. Even if I told him the whole story. There's a separation that prevents his logic from engaging with my emotions. To me, in some cases, logic is dead. It's not how you solve a problem. Before you open the book, before you begin that chapter, the subconscious mind already knows the answer. The mystery is solved on the very first page. Facts. Logic. Evidence. Rationale. They work together to obscure one's emotions from feeling the truth. But if you just close your eyes, if you just *feel* what's happened.

Then you'll know.

* * *

I am no stranger to these feelings. In my childhood, there was no murderer. There was no victim. Not one who died, anyway. I was twelve years old when it happened. I always wondered, why *that* age? From a philosophical standpoint, just, how was eleven too young, but thirteen too old?

It's important to remember this is all a random sequence of events. If humans designed the world, then I'm sure we'd all lead happy, meaningful lives. We wouldn't have made our bodies so fragile. We wouldn't have made us all so susceptible to pain. These choices were made by higher powers who didn't have our best interests at heart. Understand. Understand where you are and where everything else is. Agony may be short-lived. As long as it's someone else's.

The evening beforehand was uneventful. I could talk about the roasted chicken and vegetables. Or the History report I completed with a pen and paper. Or how the light bulb in the ceiling had gone out so I was just using the lamp on the desk. Now that I think about it, that was an event. I was living in shadows without even realizing it. Bedtime was ten thirty. My alarm would go off at six the next morning, but of course I wouldn't need it. I was already awake at three.

There were six of us in the house. Mom and Dad – baker and machinist. It was a working-class family. I had three brothers, all of whom were older than me. Percy was eighteen. Peter was sixteen. Paul was fourteen. Percy's build was a touch lean for his age, while Paul's was a touch heavier. In the end, all three came out roughly the same height and weight. Of course, you could easily tell them apart in broad daylight.

But in the dark… everyone looks the same.

The doors to the front and back were locked overnight. We had a dog in the yard – a frisky cocker spaniel named Bishop who would have raised the alarm if there were any intruders. Dad had a shotgun in the closet. If anything happened, he wouldn't waste any time jumping out of bed and retrieving it. And of course, the burglar would have my three brothers to deal with before he got to me as well. So you would think.

It was 3 a.m. when it happened, like I said. Roughly speaking. I had no view of the time. There was a towel forced over my eyes, and a knife put to my throat in case I screamed. Which I couldn't do of course.

I don't have to say what happened after that. You already know everything. If it hasn't happened to you yourself, then it's happened to someone you know. This isn't some situation of million-to-one bad luck. You put me in that house with those three adolescent males and it's just a matter of time before something happens.

Oh, sure. Not *your* child. Not the child you love. He didn't think his sister was that pretty. Or he just knew how to restrain himself.

I suppose it's easy enough to believe it wouldn't happen, based on it being family and that it'd be such a sick thing to do. And that may be the case. But it shouldn't be the default assumption.

My brother wasn't visibly sick. My brother wasn't visibly insane.

In fact, he was so normal. That sitting with him at the breakfast table the following morning before school, I had no idea whether it was…

Percy.

Or Peter.

Or Paul.

CHAPTER 42

So what happens after that? It's the zillion-dollar question nobody asked. Because I didn't tell anyone about it. The secret belongs to me and the universe. I am not a rape victim. I am not an incest survivor. It's not part of my identity. Because telling someone that story would be the same as bringing them into that room with me. It's a place no one should ever go.

I coped on my own. My healing came from within. I should point out that I was never religious. That was more my parents and their generation. My generation started searching for a higher power in the horoscopes section of the daily newspaper. Those who were even more desperate called the psychic hotline. What's going to happen to me today, star sign? Where will I be in five years, tarot cards?

Give me spiritual advice. Give me an answer to end all suffering.

When will I be happy, God? When will the pain go away?

I'm thirty-three years old now and I should know better.

This morning, I was in that room. I saw where the desk was facing. How the blankets and sheets were in disarray.

That little boy had gone to bed last night.

And someone had come in and–

"Ashley," Gordon called from the common room doorway. "Briefing in five."

By the time I looked up, he was already gone. I looked back down to my tablet device to check to see how long was left on the video I was watching. Around two and a half minutes. I could make it to the end.

As I've been saying though, I've already seen it. I've already asked these questions.

And what questions were they, nobody asked.

Well, since you want to know, I'm just watching this twenty-year-old bimbo pull cards from a tarot deck, to give a simultaneous reading for her 1.5 million subscribers and whoever else might be watching.

She asks you to think of a question and then gives you a choice of three cards at the beginning of the video, and you pick which card is calling to you and click on the designated timestamp.

And I know, I should be way too smart to fall for this. But I just keep thinking about the little boy in that room this morning. I think about what those sisters have done to him.

And I just have to ask the question.

How was seven too young, but nine too old?

CHAPTER 43

I landed in the briefing area a little after 1 p.m., which is where my lunch would have ended naturally anyway. Gordon was already there, as well as our boss Captain Frank Roper. I could see they were going over the various reports that had already been made, including the one from forensics. But it was early days yet. We were still waiting on the autopsy report from the coroner.

Neither of them had been to the actual crime scene, whereas of course I had. They hadn't seen Georgie's blood all over the walls.

Depending on how the investigation developed, there was every chance it wouldn't need to be revisited. The CCTV surveillance at the property painted a pretty clear picture of what occurred.

"Ah, Detective Irving," Roper said, motioning for me to join them. "Good afternoon. Thanks for doing most of the legwork for us this morning."

I pulled up a chair. "Afternoon, Captain. What's the present status?"

"Everyone to be interviewed has arrived and has been escorted to Level 3. We're just going over what our tactics will be. Have you formed any opinions about the case you want to share with us before we begin?"

I sighed, hesitant to launch right in. I waited until I had the full attention of both men. "Where are the girls?"

"They're not together, if that's what you're wondering. We broke them up into different rooms, each housed with at least one of our officers while we wait. There's still some confusion though as to whether we can definitely say that one of them is responsible."

I nodded. "You want to know how the girl got back inside."

"Any ideas?" Gordon asked.

"Well, there's always ideas," I said coyly. "The obvious one that can't be ignored is that somewhere, somehow, there's a fourth child."

"A little convenient that, isn't it?" Roper said, crossing his arms. "I mean, there was a fourth child, up to very recently."

"Well. Whoever the extra child is, they're not pretending to be the deceased one," I said.

"How do you figure?" asked Roper.

I looked at Gordon. "It's self-explanatory, isn't it?"

Gordon agreed. "The girls identify themselves through their names and colors. Daisy, the one we found in the alley, wore yellow. The girl on the tape wears pink."

"Lily," I added.

"Lily?" Roper repeated.

"The girls had a name for her. She came up when we spoke to them after Daisy was found. There was footage of a girl in pink in the back of Officer Watts's squad car. With the deceased, incidentally."

"With George Hart?" Roper cried.

"No, with… with Daisy." I looked to Gordon. "Haven't you given him all of this?"

"I get a bit lost in the color details," Gordon muttered.

I frowned. "That's really just the basics of this thing."

"Alright, alright," Roper said, getting up. "I just want to be clear about this. Have we ascertained who this Lily girl is?"

"No," I answered. "We think it has to be one of the other three girls."

"Well, do you know for sure?"

"Both of the parents – Sarah and Nicholas Greene – have denied the existence of a fifth child."

"I want to see their birth certificates," Roper said, waving his finger. "Get onto that, Gordon. Get me the name of the hospital and doctors who were present in the delivery room."

"Ah, okay," Gordon said mildly. "You do understand that we still think Lily is one of the other three? I mean, all she has to do is put a necklace on–"

"But we want to be a hundred percent sure of it, don't we?" said Roper. "I mean, Christ. These girls are eleven. How hard do you want to go without knowing for sure one of them really did this?"

"Point taken."

"Where are the parents?" I asked. "Nicholas and his partner, I mean."

"We've got them here too, same floor. Nicholas will be of course sitting in with you during each of his daughters' interviews," Gordon said.

"Alright." I paused. "What happens to the girls if we don't get enough to charge one of them?"

"We obviously can't keep them here forever," Roper snapped. "And especially not while we still have the killer on CCTV walking away from the house and presumably not getting back in."

"Isn't that just the cherry on top?" I mused.

Roper looked furious. "I don't know! Is it?"

I smiled. "When you really think about it. Even if we can prove there's no fifth child, if we can't explain how they got back into the house, then we won't have a leg to stand on."

"I thought you said you had ideas," Roper said bitterly.

I shrugged. "I'm not there yet."

CHAPTER 44

I don't have children at home. I'm not a mother. Any attempt to bond with the girls is going to be superficial. I can't pretend to understand them. I can't make them believe I know what they're going through.

Of course, I'm also not a junkie, or a drunk, or a criminal. I don't need to relate to evildoers in order to get what I want from them. I just have to find a way to figure them out.

"You know even if those girls keep tight-lipped," Gordon was saying on our way over to the elevators, "we should still be able to put a line through this."

"You think we'll solve this today?"

"There's just so much we already know. We have the girl on video, for Pete's sake. We know it's one of them. We just have to put together all the peripheral stuff. Like whom they were meeting at the gate. And where they went after the murder."

We stopped at the elevators, and I hit the button. "I'm sorry, I don't share your confidence," I said. "What we've got is a contradiction of fact. It's not something we can just put a line through."

Gordon shrugged. "So they found a way to avoid the cameras."

I nodded. "How?"

"They can tell us."

"Okay."

He frowned at me.

The elevator doors opened, and we stepped inside.

"Well, what's your best guess then?"

I reflected. "There's only two outcomes."

"Being?"

I pushed the button for Level 3 and the doors closed.

"The first being that the footage isn't accurate," I answered. "Don't worry, it's being tested as we speak. We'll be notified of any irregularities upon detection."

"What's the second outcome?"

"They found a way to move through the surveillance's blind spots."

"That's what I said. They avoided the cameras."

"Okay. And you want me to guess how they did that?"

"Sure. Why not?"

I exhaled.

The doors opened and we stepped out.

"You like facts, don't you, Gordon?"

"Who *doesn't* like facts?"

"Well, if we're going by facts, then we know they didn't re-enter through the kitchen door. Or the front door for that matter."

"What about the windows?"

"It's possible they could come through a window on the ground level. Except according to the house staff, the windows were locked. And then there's still the matter of how they managed to get up the stairs, which they would have been spotted doing."

"So then, maybe they climbed up to the second level and found a way in there."

We stopped outside one of the interview rooms.

"And supposing we were able to figure out how they did that," I said, "why allow yourself to be caught on camera during the crime, but then go to all this trouble to make it impossible that you could have done it?"

"Well, it's certainly giving us some problems."

I shook my head. "These girls are only eleven. They're not criminal masterminds."

Gordon sighed. "I know you like to go by your woman's intuition."

"I'll pretend you didn't say that."

"Humor me. What's your gut telling you?"

I smiled. "What? Putting logic aside?"

"Sure."

"I suspect as we get into this thing, it's going to look like someone else is responsible. Either that, or it's all three of them, working together."

"Or working with their mother from prison, perhaps?"

I nodded. "Whatever the truth is, there's one thing we do know. One of those girls went into that boy's room last night. And before this day is out, you and I will be sitting face to face with his killer…"

CHAPTER 45

I still feel his weight on top of me when I wake up some nights. For a split second, it's happening all over again. I'm drowning in the bed. I can't call for help. I can't push him off me.

I can't see a thing.

But then of course, I realize it's the current year, and that night has passed. He can't hurt me anymore. Which of course is a complete lie. Never mind the fact that he's given me chronic night terrors. My brother, the bastard, actually got away with it. And regardless of which brother did it, I know…

He's happily married.

He has a secure job.

He's made my parents proud.

There is no distinction between him and the two brothers who didn't rape me. I wonder if I'll die not knowing which of them it was. Or if I'll wake up one morning and suddenly see the truth.

"What's happening?" Nicholas Greene demanded upon our entry to the room. "What have you done with my girls?"

"Don't worry, Mr. Greene," Gordon reassured him. "They're close by. You'll be with them shortly."

"You can't question them without my being present," Mr. Greene continued. "I know the law. My attorney's going to rip you apart when he gets here."

Gordon turned to me as we took our seats opposite Greene. "He's been told, hasn't he? What's in the footage?"

I forced a smile. "I'm sure Miss Hart would have expressed that information."

"What are you talking about?" Greene demanded.

"Surely, she would have told you what she saw," I said.

He shook his head. "Her brother's just been killed. She's having a breakdown."

I gave a short laugh. "Mr. Greene. Thanks to your surveillance recordings, it is crystal clear that one of your daughters is responsible for George Hart's death."

"I don't believe it," he muttered.

"It's not the end of the world," I remarked. "She's still a child. She can be helped. She can still have a future. But you've got to help us."

He looked up, fearful.

"We're on the same side," Gordon offered.

"Two of your daughters are innocent of this crime," I pressed. "Right now, they're going through an unwarranted ordeal. You want to help them at least, don't you?"

Greene swallowed. "I want to see the footage."

"Not today," Gordon replied.

"Why the hell not?"

"You'll just have to take our word for it. Or Miss Hart's."

Greene shook his head. "What does the footage show exactly?"

"We have one of your daughters entering George's room, after nine o'clock last night. She then exits, holding a knife dripping with blood. She left it in the kitchen sink."

"Were there prints on the knife?"

"Negative. It was wiped clean."

"So, you're telling me… you're one hundred percent."

Both Gordon and I nodded.

"Her sisters are trying to protect her," I explained. "It just so happens, one of the girls was with Miss Hart at the same time George was being murdered."

"All three are claiming to be that girl," Gordon finished.

"I don't understand." Greene sighed. "Why would they kill Georgie? Nothing like this has ever happened before. Unless you count what happened to…"

I leaned forward. "What happened to whom?"

"Well, Daisy, of course," Greene answered. "Are you still sure Sarah killed her?"

"We can't say that what happened to Daisy has anything to do with–"

"I'm just thinking out loud here," Greene continued, "but if you've got two children who were stabbed to death, and you know for certain one of the girls was responsible for one of the murders – how do you know she's not responsible for the other?"

CHAPTER 46

"Daddy!"

Rose got up from the table and rushed to hug her father as we entered the room. I moved around them and the female officer making her way to the other side.

"Hold on," I said tapping her shoulder.

The officer turned.

"Did she *say* anything to you?"

"Who, Rose?" the officer replied. "She wouldn't stop talking."

"About what happened last night?" I asked hopefully.

"It didn't come up."

I turned back to the table and caught a glimpse of Gordon chuckling to himself.

"What?" I hissed.

He shook his head, ever so serious.

The door closed and Rose ran back to her seat, dragging her father in tow.

"I get to answer all the questions now, don't I, Daddy?" she was saying. "And then we get to go home?"

"This isn't a game, honey," her father muttered.

"Of course it is," Rose sang. "And when we get home, Georgie Porgie will wake up and make us some pudding pie!"

Both Gordon and Mr. Greene's jaws dropped. I was a bit startled as well but got my senses back quicker. As Rose danced her way back into her chair, I put my fist out to her face and snapped my fingers.

Rose shook in surprise.

Then her eyes locked with mine.

"Georgie's not waking up," I said fiercely. "Georgie's dead."

The girl's face tensed and she glanced up at her father.

He patted her on the back for reassurance.

"We know one of you killed him," I said. "But until we know who, no one gets to go home."

Rose rubbed her lips together. "Why do you think we killed him?"

"There's surveillance," I began.

"In Georgie's room?" Rose said quickly.

I looked at Gordon.

"You know about the surveillance, Rose," Gordon stated. "Don't play dumb."

"Easy now," Mr. Greene said. "There's no need to be making baseless accusations."

I turned to Rose. "Did you know about the surveillance?"

Rose shrugged. "I was just asking a question. Was there surveillance in Georgie's room? There wasn't, was there?" she fired off.

I failed to answer immediately.

"You see? I knew it," Rose said defiantly. "If you can't see what happened in that room, then you don't know what happened. And you don't know it was one of us."

"There's a camera outside the room," Mr. Greene said. "We can see one of you went in there with a knife."

"Can you?" Rose asked.

I looked at Gordon, but he seemed lost.

"Can you," Rose stated.

I looked for Mr. Greene. "I need a minute with my partner. Okay?"

Mr. Greene shrugged.

I stood up and motioned for Gordon to follow me.

We exited the room.

"Everything alright?" the female officer standing outside asked. "Should I go back in?"

"No." I shook my head. "We're just taking a break."

"What's happening?" Gordon asked, joining me.

"Come on," I said.

We walked along the corridor together.

"Ashley," he tried again, "for God's sake."

"We're going to the crow's nest," I said. "Okay?"

"What for?"

"We're going to watch her with the father for a few minutes, while we figure out a new strategy."

"I don't understand," Gordon replied. "I thought *I* was leading this investigation."

"It's a team effort, as always," I shot back. "But please tell me you picked up on what just happened in there."

He shook his head. "Okay. You got me."

We stopped outside the observation room, or the crow's nest, as it was referred to. I peered through the blinds and saw a plain-clothes woman with curly gray hair and glasses at one of the computers.

She didn't see me.

"Who's that?" I asked Gordon.

"I don't know," he answered.

"Alright. I'll just spell it out to you quickly then."

"I'm listening."

I took a breath. Reflected.

"The surveillance showed the girl coming out with the knife."

"Yes?"

"The knife, dripping with blood."

"Yes," Gordon repeated.

"But the surveillance *didn't* show the girl going in there with the knife."

He blinked a couple of times. "It was under her jacket."

"So we believe."

"What the hell are you getting at? Are you trying to say that the girl went into the room and pulled the knife out of Georgie, who had already been killed?"

I smiled. "I'm not saying that. I'm saying that Rose knew we didn't have the girl walking into the room with the knife."

"And… you're thinking, how would she know that?"

"Precisely."

CHAPTER 47

There's an undercurrent running through this situation. It's not so much that it's invisible. It's more just that it's behind me.

Subconsciously, we're all aware. Through the graveyards of our sleeping souls, all truths are made clear. Our lives on this planet are fated. Whether that fate has meaning, of course, depends on the person ascribing it. You watch the girl on the video screen, shuffling her tarot cards. This is not a personal reading. What is happening to you is happening to somebody else.

My mind is walking through the hallway again. I can see it's dark, but not completely. Moonlight, artificial light, it comes along in bits and pieces. Never certain. Never consistent.

I put my hand to the bedroom door, and let it fall away. There's the bed. That's where they were supposed to be sleeping. Except, this isn't Georgie's room I'm standing in anymore. I'm watching myself before it happened. The seconds are ticking by.

I want to turn away. I want to push my head outside of the door.

Up there, overhead, there could have been a camera. Recording surveillance. It wouldn't be perfect, but it would have been a record of what happened.

I wonder. What would it have seen?

Who came into my room that night?

Where did he go afterward?

If I kept watching the feed, would one of the other brothers appear after? Would he turn back to the camera? Would he let me know he'd seen the whole thing?

* * *

I have to stop zoning out. It's not good for me to keep going back to the rape. You'd think I'd be over it by now. I just can't pretend I don't notice the similarities. Figuring out which of these girls killed Georgie is starting to feel like trying to crack a safe without the combination. I just wonder how it's going to feel when that door finally swings open. Rose did it. Poppy did it. Violet did it. I don't feel any different when considering those scenarios. So how much difference would it make to know which of my brothers raped me?

Round and round, the undercurrent goes…

"Dr. Simone Archer," the curly-haired woman introduced herself a few minutes earlier. "Trained child psychologist."

I peered over at her computer screen. It appeared we'd finally been sent the coroner's report.

"What are you doing here?" I asked bluntly. I saw a worrying look glaze over her eyes for a moment, before Gordon interrupted.

"I'm Detective Burke, this is Detective Irvine, Homicide Division." He glanced around at the other monitors. All other mounted interrogation feeds were switched off, apart from the rooms with each of the three girls. "I guess you've already seen us at work."

"I know who you both are," Dr. Archer said mildly. "Your captain's given me the tools and resources to investigate my own findings."

"We all want the same outcome," I said casually. "No need for you to come at this independently."

"You've seen the house surveillance?" Gordon asked her.

"Not the whole thing. Just a few clips."

"Do you have anything you want to share with us, before we get going again?" I asked.

"First impressions observing the girls – both Violet and Rose appear to be in joint leadership of the sibling hierarchy. Violet's the calm, considered thinker. She's feeding the other two on what to say and do. Poppy will go along with whatever she's told. Rose is obviously only going to do what Rose wants to do, but semantics aside, my guess is that Violet was the girl who spoke to the mother and came down the stairs later, while Rose was the one who actually went into the boy's room with the dagger. Which would place Poppy in her room, making her completely innocent."

Gordon chuckled to himself. "Do you have any evidence to back up your theory?"

"These are just my impressions from observing the girls with the officers," Dr. Archer answered.

"That may well be the scenario that's played out," I said. "One of the girls was an accomplice, one was the killer, one stayed out of it. But how do we know for sure that Poppy wasn't the murderer, and Rose stayed behind? I mean, you can just switch the girls around and the scenario still works."

"True." Dr. Archer shrugged. "That's why I'd like to speak to them all myself, one on one."

"We haven't conducted our investigation yet," I protested.

"Time is running out," Dr. Archer said. "How long do you think it will be before Mr. Greene lawyers up and shuts this whole thing down?"

That stopped us in our tracks.

"Speaking of Mr. Greene," Gordon remarked, "he posed an interesting theory."

"Oh?"

"That perhaps we made a mistake with the first murder."

Dr. Archer raised an eyebrow.

"That maybe Sarah Greene was innocent," he continued. "That maybe whoever killed Georgie, also killed Daisy."

"Well, I guess that's a possibility," Dr. Archer replied. "But we don't want to get ahead of ourselves. We still don't know exactly what happened to Georgie."

I raised my hand, wanting to interject, but Gordon beat me to it.

"We know what happened," he said. "We don't know the details."

"So let me talk to them," Dr. Archer persisted. "I know I can get through to them."

We both looked at each other.

"No, Gordon," I said.

He nodded. "Yes, Ashley. Yes."

CHAPTER 48

So then. Time to be a fly on the wall. Nicholas Greene and a couple of officers were brought to join me in the crow's nest, while Gordon went off to chase down those birth records the captain wanted. I could handle things from here. If it ever went south between Dr. Archer and the girls, I'd pull the plug. In the meantime, it would be interesting to see if she got any further with them than anyone else had been able to.

We were watching on a brightly lit monitor which was set squarely on Rose. Before long, Dr. Archer entered the room and sat somewhere out of view.

She picked right up where we left off.

"Before we get started, I want to advise you, you don't have to tell me anything you're not comfortable with."

"Are you with the police?" Rose asked.

"Oh, I'm sorry that wasn't clear." I heard the doctor flip through her documents. "I work for an independent body. That means I report my findings to the police, but I don't technically work for them. I'm not here today to accuse you or anyone else of anything. The fact is that you and your sisters are in an unfavorable situation at present, and I consider it my job to get you out of that situation."

"Untrue," I muttered out loud.

Mr. Greene had his hands in his pockets and was standing awkwardly.

"Sit down," I said to him.

He glanced at me a moment, but remained standing.

"If I talk to you, will they let me go?" Rose asked. "Or am I going to have to talk to you, and those other people?"

"The other people are watching us right now," Dr. Archer answered. "You see that little black globe in the corner there? It's recording everything in this room."

I glanced back at the two officers and rolled my eyes.

Not a great strategy, doctor. But keep going.

"Can't you just turn it off?" Rose asked.

"I can," Archer replied. "But then you would have to talk to those other people all over again. If we keep it on, then hopefully you can just talk to me. Would you prefer that?"

"Talk to you?"

"It's your choice, dear."

Rose leaned back in her chair, pausing a moment. "I'll talk to you."

"Excellent," Dr. Archer replied. "So, are you happy for me to ask questions? Or would you just like to tell me what happened by yourself?"

"Well, I'm not making any confessions," Rose gushed. "And I'm not blaming anyone else."

"I'm not asking you to."

"I suppose I could tell you some things."

"About?"

"Last night."

Dr. Archer tilted her head. "What sort of things?"

"I don't like Dad's new girlfriend."

"Why not?"

"As soon as we get into her car, she's just blah-blah-blah rules this, rules that. Like, really mean about it… Then she served us a really disgusting asparagus dinner, while her brother was sitting there eating normal food at the same table."

"You mean, Georgie?"

Rose leaned forward. "Except, it's not her brother. Georgie's her son."

"What the…" Mr. Greene gasped. "Why is she saying that?"

"Shut up," I advised him.

"Who told you Georgie was her son?" Dr. Archer asked.

Rose smiled. "Wouldn't you like to know."

CHAPTER 49

There's an outside presence involved in this. Someone is helping the girls, I just can't see who they are yet. I can't make them out at all, but I know they were in the car last night. I know they're in some way responsible for what happened to George Hart. Who could it be then? Who has the motive? Could it be Sarah, I wondered? Sarah whom we'd locked up and shackled away in prison? That car hadn't been driving itself. Someone else was behind that wheel. Who else were the girls close to? Who had followed them from the train to the house, and waited for the servants to leave before driving up?

For a fleeting moment, I thought about the woman who had supposedly abducted Daisy all those years ago. I wondered if she was still around. What her place was in all this.

Rose knows more than she's letting on. I can see it in her eyes. She knows everything that happened last night. I think she is the one who killed Georgie. It would have happened exactly as Dr. Archer professed it to be. Violet the thinker. Rose the doer. Poppy the innocent.

We still didn't have them though. We didn't know how Rose got back into the house.

"Did you kill that boy, Rose?" Dr. Archer was asking on the screen. "Who was in that car outside the gate? Did they put you up to it? Did they give you the knife?"

"No comment," Rose replied tonelessly.

"Were you jealous of him?" Dr. Archer went on. "Was it payback for how Jessica treated you?"

"I don't like you anymore. I want my dad."

Mr. Greene immediately went for the exit.

I rushed after him. "Hold up."

"No," he snapped. "Back off."

He pulled open the door and I followed him into the corridor.

"You may not like it, but it doesn't look good for her," I explained to him. "She keeps dropping hints that she's involved."

Mr. Greene pulled out his phone and made a call.

Ahead of us, I saw Dr. Archer exiting Rose's interview room.

"Where the hell are you?" I heard Mr. Greene say as he went ahead. "You know they're tearing my girls apart, don't you…?"

"Hello, Nicholas."

I watched as Mr. Greene seemed taken aback by Dr. Archer's appearance. He looked at me for a moment, before pushing past her to be with his daughter.

I signaled to the doctor and we ended up opposite each other.

"Have you two already met?" I asked.

"Some years ago." Dr. Archer gave a small smile. "Back to Rose, it's not her."

"What?" My jaw dropped.

"She didn't kill the boy."

"How the hell do you know that?"

"The attachment to the father for one thing," Dr. Archer replied. "But obviously it's more than that."

"I'm not following."

Dr. Archer nodded. She checked her watch. "Before Rose shut down, she volunteered a fair amount of information. She offered up what could be construed as motive."

"And?" I demanded.

Dr. Archer shrugged. "If it's true that George is Jessica's son, and he was killed because they wanted to get even with her, why would Rose tell us so plainly?"

"Because she's eleven," I countered.

"Who do you think told her about their relationship?"

"No idea."

"I would want to ask Jessica that. If Mr. Greene was unaware at least, Jessica might know who might have told the girls."

I exhaled. "The same person who was in the car outside the gates?"

"We might almost be there," Dr. Archer said. "I think your next move should be talking to Miss Hart. And while you're focused on that, I could check on the other two girls and test them. See what they know about this."

I hesitated. "You're not trying to drive me out of this, are you, doctor?"

"I can wait for you, if you prefer," she replied. "Of course, Mr. Greene's lawyer will be here any minute, and who knows who'll be talking to us then?"

"Good point," I conceded.

CHAPTER 50

How do we see ourselves? Are our perceptions accurate? There is a bias behind all things. You might even call it biological.

The person standing before us in the mirror is not our true selves. This is a skewed reality, where everything is backwards – who we are, the words we say. It is no secret; we sound and appear quite different through the eyes of others.

Miss Jessica Hart is not a broken woman. I have seen broken women. I have, myself, been broken. What I'm looking at right now, is a person consumed by thought. Artificially, her composure is shattered. Her cheeks are sunken, and her eyes are red. She trembles. The body's gone inward. But what Jess doesn't realize is, I can see the spine inside her.

She is supported by a tower of bricks.

"I've been such a fool," she recited disdainfully, "to leave my Georgie out where those girls could get to him. This is all my fault…"

Now she makes eye contact.

There is an expectation foisted on me to tell her she's not to blame. But of course, I won't be saying any such thing. "Are you Georgie's mother?"

She lowered her eyes. "So, I take it my parents are here then?"

"Have you spoken to them?" I asked.

"No." A pause. "Where are they?"

"I haven't spoken to your parents, Miss Hart."

She grimaced. "So… you just guessed it then?"

"It came from one of the girls."

"You must be joking."

"Nope."

Miss Hart reflected. "What did they say?"

"That you're George's biological mother. Mr. Greene was upset by the revelation. When questioned further, the child wouldn't say who told them. Only, whoever it was, may have been the one who wanted the boy dead…"

"The car at the gate," Miss Hart remarked. "They put them up to it."

"And it's true then, you are George's mother?"

"Yes."

"Who knew? Did Nicholas? Did George?"

"Just my parents. I was but a schoolgirl when I gave birth. It wasn't appropriate for me to be raising him as my own."

"But you were trying to do that now?"

"Trying to."

I took a breath. "No one else knew about this apart from you and your parents?"

"I don't think so. Of course, there's always the possibility…"

"Of what?"

"That I might have been overheard referring to Georgie as mine over the phone. When I'm excited, my voice tends to carry."

"I hadn't noticed."

"Ha-ha."

"So, who might have overhead you then? Are there any specific conversations you can recall where you might have been overheard?"

Miss Hart composed herself. "I don't know. I suppose maybe at work. There's always people going in and out of the building. I'm out front, at the admin desk, so… I may have taken a call when I thought there wasn't anyone around, when in fact there was."

"Do you suppose Mr. Greene might have heard you? Or the children themselves?"

"Doubtful. Of course, maybe it didn't happen at work. It may have happened at the house. Chantley House. The servants… maybe…"

I watched her eyes shift.

"The chef's assistant – Natalia. She's always had it in for me. She's jealous and wants Nicholas all for herself."

"She does?"

"Well, it's as good an explanation as I can come up with. She's here, isn't she? You brought her in for questioning with the others, didn't you?"

"I'd have to check."

"Well, do that. Please."

I made a note of it. "Miss Hart? Is there anything else you can think of that would help us with this investigation?"

"Just be careful of those girls," she said.

CHAPTER 51

Have you ever heard the phrase 'One True Path'? It's like you're some adventurer, collecting items in preparation for a final battle at the end. Only, if you go through the wrong door – east instead of west, right instead of left – you wind up missing out on the Master Sword to defeat your last opponent. The trick of it is, no one comes along to interrupt you at that point. The game's over and you don't even know it. All there is are the gray clouds beginning to gather in the sky above you. The eye of the storm is bearing down. You know nothing and it knows all.

Have you seen it yet? Have you seen my mistake? I have no idea what is happening in this world outside of me. I began the afternoon with a tiny flashlight in a narrow cavern. But now that light has been smashed to pieces. I can't find my way out of here. I can't see what's in front of me.

"Captain," I called as I saw Roper walking across the opposite wall.

He stopped without turning, and I caught up. "Detective Irvine. Have you been making progress?"

"In a way," I answered. "I was just talking to the boy's sister, Mr. Greene's partner. She's actually his biological mother."

"Alright."

"It's – according to her – supposed to be a secret. But one of the girls – Rose – showed off that she knew. We believe that whoever told Rose could have been the driver outside the gates last night."

"What else are they saying? Do you have any idea who put them up to this?"

"Miss Hart was saying one of the staff had a grudge against her. She may have overheard a conversation, then relayed that information at some point back to the girls."

"Seems like a lot of maybes," Captain Roper remarked. "Where's Burke? Is he with the girls?"

"I haven't seen him for a bit. He went to hunt down those birth records you wanted, to make sure there wasn't a fifth sister."

Roper sighed. "Alright. Check back with him and come see me in my office at 3 p.m. I want a comprehensive report of where you're at."

"Do you know if we have the chef's assistant, Natalia, here?"

"No, I don't know. Check with Detective Burke. But seriously, I'd be using whatever time you have with the girls themselves, because we can't hold them here forever."

"Even though one of them is a murderer?"

"If we don't know which one is the murderer, Ashley," Roper said wiping his forehead, "then we don't know anything…"

CHAPTER 52

Her name didn't come up. I don't know how, but it didn't. She was there, weaving in between the captain and me. With me seeing one half of the shadow and him seeing, presumably, the other. But of course, there was no other half, because she didn't actually exist.

Slow to react, as they say. My guards were down. I was getting my mind tangled up in this mess of a case.

The driver in the car – I had to find them. I didn't care what the captain said, they were the key to this. An adult figure, influencing the children. Connected to the mother, perhaps? I couldn't see it. It was so obvious, but I was blind. Inaccurate presumptions had already been made. Too many.

Far too many.

I clapped my hands together and turned away from the captain. I walked by Miss Hart's room, until I was at the corner on the other side; I could see the rooms where the girls were waiting.

I wondered how Dr. Archer was getting along with them.

* * *

Forget Natalia. Forget the girls. Who knows where the path would have taken me if I'd kept on walking. But I'd gotten a call from Gordon, and I was asked to go down to floor B3, as in the basement, where he was with the guys in forensics.

It had just gone 2 p.m. We didn't have a lot of time before we had to update Roper at three.

"So, how'd you go?" I asked, entering the dimly lit room. "Were there five children delivered at the birth?"

"Negative," Gordon replied, glancing back from his chair. "Just the four girls, as expected."

"Well, there goes the captain's theory," I muttered.

"Sounds like quite a delivery," the forensics guy sitting with Gordon joked. "Wish I could've been there."

"Cut the shit," I snarled at him. "We're on a deadline here. What have you brought me down here for?"

Gordon motioned to the screens on the table.

It was the multi-angled surveillance from Chantley House.

"Play it," Gordon ordered.

I watched a fifteen-second clip of the three girls walking up the stairs with their suitcases.

"That's when they first arrived at the house," Gordon explained.

"Okay," I said.

"Next one," Gordon instructed.

Another fifteen-second clip of the girls coming back down the steps. "What am I looking for?" I asked.

"You didn't notice anything?" Gordon replied.

I blinked cynically. "Play it again."

"Do the first one again," Gordon said.

Up the stairs.

Down the stairs.

One, two, three little girls.

Nothing unusual.

Yet.

"Nothing?" Gordon asked.

I sighed. "You got me."

"Play the next one, Ray."

Ray did as he was told.

Back up the stairs again. I'm not seeing anything strange with it at all. The girls are behaving… normally.

"There's more," Gordon explained. "Them going up, them coming down. And it happens every time without fail."

I scratched above my eye. "You gonna tell me what it is?"

"Play the clip after the lights go out."

Here we go again.

It's Lily, the girl with a pink necklace, walking out the girls' wing, towards the stairs.

And then, I finally saw it.

CHAPTER 53

They thought they had it figured out. Take away their colors and the girls are anonymous. But as we watched the three of them ascending the stairs upon their arrival, one of them is seen dragging her hand along the banister, behind the other two.

When the girls are coming down later that evening for dinner, one of them is, again, dragging her hand along the banister.

Up and down. Every time.

The other two go nowhere near it.

And finally, beyond all thought or reason, I now see the girl who is leaving the house – the girl who is returning up those same stairs, yet again, to pay Georgie a visit.

She's dragging her hand across the banister…

* * *

"There's a number of problems we'll still have either way," I was saying in the elevator a minute later. "Who was in the car at the gate? How did the killer get back in? What really happened in the alley? We still won't know any of that."

"It'll come," Gordon assured me. "One by one. Once we know which of the girls to focus on, it's just a matter of time."

"I hope so."

I really, really do.

After that surging euphoria – our lightbulb moment – a gaping void of uncertainty began to form. Supposing our test works, we'll know who did it. But we still won't have proof, or the answers to anything…

"It's a start," Gordon continued. "It's something to go on. Before you know it, we'll have this thing wrapped up."

The elevator doors opened. We stepped out into the corridor.

"Do you think Mr. Greene will go for it?" I asked.

"Sure, why not," Gordon said casually. "If we can clear two of his daughters, then that's got to be in his best interests, right?"

"Right."

In a way, it's funny but I have to remind myself one of those girls is completely innocent and only one wielded the blade.

Soon enough, we were turning the corner and approaching the officer standing guard outside the girls' rooms.

"Is Mr. Greene around?" Gordon asked.

The officer directed his thumb. "Interrogation 3A."

Violet's room.

We walked by the other two rooms and entered 3A.

Mr. Greene and his lawyer were sitting around Violet, going over various documents.

"Finally." Mr. Greene sighed. "Do you know how long we've been waiting here?"

"Mr. Greene, is it alright if we speak with you in private?" I asked.

"Regarding what?" the lawyer fired back.

"Look, if it's necessary," Mr. Greene said. "Is it necessary?"

"It will only take a second," Gordon replied.

Mr. Greene stood.

"Nicholas, as your attorney, I don't advise–"

"Just, cool it," Mr. Greene muttered.

"I'll stay here," I said to Gordon.

He nodded.

Mr. Greene walked by me, and Gordon followed him out of the room.

I turned my gaze to Violet in the chair. "How are you keeping, dear?"

She tried to sit up. "We didn't do this."

I crossed my arms. "We've got the surveillance. We know one of you did it."

"Violet, you don't have to answer–" the lawyer began.

"No, you don't," Violet said sternly. "And we're just laughing at you."

"What's that?" I replied.

"We're laughing because you can't see inside that room."

A chill ran down my spine.

The door suddenly opened with a bang.

"Ashley, get out here!" Gordon yelled.

CHAPTER 54

The door to Interrogation 3B was wide open. The room itself was completely empty. It hadn't taken long to find out Dr. Archer had taken Rose to the bathroom. Which would have been fine if it hadn't happened more than twenty minutes ago.

"Dear God," Mr. Greene exclaimed as he and the other police officers poured over the crow's nest surveillance.

I watched Gordon's face from the door.

"Well, where are they?" I demanded.

He shook his head. "They're gone."

And like that, two sides of a book are snapped together.

Gordon and I were soon sitting in Captain Roper's office, getting the living daylights blasted out of us.

This whole time. She wasn't real.

Dr. Archer was an imposter.

And now she'd taken Rose.

Why?

"I don't care what you have to do," Roper was saying, "if you don't locate that child within the next hour, I'll be pushing a recommendation for your immediate dismissal. Heads will roll for this. And it damn sure ain't gonna be mine."

Gordon got up and stormed out of the room.

I put my hands together and leaned forward to face Roper. "This isn't an ideal situation, I'll give you that–"

Roper struck a match and lit a cigarette.

"–but tracking this woman shouldn't be impossible."

"You're wasting time," Roper said sourly.

"I just feel that we should take a moment to breathe. If we can ascertain who she is and what her intentions are, then perhaps we can tidy this up a lot quicker than we'd previously thought."

"All I know is, Mr. Greene's attorney is standing right outside the window behind you, and he is going to run a tractor through this place if we don't produce that child. I mean, I can't even protect you from criminal litigation, let alone a civil suit–"

"I need time with the other two girls," I said.

"What?"

"Just me and them. No outside influence."

"Have you gone mad?"

"You don't understand, Gordon and I, we almost had this thing. I just have to talk to them, and I'll convince them to tell me where the woman has gone."

"What makes you so sure they even know that information?"

"Trust me," I said. "They know."

CHAPTER 55

Our station's largest interrogation room is situated downstairs, on the ground floor. The chairs are bigger. The carpet is softer. The walls are brighter. At the back, there's a two-way mirror. Behind it, Mr. Greene, his lawyer, Captain Roper and a cluster of other officials are watching. Inside the room itself, sitting together on one side of a long table, are Violet and Poppy. We brought them down here, so I could speak to them together.

Of course if things go south, I stand to lose everything.

"Hi, girls," I said cheerfully upon entry. "I brought food for you."

Sandwiches, cake, fruit, chocolate milk. We raided the staff room fridge and put together a platter. I set the tray down on the table between them and let them inspect the food.

Violet took a plum.

Poppy took a piece of cake with blue icing.

"You remember me, don't you?" I began. "Of course, we just spoke before, Violet. But I've seen you girls on a few occasions now. First at the school. And then when we had to ask you about your mother. It hasn't been easy, I know."

I paused a moment.

They chewed slowly.

"I know I've said my name before is Detective Irvine, but from now on you can just call me Ashley."

"Where's Rose?" Violet asked. "Aren't we waiting for her?"

"She's with Dr. Archer," I answered.

Violet went still.

Poppy lowered her head a little.

"You know Dr. Archer, don't you?" I continued. "She did speak to you both briefly, a short time ago, yes?"

"So?" Violet said.

"We've got it all on tape of course. So we know what was said."

Violet put her plum down. "Where's Dad? Shouldn't he be here?"

"He's just behind the glass there, watching you."

"He has to be present," Violet declared. "You can't speak to us otherwise. It's the law."

"This isn't an official conversation," I combatted. "You're both free to leave once you've finished eating."

Violet looked to Poppy. "Are we going then?"

Poppy was still eating her cake. "I'm hungry."

"Yes, but–"

I pulled up the chair opposite them and sat down. "So, here's what we know. We know Dr. Archer isn't Dr. Archer. We know that the three of you know her at least in some capacity, outside of today. We think that it was Dr. Archer's idea to hurt Georgie. And also, we think she was behind your sister Daisy's death." I leaned forward. "When you were in the store that night, when you were with your mother as she bought the pink handled knife – that wasn't really your mother, was it?"

Violet shook and shuddered, like she was about to call out for help. But Poppy put her cake down and touched her sister on the shoulder to quiet her.

"We're not safe here," Poppy said.

"What do you mean, you're not safe?" I queried.

"Shut up!" Violet punched her.

"It's not safe to talk," Poppy answered.

"Do you mean because of Dr. Archer? Because she's not here anymore. She left."

"Did she take Rose with her?" Violet asked.

My face faltered.

"I knew it," Violet hissed.

"We need to get out of here," Poppy said to me.

"Why?" I demanded. "What are you afraid of?"

Ringtone activated.

I checked it. Gordon was calling.

"Hold on one sec."

I stood up and took the call.

"Ashley?"

"Yeah, hello, what's up?"

"Are you still at the station?"

"Of course. Where are you?"

"What's going on with the girls there?"

"I've got them right in front of me. They're just eating some lunch on the ground floor."

"Alright, listen. This is going to sound nuts, but I need you to get them out of there."

"What the hell are you talking about?"

"I got a call from Dr. Archer. I'm on my way to meet her and Rose as we speak. There's a reason she took Rose out of there. And it's not what we were thinking."

"Well, don't hold me in suspense."

"Dr. Archer works at the girls' school. She's been talking to the girls for weeks about what's been going on at home, and the things she was saying, it's just…"

My feet shifted on the floor below me.

"Dr. Archer had an idea something was wrong, but it's only just now that Rose has told her the whole story."

It's a story we've all heard. It's a place we've all been. But looking at the girls, I just wished he wouldn't say it.

"The father, Nicholas Greene, is behind everything. Daisy. George. He stopped the girls from telling the truth about what happened in the alley. He forced Rose to pretend she was the killer for the cameras. And that's not all.

"In Rose's own words, he's been sexually abusing the girls…"

CHAPTER 56

This changes everything.

With the phone falling from my ear, the call ended, my eyes are drawn to the children at the table. I'm no longer dealing with perceived danger. I'm no longer dealing with manipulation. Just look at their faces – these girls have been through hell.

Of course, no one wants to jump to conclusions. This is merely a shifting of the focus, a reorganizing of priorities. If the girls did have a hand in George's death, then maybe they weren't to blame…

I turned to the mirror. "Captain? I need to speak with you outside." Then to the girls. "Sit tight." I stepped into the corridor at the same time as Captain Roper.

He swiftly approached. "Who was that on the phone?"

"Gordon," I answered. "Did he call you?"

"No." Roper shook his head.

"The situation has altered. Gordon's in contact with Dr. Archer who still has Rose and is claiming to be the girl's counselor from school. She believes the girls to be in danger, and basically Rose is making a ton of accusations about the father."

Roper crossed his arms. "Does he have their location?"

"He's supposed to be meeting up with them. But look, Rose isn't just incriminating Mr. Greene with what happened to both George and Daisy. There's apparently been some… sexual abuse."

"What?"

"Mr. Greene is abusing his daughters."

Captain Roper rolled his eyes. "This is what the imposter has been saying?"

"The accusations are serious," I reasoned, "no matter where they come from."

Roper shook his head. "You just tell Gordon to arrest that woman and get Mr. Greene's daughter back here, posthaste."

"Sir?"

"Don't look at me like that, Ashley. I hope you're not taken in by this rubbish."

"Rubbish?"

He moved in and took me to the side. "Mr. Greene is an upstanding member of the community, and I don't care who that lunatic says she is or what he's done – she's committed offenses by fraudulently gaining access to our classified areas; disrupting a homicide investigation; and kidnapping a minor under the age of fifteen."

"That may be the case," I said, "but what happens to Mr. Greene while this is going on?"

"What do you mean, what happens to him? He can take the girls home before any of us are subject to lawsuits regarding the unlawful detainment of his children. After all, you still don't know which of the girls killed George, do you?"

"It's looking like Rose was the one who entered the boy's room on the surveillance," I confessed, "as we always suspected."

"Do you have any proof?"

"The wheels are still in motion. Gordon and Dr. Archer–"

Roper shook his head violently. "There's just no getting through to you, is there?"

He put his back to me and pushed open the door to the interrogation room. And then he made his way back in the direction of the observation room.

"Um, excuse me," I called after him. "You're not really turning these girls over to an alleged child-abuser, are you?"

Roper glanced back at me. "That woman is a liar."

* * *

He doesn't believe. He doesn't believe her. He doesn't believe the girls. Why should he? Nothing like this has ever happened to him. He hasn't seen what these so-called 'upstanding members of the community' are capable of. He left me there frozen. Paralyzed. I can't comprehend this. Are all the stereotypes true? Are all these privileged white males really just covering for each other?

All I know is, I didn't speak up. I didn't tell anyone what happened to me. I was too afraid.

But times have changed.

"Girls?" I said, poking my head back into the room. They were already standing. I motioned quietly. "Come on. Come along."

They followed my lead.

I anxiously looked down the corridor. No sign of them yet. I bent down on one knee as the girls approached.

"Rose has told us what's happened," I said. "If you want my help, I won't let him get anywhere near you."

And then, simultaneously, both girls put their arms around me.

I couldn't believe it. The hopelessness that had been following me around all these years. It was right there, in front of me.

CHAPTER 57

Every action has consequences. Every wrongdoing. Every fault. Every mistake. Break the rules, and you will be judged. You will be punished.

There are no questions. There is no nuance. This is how the country is run. It's all there, in print. Empowered by law. Empowered by the state. Empowered by God. Something has to go very wrong in a person's life for them to find themselves going against the rule of law.

In my case, I had to be raped. We wouldn't be here if I wasn't.

So, what happens next is a blur. The men behind us are still busy with one another. No one has seen the girls sneak out to be with me.

And now we're walking. Quickly. One foot after the other.

At the turn of the corner, I immediately broke into a sprint.

"Detective Irvine!"

They know.

"Come on, come on!" I pleaded to the girls.

They raced along with me.

I hit the button to the elevator and luckily it was already on our floor. The doors parted and we stepped inside. I hit the button for the basement, and the doors shut before anyone else made it to the other side of that corner.

"What are we doing?" Violet asked. "Aren't you in trouble now?"

I shuddered. "Uh – yes – probably." A pause. "I don't know what I'm doing. I'm just getting you away from here. Is that okay?"

I felt Poppy's fingers take hold of my hand. "We trust you."

I swallowed.

It's okay. It's going to be okay. It'll all work out.

You're doing the right thing…

The elevator doors opened. We stepped out into the basement garage.

"Alright, hurry now," I ushered them. "My car's parked just over there."

We skipped along together in silence.

I went for my keys and unlocked the car from a distance.

Ringtone activated.

Approaching the car, I pulled out my phone. It was Captain Roper, of course.

"Alright, girls, get in," I said, picking up pace.

I forced my way into the driver's seat and shut the door, the phone still ringing.

I turned the ignition. The engine hummed.

"Are you going to answer that?" Violet inquired.

I set the phone down and took hold of the stick. "Not just yet."

* * *

Two minutes later, and the station was long gone. We were on the road. I reached over, and tentatively took the captain's call.

"Hello?" his voice came in politely. "Are you there, Ashley?"

"I'm here, Captain."

"I want to apologize to you for earlier," he said, continuing his meek tone. "I know I was very dismissive of that accusation, but since then, I've had a chance to think. We've put Mr. Greene into interrogation and are ready to proceed with his interview as soon as you're ready."

I couldn't believe what I was hearing. "You do know, I've taken the girls, don't you?"

"Yes. The girls are presently in your care."

"And I'm no longer in the station."

"That's not important. You just take your time, wherever you are. And then when you feel comfortable, please come back and we can get started with Mr. Greene's interview."

I hesitated. "That sounds great–"

"Excellent. I'll contact child services now and have someone ready to pick up the girls on your safe return."

"Alright." I sighed. "I'll… I'll be back in a few minutes then. You're really not mad at me?"

"We'll talk about that when you come in."

"Okay."

I set the phone down. We were approaching a set of traffic lights. I reluctantly hit the indicator so as to make a U-turn.

"We're going back?" Poppy asked, leaning forward.

"I think he's had second thoughts," I said. "He's going to take me seriously now."

"Yeah sure," Violet said sarcastically.

"What?" I muttered.

"You just abducted two children, and he's going to take you seriously?"

Dizziness. A flash in my eyes.

Tick-tick, tick-tick, tick-tick, tick-tick.

The girl was right. Captain Roper was just saying what I wanted to hear.

Oh God. I'm so dead.

I snapped the indicator off and proceeded forward with the green light.

"Why don't you try calling your partner?" Violet suggested.

"What? How do you–"

"He knows where Rose is, doesn't he?"

I sighed. It wasn't a bad idea. I picked up the cell and put it to my ear.

Ringing. Ringing.

I watched the girls in the rearview mirror. Violet was whispering something in Poppy's ear.

"Ashley," Gordon answered. "Dear God, what are you doing?"

"Roper was going to turn them over to the father," I said. "I couldn't allow it."

"You know he's actually authorized me to use deadly force against you, if we happen to cross paths."

"He… he… that lying son of a–"

"Yeah, I know. But still. You're just making it hard for yourself."

"I don't care what happens to me."

"Well, look, you should maybe drop the girls off at their school. Just so you know, there isn't a SWAT team on the move to bring you down."

"What about you? Have you located Rose?"

"I'm on my way there right now."

"On your way where?"

"Dr. Archer's house. I haven't given the address to the station yet. I need to make sure Rose is safe, and then bring the woman in quietly."

"Wait," I whispered. "You believe her, right?"

"Believe who?"

"All that stuff about the father?"

"I don't know what I believe. Maybe I shouldn't have told you."

I shook my head. "What's the address?"

"No, Ashley, come on–"

"Look, you're either with me or against me!"

"Jesus. What… what are you going to do when you get here?"

"What am I going to do? What am I going to do?" I said breathlessly. "I'm going to listen to their story…"

CHAPTER 58

The following is a statement I, Rose Greene, make on behalf of myself and my two sisters, Violet and Poppy. I do this with the guidance of my counselor Dr. Simone Archer, whom I have been speaking with about these experiences over the past few weeks.

I make this statement to document the systematic abuse I, and my sisters, have suffered under our father, Nicholas Greene. I also hope this sheds some light on the circumstances surrounding our abandoned sister, Daisy Greene, and also George Hart.

To tell my story, our story, I need to start from the beginning. As I mentioned earlier, we began as four sisters, not three. Our parents,

Sarah and Nicholas, did not have a happy marriage. They were not prepared for the responsibility of looking after four children.

I remember Sarah driving us children out to a playground far away one day. She said we had to pretend we saw a woman with a gun in the park. She said to imagine her. She said if anyone asked, we had seen her. I was very confused and none of it made sense to me. I thought it was a game. But I also knew one of us was going away that day. When we went back home, we left one of us behind.

All photos of Daisy began disappearing in the house. Sarah was trying to make her vanish, as if she never existed. If she caught any of us speaking her name, she would run a cold shower, strip us naked, and force us into the freezing water until we swore we didn't know who Daisy was.

Although he never said, it is my belief Nicholas was upset with Sarah for giving Daisy away and making the false report to the police. They divorced soon after.

All my life, and all of Violet's life, and all of Poppy's life, and all of Daisy's life, Nicholas had been molesting us as far back as any of us can remember. We didn't know it was wrong. Looking back, my feeling is that Nicholas was afraid that if Daisy found new people to look after her, she would one day remember what he'd been doing to us, and they would come after him.

Sarah is not a participant, but rather an enabler of the sexual abuse. As the three of us grew older, the abuse escalated. We were eventually expected to behave with our father as a wife would with her husband. Sarah knew everything that was going on, but Sarah refused to ever speak about it.

The abuse continued. I thought it would never end. I was afraid of how it was changing me. I was thinking about things I shouldn't have been thinking about. But I was also afraid of being abandoned in the park, just like Daisy had been. Sometimes, I would fantasize about being Daisy. If maybe I changed the color of my ribbon, I could somehow escape.

Over a number of sessions, I have been speaking about problems at home with Dr. Archer, but this is the first time I have given her all the details. Had she known about the sexual abuse from Nicholas, she would have contacted the police immediately. I deliberately withheld these details from her as I was too afraid to speak up. I didn't realize people would die because of it.

A few weeks ago, I woke up one night to someone banging on my bedroom window. I went outside to see who it was, and Daisy was there. She had tracked us down.

Daisy wanted to come inside and wake up our other sisters and Sarah, but I was too afraid to let her back into our world. I didn't want what was happening to us to happen to her.

I tried to lead her away from the house, which is how we ended up at the grocery store together. I was just stealing things to make me look pretty, and when the security guards came, I took off my red hair clips, and told them my name was Lily.

Daisy's new mom came to meet us at the station, and she lied about being Sarah to protect Daisy. She was a nice lady, but I only met her once. She drove me home a bit after.

When I got home, Sarah was awake. She demanded to know where I'd been. I should have kept my mouth shut, but I was just so happy to see Daisy again, I blurted it all out. Sarah went crazy at me. She said if I ever saw Daisy again she'd kill her. I didn't understand why, but now when I look back at our lives… Sarah was still in love with Nicholas. She was still hoping for a way back to him.

A short time later, Sarah changed her mind. She said she wanted to meet Daisy and just have a talk with her. So the next time she came knocking on my window, I went and got Sarah, and all five of us went out for ice cream.

Things seemed to be going okay. They were getting along. Then at the end, Sarah said she wanted to buy Daisy a present. So Daisy had to wait in the car while we went into the shop to get her something.

I didn't see Sarah purchase the knife. I had no idea what was happening. But Sarah made sure we were all there in the alley when she gave Daisy her present.

After that, I stopped thinking of her as my mom. She was just Sarah. The next morning, we got up and she'd made our lunches and everyone was acting like nothing had happened. What could we do? If we went against Sarah, we'd be next.

After the police visited the school and took Violet away, I knew what it was about. I went to see Dr. Archer and told her what had happened to Daisy. She said that I didn't have to say anything while Sarah was in the room with the detectives, but that I should wait for another time to come forward. I also had to talk to Violet and Poppy and make sure they were okay to tell the truth.

We told the police about Sarah later that night. The detectives were good people who listened to us. But of course we couldn't tell them why she killed Daisy. We hadn't even told each other what Nicholas was doing to us individually. It is so hard to talk about.

We then found out we were going to stay with Nicholas's girlfriend, whom we hadn't met before. I didn't know if she would be good or bad, whether we'd be able to talk to her. But when we got there, she was just the worst person ever.

After a brief dinner, we retired to our rooms which were in their own wing. It was there I finally had the courage to talk to Violet and Poppy about why Sarah had killed Daisy, and what our father had been doing to us.

It was dark outside the house. All three of us were in bed, and all the lights were off. I could hear Jess playing music upstairs and it was loud and weird. I couldn't sleep.

I should have mentioned that before we got on the train to meet Jess, Nicholas had given us a cell phone for emergencies. I happened to have the phone in my possession, and I heard it go off in my bag. I got up from my bed and had a look at the phone. There was a message from Nicholas telling me to go outside, which I did.

He was in the car by the gate. He was very upset and angry. He said that Jess had gotten into a fight with her son George – whom we'd just met as well for the first time that day – and she'd stabbed him to death.

He then handed me a knife with a pink handle and told me to go upstairs and stab George's body with it to make it look like I'd killed him. He said that the surveillance would see me but because I wasn't wearing my ribbon – just my pink beads – the cops wouldn't know which of us did it, so we'd all get off.

Of course, I said no. I begged him. I pleaded. But he opened his glove box and showed me a gun there and said if I didn't do it, he would come in the house and shoot everyone.

I was trapped. I was outside my body. But I had to do what he said.

So, I went back into the house, I climbed the stairs, I opened the door to George's room. And I saw him in the bed.

He was dead. I swear it to you. I could barely put the knife into his skin. I barely nicked it. Then I just came out and went downstairs to throw the knife away.

I unlocked the kitchen door and stumbled outside. I couldn't see straight. I was so ashamed of what I'd done. But I was afraid. I was afraid of Jessica. I was afraid of Dad. I was afraid Sarah's lawyer would find a way out of her charges and she'd come looking to kill me too.

So I ran. I kept on running. Through the trees and the grass. I didn't think I'd ever be going back. I just wanted to be like Daisy. I wanted to be gone from the family. Gone from the world.

But of course they still had my sisters. Violet and Poppy were their hostages. If I didn't go back, Nicholas could punish them with his gun. So after an hour or so, I started walking back.

I went around to the side of the house and threw small rocks up at Violet's window. She opened it and I called for help

We were too afraid to wake Jessica up, or get caught outside our rooms, so Violet fastened some bedsheets together and threw them out the window for me to climb up.

Once back inside, I went straight back to bed and tried to sleep. Of course, I couldn't. Not after all that. I knew that I had to tell someone what had happened, but if Nicholas or Jessica found out I'd be done for. So, when Dr. Archer from school showed up at the station, I just had to play along with it until we were alone together.

My sisters will need to give their own statements when they are ready to do so. I know there will come a time when I have to tell someone the exact details of each sexual experience I have had with Nicholas, but that is so traumatic I can barely find the words.

I owe Dr. Archer my life. She did not kidnap me, as I went with her voluntarily.

My father Nicholas Greene is a rapist and pedophile.

My mother Sarah Greene is a killer.

My father told me Jessica Hart was the one who killed George and I believe him.

I beg the police to protect me and my sisters from these monstrous people. And again, I thank Dr. Archer, without whom none of this would be possible.

Yours sincerely,
Rose Greene

* * *

It's the sound of a leaking tap in the kitchen. Little drops of water falling. Splashing into the sink. No one in the living room can contain themselves. Dr. Archer has one arm over Rose on the sofa, but her whole body is shaking. Poppy is sitting on the other side of Rose, sobbing uncontrollably. Violet, in a nearby recliner, has gone as white as a sheet.

"Where's the bathroom?" she asked.

"Down the hall," Archer whispered. "Last door at the end."

Violet leaps from her chair and rushes away.

Gordon is standing by the front door, and he doesn't look much better. His cheeks are red, his eyes swollen. We are all horrified. The story has cut me up into a million pieces.

But not Rose. She is the strongest in the room. Although the words she read aloud were prepared in advance, I can be sure they were her own by how she read them.

What has happened to these children is an absolute tragedy. There is no longer any doubt in my mind I have made the right decision by bringing the children here. Every word Dr. Archer has said is true. We confirmed her identity before entering the house. She does work at the school and has been counseling Rose and her sisters. I must admit, a part of me has tried to stay skeptical. It would be so easy to believe Rose has made all of this up, if I hadn't listened to every word of the story. If I hadn't seen her face as she told it.

What Nicholas and Sarah have done to these children is beyond the sickest of all nightmares. It makes my own abuse seem trivial in comparison.

I am ashamed I ever doubted them.

I am ashamed of every second.

"Well, that's all there is," Dr. Archer informed me. "But you're welcome to ask the other girls questions to verify Rose's statement."

I looked at Poppy, who was still a mess. Rose was trying to comfort her. Violet could be heard throwing up out the back.

"We don't have any questions for now," I said humbly. "Unless, Gordon…"

He stepped forward.

I watched as he approached Rose and got down on one knee.

"I'm so sorry what's happened to you," he said to her.

"That's okay," Rose murmured.

"I don't know what happens from here, but I'm going to do everything in my power to set this right with the department." He turned to me. "I'll make Captain Roper see reason."

"It's easier said than done," I said sourly.

He stood back up and turned to Dr. Archer. "Would we be able to get a copy of that statement?"

"I can email it to you," Dr. Archer confirmed.

"Alright." Gordon gave her his details. "I'll make sure no one comes back here before you've spoken to me. You will need to come back into the station tonight, but I'll try and make it as brief as possible."

"What about their father?" Dr. Archer demanded.

"And Jess," Rose added in a hushed whisper.

"With this statement, he won't be setting a foot near those girls. I can promise you that." I got up and approached them. I looked to Poppy specifically. "Are you sure you're alright here, darling?"

"Yes, thank you," Poppy answered.

"I don't know what's happening with my situation," I confessed. "But I'll do everything I can from wherever I am to see that you guys are okay. And justice is served."

"We'd really appreciate that, thank you," Dr. Archer said, standing. "And sorry about earlier."

I nodded.

"I'll walk you out," she said.

We began exiting the room and Gordon was asking Dr. Archer another question or two, while she opened the front door. I looked back at Rose and Poppy, one last time, just to make sure they were okay.

"Bye-bye." Rose waved.

I waved back. I approached the front door, just as a small object came out of nowhere, colliding with my leg.

"Whoops," Violet said from the adjacent passage.

I bent down and picked up the red ball.

"Is this yours?" I asked her.

"It's Rose's… I mean, Daisy's… I mean… Um…"

Everything is blurring together. "Do you want it?" I offered.

She slowly nodded. I bounced it on the floor, and the child caught it.

CHAPTER 59

So here we are then. The place where it all started. I should have seen this coming, I should have seen those girls for who they truly were. They were… survivors. Like I'm a survivor.

"What's this?" Gordon asked as I jumped into the passenger seat of his car. "Where are we?"

"It's the house I grew up in," I said. "My childhood home."

I made him come here, without telling him what it was.

"My family don't live there anymore."

"So why are we here?" he asked, dumbfounded. "What's this got to do with anything?"

"I'm not going back to the station with you," I tried to explain. "I brought you here because I have to tell you something. Something I've never told anyone."

"Oh, Ashley…" His voice quivered with emotion.

"I was raped in that house."

He looked away from me, in its direction.

"I was twelve years old."

He cursed quietly.

"I remember it was three o'clock in the morning. He jumped on top of me and put something over my eyes so I couldn't see his face."

"Was it… was it your father?" he croaked.

"I could tell by his weight that it wasn't. I had three brothers. So, any one of them. But I never knew which one it was."

"Did you report it?"

I grabbed his arm. "Will you look at me, please?"

"Sorry."

"So, what did you want to ask? Did I report it? Are you trying to make a joke or something?"

"No, I'm… Are you reporting it now?"

"Are you not listening?" I yelled at him. "I haven't told anyone about this. You're the only one."

"So why now?"

"Because I learned something today. I learned that it isn't just me. It's never been just me." The tears poured out. "Every day, this is happening to someone. And… And no one believes them. Because children have no power. Not over you men."

"Hey, what the hell did I do?" Gordon protested.

"Nothing. I hope."

His jaw dropped. "Come on, Ashley. That's not fair."

"You want to talk about what's fair? Right now, my own friends and co-workers are looking to put me down, because I tried to save some children. Our boss – that miserable excuse for a human being – he ordered you to kill me on sight. That's what you said, correct?"

"I'm not him," Gordon said defiantly. "I'm on your side."

"What about their side?"

"I'm on their side too! What makes you think otherwise?"

"Nothing," I sobbed. "I just. I need to be heard. I need you to listen."

"I am listening, Ashley."

"It's not my fault they did it to me."

"No, no one's saying it's your fault."

I shook my head. "You don't know my family."

He sighed. A moment's pause. "I'm sorry it happened to you. I mean that with every fiber of my being. It makes me sick, it really does."

I nodded and fell into his arms. He held me. And I cried.

I cried some more.

But never for myself.

Only.

Only for those girls.

CHAPTER 60

It's getting dark outside. I'm on the bed in a motel room, watching the local six o'clock news. Gordon does not appear. Captain Roper is helming the press conference and taking all the credit for Mr. Greene's arrest. He has yet to be publicly identified. But it will happen. It will happen real soon.

"And can I just make a plea to Detective Ashley Irvine, if she's watching," Roper continued, on camera. "Ashley. I'm sorry things turned out as they did. Turn yourself in, as soon as possible, and you'll see you have the full support of the department and myself–"

I shut the TV off.

That's that then. I'm not going back now. They'll have to drag me kicking and screaming.

I've been watching pick-a-card videos to kill the time. I have my whole life in front of me. The shadows of the past have surfaced, but they will be dealt with, and the experience will help me to grow over time.

There are still wrongs that need to be righted. If only I could find the courage. If only I could find the strength. I have their numbers after all.

Percy.

Peter.

Paul.

I could call them all up right now. I can ask them the question I've never asked. Maybe… If they confess what they did… If they say they're truly sorry… If they say they love me… Maybe…

I'll be able to move on…

* * *

I wake up and my head is killing me. It's completely dark in here. I can't see a thing. Except… the bedside table clock: 3 a.m. I drank too much, I passed out. Did I… Did I call my brothers?

Hey. What's going on with my wrist? It's both of them! What is that? It can't be…

Zip ties?

"Hey!" I shouted. "Hello…? Is someone there?"

Silence.

I'm trying to break free of the ties, but they won't budge. This is no accident.

"Hey!"

I feel them now. They're on the bed with me. Slowly, but surely, they're climbing on top of me. I try to kick them off but already I feel the knife at my throat.

"No!" I yelped.

"Shut up."

I know that voice. I'm completely bewildered. My eyes are now adjusting to the dark. I can see where they are. I can see their face peering over mine.

"Wait," I said. "Is that you, Violet?"

And again, "Or is that you, Rose?"

And again, "Or is that you, Poppy?"

And then my thoughts collapsed.

"You'll never know," she said, and cut my throat.

PART IV

Violet

CHAPTER 61

Purple is my color. Purple is my soul. I am Violet Greene. Violet is the flower. Greene is the stem. Life is a garden. My pot moves from place to place.

Sometimes it's winter. Sometimes it's spring.

Sometimes I'm in the light, and other times I'm in the shade.

There's all sorts of environmental conditions out here, where I have to adapt. I have real potted violets sitting on my study desk for decoration. If I take proper care of them, then they'll be with me for a long time. Of course, there's always the chance they'll outlive me.

One of my sisters hurt Georgie.

And I don't want to be next.

* * *

That's right, I didn't do it. I didn't stab the boy. I'm not asking anyone to believe me. It's merely a statement of fact. I don't see the act itself as damning. It is not the manifestation of evil. My sister didn't make the blade. She didn't make the boy, for that matter either. Or the house. Or the bed he was sleeping in. That anyone would feel it's their place to judge her is humorous to me. She was only eleven, after all. You adults had a hand in this too.

Really, I don't mind. When people look at you like you're a potential knife-wielding maniac, it actually gives you a certain type of status. You're allowed to have grievance with them. Why are you staring at me? Do we have a problem? Is there something you'd like to share?

There was this one girl – Kristen – who mistook our notoriety for weakness. In our first year of middle school, she rounded up some of the 'cool' girls to make fun of me. I'm just Violet after all. I'm the bookworm. I'm the sister with the reading glasses. It's gotta be one of the other two. I'm the least likely to have done it.

So, that one recess, where Kristen and her goons cornered me in the locker bay… yelling in my ear… knocking my books to the floor… That's where I showed her who she was dealing with.

"Harry and Madeline. Amie not spelled with a *Y*, but with an *I* and an *E*," I said. The names of her parents and baby sister.

"What?" Kristen gasped. "What the hell are you–?"

"Number Six. Porterstop Lane, New Hansville." Her home address.

"Who told you where I live?"

A silent wave, moving through the girls.

"No one told me," I answered truthfully. "I followed you home last Friday."

"You… freak…" she mumbled.

I took off my glasses. "Pick the books up, and we'll forget this ever happened."

She hesitated, and I grinned. "I'm not asking twice."

Kristen bent her knees and handed me the books.

* * *

You get the point now, don't you. You can see how my personality and reputation has developed over the years. In the beginning, when the new kids meet you, you're a little famous, and you're a bit weird. Some people are afraid, and many stay away. I'm always honest with people though. Don't mess with me, and I won't mess with you. I'm not here to hurt anyone. I'm following the compulsory academic path as directed by the school curriculum. And it should be noted I'm attending public school and getting the good, solid, cheap education I deserve. It's not what my father would have wanted, or my mother for that matter. But you know what happened to them, don't you? They're both doing twenty-five to life. Mom for Daisy. Dad for the rest of us. The only one who got away was Jessica, who had two mistrials before finally being found not guilty. A lot of people still think she killed Georgie. But there are those in the community that doubted Rose's testimony. They believe one of us girls killed Georgie.

And, of course, they would be right.

CHAPTER 62

The cameras didn't lie. One of us left the house that night. When they came back, they went straight for Georgie's room. They went there with a knife.

My two sisters. Would you believe me if I said I didn't know which of them did it? Of course, if there was anyone who knew, then it'd have to be me, right? Hell, even Jessica's defense team tried to make out I was the one who instrumented the whole thing – the brains behind it, as it were. They couldn't accept the killer acted alone. They also couldn't accept that these identical triplet sisters didn't have that special kind of bond where we read each other's minds, feel each other's thoughts.

It's not like that. We have no difficulty lying to each other, any more than anyone else. One thing I think we do have a shared understanding of is that it's a game. All of it – Daisy, Georgie, the parents, our lives. It's a game where everyone's after the same thing.

When the sun comes down, we'll be on top.

My sisters aren't my enemies, but that doesn't mean we're always working together. Go back to the start of the school year, which is indeed our final year of high school. First week in and I'd already made the rounds to ensure I was nominated for class president. I'd been a prefect last semester, and my marks were exceptional in all my subjects. I was part of the debate team, helped in the library at lunches and volunteered for community clean-up on holidays and weekends.

Yes, that's me. Violet – straight-A student and teacher's pet who sits in the front row of every class.

Asking around, I was apparently going up against two jocks, that is, the future prom king and his best friend – both insanely popular, sporty, outgoing types – who would surely slaughter me in any vote; which is why I spent the summer two-timing them without each other's knowledge.

In my speech titled *Boys will be Boys* I was to talk about the pressure teenage girls are placed under by our adolescent counterparts. I didn't want to be with both these boys. I kept saying no but they kept pushing.

I'd go on to describe their bodies – the pale skin under their clothes where the moles and birthmarks are. I didn't have sex with either of them, but I took it just far enough so that I could basically make an argument to the student base that they were both potential rapists.

Before we assembled in the auditorium to give our speeches, I checked in with our student coordinator, to make sure I was the last nominee to give their speech. I knew as the nominees had yet to be publicly announced, there was a chance either of them could have withdrawn, in which case I would alter my speech to not include the withdrawn candidate.

We were only given ten minutes each on the podium to make our case as to why we should be president, but in any instance, I was going to make every minute count.

The auditorium had a number of uses – assembly, gym class and performing arts to name a few. The podium was on an elevated stage, and there were rows and rows of seating laid out for the seventy-odd students present. I was in the front row, of course, next to the student coordinator when she wasn't on the stage. While the boys were up there, I thought I was getting a clearer picture of what was going on. I was listening to every word that was spoken. It's how I've never fallen behind in class, how I always make sure I'm engaged, and on top.

Here's the thing, though. When you sit up the front, you get the best view of the teacher but you miss everything going on behind you.

"Our next nominee," the student coordinator was saying as I slowly prepared to stand up, "is a very brave and courageous young woman, who has a larger-than-life personality. She's friendly, she's talented, she makes everyone she comes across smile. You all know who I'm talking about – she is no stranger to this stage at all. Please give it up for… Rose Greene!"

Like I said, we weren't enemies.

"Thank you," Rose said, taking the podium. "My speech today is entitled *Boys will be Boys, and Girls will be Girls: or how I watched on in horror as my sister manipulated two boys in a bid to scrap their nominations.*"

But we weren't very good friends either.

CHAPTER 63

I sit at the front. Rose sits in the middle. Poppy sits at the back.

We're on the school bus, on our way home. No one drives yet. I guess that comes later, when we have the money, when we have autonomy. In all honesty, I should be making moves to ensure I'm driving sooner rather than later. Not that I'd let the other two leech on me for rides anyway.

"So?" a voice piped up in the seat behind me. "What happened?"

I turned my head sideways as Leanne Lu leaned over. "What happened with what?" I asked innocently.

"You've been talking about being nominated for class president for months now," she gushed, "but Kim and Kasey said you pulled out at the last minute."

"I take it you weren't in assembly this afternoon."

"I was helping Ms. Yarran clean out the python tanks."

"Of course, you were."

She eyeballed me. "Come on. You know I'm gonna find out anyway."

I shook my head. "Rose foiled my evil plan. Made a laughing stock out of me. She's gotta be odds-on favorite to get voted in now."

"Oh no." Leanne grinned.

"It's not funny," I snapped. "Although I do have to give her credit for outsmarting me on this occasion."

"Ah well. I'm sure being class president's not all it's cracked up to be."

"I have the skills, I have the work ethic, I have the strength to invoke positive change and get things done," I said, venting my frustration. "But when it comes down to it, it's just a popularity contest. And who is popular among the idiots?"

She shrugged.

"Well, not smart people, I'll tell you that," I said. "But this isn't over. I will get the better of her before the year is out."

"I'm sure you will, Violet," Leanne said teasingly. "I'm sure you will…"

CHAPTER 64

Of course, one has to be careful. There's every chance in the world it was Rose who went into little Georgie's room that night and stabbed him to death. She admitted it was her who went into the room at least, and of course, down the stairs to visit our father in the car outside, if that was really him who was out there.

One thing, one very strange thing, that Rose lied about in her testimony was that upon her returning to the house, I was apparently the one who fastened a bedsheet to toss out the window for her to climb back in. I did no such thing. In fact, the very physics of Rose climbing up the house in the middle of the night seem quite improbable to me. So, the alternative isn't simply that it was Poppy that let her in, but that how Rose got back into the house is a completely different story all together. I am not sure how she managed to do that. I am not sure why we don't know how. If the crime was already committed, what was there left to cover up? What secrets had yet to be disclosed?

It's funny. For all her lies, Rose doesn't strike me as a violent person. She's far too… extroverted to do something like that. Let me explain. Rose isn't someone who bottles up her emotions. She's like a barking puppy when it comes to getting what she wants. She's persistent, determined, confident. She has a sense of humor as well. She likes to make fun of people. To their face.

I'm not here to point the blame at anyone, but people want to know. I said I didn't know who stabbed Georgie, and I stand by that statement, but it doesn't mean I don't have suspicions.

"Yo! Call us when you get home!"

"We're staying out all night tonight, ha-ha!"

"We love you, Poppy! Whoo!"

Poppy's friends from up the back of the bus. Who would have thought she'd wind up with more friends than any of us? Well, I suppose that's not true. I'll correct. Rose has a million friends but they're all artificial. She has no deep and meaningful relationships. I hear what people say about her behind her back. She's got the power, but no one wants her to succeed. For myself, I really just have Leanne. We're both losers, I guess. There's a few other girls we get along with, but I don't see them outside of school. I know there's plenty of boys who'd want to date me, and I could be part of the cool crowd, if it's what I wanted. But that's not true to me. To be honest, I just hate them.

Then there's Poppy, the biggest mystery of all. In class, she has the teachers completely fooled because she comes across as extremely shy, just meek and subservient. But there's a whole other side of her, where she's friends with all the outcasts. The smokers, the drug-users, the goth types. When she lets her hair out, you'll see the dyed-blue streaks that are otherwise hidden when she has it back. She also has a pierced belly button and a tattoo of a peacock on her back, which she thinks no one knows about.

"Love you!" Poppy called, waving as the bus drove away, as we walked.

"Did Zowie just say you were going out tonight?" Rose asked her.

Poppy smiled and shrugged her shoulders.

"You know she hangs around those gangbangers from the other side of town," Rose continued. "I heard there was some party they were at where a guy got shot and died."

"Why'd they shoot him?" Poppy asked.

"I don't know," Rose said, flustered. "He probably tried to rip them off or something."

"So, who did I rip off?" Poppy laughed.

"Don't be stupid," Rose scolded. "You'll get picked on and bullied like you did back in middle school. You think you're all tough now, wait till they drop speed or cocaine on the table and tell you to snort it–"

"You're just jealous," Poppy said.

Rose's jaw dropped. "Jealous? I don't think so! Come on, Violet, back me up."

"Yeah, I'm not talking to you," I said.

"Geez, what's your problem? You take everything so seriously! You don't even have any friends at school. No one was going to vote for you."

"Did you hear something, Poppy?" I asked, meeting my sister's eyes.

"No, not really," Poppy murmured. "Apart from the breeze. It's pleasant."

"Okay, fine, you guys can go to hell," Rose said storming ahead. "Hope you'll remember this, next time you need something from me!"

I chuckled to myself as she marched away.

"She has problems," Poppy remarked.

"She is right about Zowie's friends though," I replied. "Just be careful."

"Nothing bad will happen," Poppy said dreamily.

"But you know how sad we'd all be if anything did."

"That's just because you love me," Poppy said. "As I love you, sis."

I smiled. Poppy was pretty cool these days.

Even if I did think she was the one who stabbed Georgie.

CHAPTER 65

There's a lot of blanks, aren't there? A lot of stuff being left out. A lot of stuff I'm not saying.

My message to you is that I'm not trying to deceive. Sometimes the best way to tell a story isn't chronologically. I wanted you to see me and my sisters as fully functioning seventeen-year-old high school students, right there, on the path. Trying to succeed.

Our journey is like yours. Or anyone else's when they reach this age. I'm here now, from what I understand to be a place of maturity. So here I am. Looking back to the start of the school year and beyond.

Things have not been normal leading up to this.

I gloss over. I minimize. I deduct. I delete and forget.

How far back should I go? How far would adequately explain the circumstances surrounding the woman living with us at home?

Simone is not our mother. She's not our stepmother. Simone is, among many other things, our legal guardian.

* * *

I first met Simone at the start of sixth grade. She sat in with our teacher Ms. Bright for whatever we were learning that day, and then the next day had ten minutes with every student in the class, one on one. She had a nice little office across the corridor with a big comfy chair for you to sit in, while she took notes from behind the desk. I can't remember any of her initial questions, but I think she was just feeling everybody out to make sure all the students were healthy and safe. If there were any issues we were having – whether that be at school or at home – then we were encouraged to discuss them with her. At our first meeting, I didn't have anything to report. I'm sure I was my ever-charming self and would have been able to persuade any trained counselor that everything was fine… but, of course, Simone had a hidden agenda.

A day or two after that, I was called in for a second, longer meeting. I was feeling fearless with nothing to hide right up until she said she'd spoken to my sisters, and at least one of them had said how things were not okay at home.

"What? Why wouldn't they be?" I said defensively.

"That's why we're here, Violet," Simone replied. "That's what you need to tell me."

It's not good for a person to keep secrets, especially not children. Up until that point, I wasn't thinking about it, but of course, there were plenty of skeletons in my closet.

I suddenly became terrified.

"Is it both of them, or just one of them?"

"Pardon me," Simone responded.

"Who said things weren't okay?"

"What difference does that make? I can see by your face, they're clearly not."

So, she wants the truth. No holding back. I found the implication alarming. These were my thoughts. My feelings. My secrets.

These things were private.

"Do you think your mother loves you?" Simone asked.

"Why shouldn't she love me?" I snapped back at her.

Fast-forward.

Push through all the years ahead of us.

It is Simone peering up at us from the kitchen bench, while our true mother rots behind bars.

"What's wrong with your sister?" Simone asked as Poppy and I came in. "Did something happen at school today?"

"Oh God," I said rolling my eyes.

"You should probably ask her," Poppy suggested.

We set our schoolbags down and took up a stool each in anticipation of afternoon tea.

"She went through here so fast, I didn't get a chance to," Simone replied. "Now what would you like to eat and drink?"

"Blueberry yogurt," I said.

"I'll have vanilla yogurt with blueberries on the side," Poppy said.

Nothing out of the ordinary here.

I'm sure Poppy and I would eat blue and purple foods three times a day if there was a wide enough selection to choose from.

"What juice do you want?"

"Black currant," I answered.

"I'll just have mango," Poppy said.

We ate our yogurt and drank our juice.

Simone eyed us carefully. "Well, how did it go?"

I blinked a few times.

"Madam… President…?"

She had her hands in tight fists ready to explode with celebration.

"You probably should ask Rose about that too," Poppy said and left the bench.

Simone waited till she was gone before moving in close to me. "Honey? What does she mean ask Rose?"

I sighed. "She managed to get herself nominated."

"Oh!"

"And she embarrassed me in front of the entire year level. So, I withdrew."

"But why? Aren't we all getting along? Isn't she happy?"

"I don't know," I said truthfully. "Maybe she should talk to someone."

CHAPTER 66

Speaking of therapy, those ten-minute sessions with Dr. Simone Archer were just the beginning of what was to come. Throughout the legal proceedings, I was subject to a multitude of assessments, the least of which being psychological. I've talked about Dad, I've talked about Mom. I've talked about Poppy and Rose. The talking is endless. How did I feel about this? What did I think when that happened? It just goes on and on, round in circles. The whole time, they're trying to make me slip up. If I say the wrong thing, the charade is over, and the abusers walk free. Of course, I didn't go in there without a plan. Our parents would never have been put away if all three of us weren't on the same page.

"'I was six years old when Dad first asked me to come into the shower with him' – eww, gross!"

Dr. Archer stared at me from the doorway, her arms crossed. I set the paper down and shifted across the bed away from it. "You can't expect me to say that to people."

"Not only will you say it to people," Dr. Archer said, "you will have it memorized. Line by line. Word for word."

"It's disgusting," I protested. "And it's not true."

"What's your point, Violet?"

"People will know. They'll be able to see on my face that I'm making it up."

"Well, obviously if we marched you in there now, but thankfully we have time to prepare. You can expect this will be a long, exhausting process."

I'm no fool, but this was the first time I realized who Simone truly was. And with that knowledge, I was at a crossroads.

"Your sisters are counting on you, my dear," she said sternly.

I nodded. "I guess there's no backing out now."

* * *

I have no regrets. You can't appeal to my better nature with your shallow morality or idiotic concepts of injustice. In my mind, Sarah and Nicholas's sole purpose for existing was to look after, provide for, and protect their four daughters, and their failing in this hurts me so much I am prepared to let the gates of hell open and shut on them. The pain and suffering I feel from them is the same as if they actually abused me. In a million lifetimes over, Sarah gets to abandon Daisy, Nicholas gets to neglect his parental responsibilities, Jessica gets to inflict her personality disorder upon us, and we girls just have stand there and take it. Powerless. Silently screaming.

So, this is it. That one time in a million where we have our guardian angel in Dr. Archer climb down from the clouds and save us, the tables are miraculously turned. We girls hold the power to hurt them. And they can suffer in our place.

Like I said, no regrets. I look to the future with cynical optimism, which means I'm watching God and if he doesn't give me the happiness I deserve, I'm going to be all over his case like a starving dog on a bone.

* * *

"Tell me about that happiness."

It's a question, but it sounds more like a command. I'm so sick of answering questions. I'm so sick of talking about myself. But having these sessions with the high-school welfare officer is still part of my agreement.

"You know what happiness is to me," I said from my chair. "I've told you heaps of times already. I need to be on top."

"Of your grades?" he said.

I couldn't help but smile.

"Of the world?"

"I'll know it when I'm there."

"Well. May I ask, what makes you unhappy?"

I swallowed. "My sister in assembly yesterday for a start."

"Why do you think she did that to you? Could it be she is crying out for attention?"

"Attention," I said dryly. "Attention from whom?"

"From you?"

"You know I think I understand Rose all too well," I replied. "She's like a bully. And then the fat kid walks past and maybe the bully and the fat kid are friends. You know, there's nothing wrong between them, but there's pressure from the other kids. The bully knows people are watching him, and he just can't help himself. It doesn't feel good in the moment. He feels horrible after. The guilt of seeing the fat kid suffer from his actions is quite distressing.

"And yet. The bully is compelled to attack. It's not negotiable. She… Rose… She just couldn't sit still and leave it."

"So what does all that mean to you?"

I shook my head. "What does it mean? It means nothing. It means she got the better of me… and in the end, the dumb people win."

"You think your sister's dumb?"

"I don't know. Compared to me, yeah. It doesn't even matter. I just assigned a made-up meaning because you asked for it."

"Alright."

Silence.

I looked up to the counselor, whom I saw was checking his phone.

"Time's up?" I asked.

"Not yet, sorry," he said, putting it away. "Another twelve minutes."

"Can I ask you a question?"

"Of course."

"You see a lot of screwed-up kids in here, right?"

"That's not a term I'm comfortable with using."

"I was being polite."

He smiled uneasily. "What's your question?"

"Where do I rank on the scale?"

"Scale?"

"Am I like… Just how messed up do you think I am?"

"I don't think–"

"How messed up?"

He put his hands together. "I don't think you're messed up. I think you've suffered through some extreme trauma and you are still healing from those experiences."

I made a face. "So, in other words, you haven't been listening to me at all?"

"I can see that you're angry. And I'm sorry if I'm not helping you the way you'd like."

"I don't want your help."

"That's okay."

"Because we're just ticking boxes in here anyway."

He leaned forward. "You know what, Violet? I do think you want my help."

"Oh really?"

"There's something going on in your life that you're not telling anyone about. Something you need to discuss with someone. I can see it. And it's not that Rose embarrassed you yesterday. I know you don't care about what the other students think, the way you're pretending to."

My jaw dropped. "That's the truest thing you've said in here."

He laughed heartily. "Well, thank you."

"If I tell you what it is, will you promise not to repeat it?"

"We're in confidentiality here, you know that."

"Alright."

I leaned forward.

He moved in closer.

"I've been crushing on you so bad, Ned. You got the hottest body, and I've just been thinking about sucking you in here cause no one would even know–"

"Alright," he said, standing. "There's the door. On you go, Violet."

"Oh, okay." I stood up then flashed my pearly whites before turning the handle. "Same time next week?"

"Out."

I nodded. Because there weren't really any more words for how good it felt.

To take their power away.

CHAPTER 67

Actions have consequences. I know I'm not going to get away with that. It is tempting to think, just because you're able to forget about something, that the universe won't remember either. Every tree that falls in a forest makes a sound. Even if there's nobody around to hear it.

I understand, of course. I understand the sentiment. It is so appealing to buy into the illusion. But here's the truth. Life is not based on anyone's perception, collective or otherwise. I admit, the belief fluctuates. I can't always get a complete grasp of it. But then there are times where I'll lose something in my otherwise perfectly organized bedroom. It starts when I go to pick it up, and not find it in its usual place. How? How is it gone? I'm always on the look-out for that glitch in the matrix. That moment of realization where my mind exists beyond the universe. But that's not the truth. Because every time, without fail… Every time that missing item turns up exactly in the place it's supposed to be.

God is watching us, boys and girls. And he's not some man or woman living in a faraway, magical place. God is our environment. God is the air we can't see. God is the definition of our true selves. We, being the land mammals. Who learned to speak.

"Who did what?"

"Her – there. Walking away. Violet Greene…"

The teachers are watching me. Eyes on my back. Every move becomes so important now.

"But nothing happened, right?"

"Nothing. Look, I told you–"

"You didn't touch her, did you? Ned?"

Actions. Consequences.

"No, of course, I didn't…"

It's too late now. It can't be taken back.

We're all finished.

* * *

Tap, tap, tap. My pen. On the table. Loud enough for Leanne to look up. Not so loud to disturb the others.

"What?" she mouths at me.

We're supposed to be writing our essays, and the teacher is walking close by. I grabbed a piece of scrap paper and jotted down some words.

> *I'm not giving up. We must defeat Rose.*

I passed it across to Leanne. She read it and looked up. I saw weakness in her eyes. She sighed and tore off a bit of paper to write me a note. I gazed around the room to make sure no one was watching. Leanne passed me a note and went back to her essay.

> *That's exactly what she wants. Just leave it.*

I clenched my teeth and tore off another piece of paper.

> *I have a plan. I need your help. Are you in or out?*

I pushed the paper over to Leanne. I waited and waited and waited for her to turn away from her essay.

"Are you finished then, Violet?"

I looked up and saw the teacher approaching me. "Uh, no," I replied softly.

"Let's see how you're doing."

I made a face as she leaned over my shoulder to inspect the work in front of me.

"Great start, love where it's going," she said enthusiastically. "Just remember to include item four."

"Yes," I muttered. "I haven't forgotten about it..."

The teacher moved along. When I looked at Leanne again, I saw she'd replied to my note.

What's your plan?

A smile touched my lips. I avoided her gaze and went back to my essay.

CHAPTER 68

There's an old toolshed right on the edge of the school's perimeter. You have to go right past the outer buildings and walk through a cluster of trees before it even becomes visible. It got broken into last year. No one seemed to care. There was a bunch of equipment and furniture in there gathering dust that subsequently got removed. Now it's just a void of shadows and concrete.

Walking back to the schoolyard, I checked the time on my phone. Still fifteen minutes before the end of lunch. I wasn't going to be late for assembly after.

Rose, on the other hand...

"Hey."

Ignore the whispers. Avoid the airborne fruit. Very soon, this will all change.

"Hey."

Rose's attention doesn't come easily. She's giggling with a bunch of other girls watching a stupid video on her phone.

"I said, 'Hey!'"

Rose looked at me and grimaced. "Don't I see enough of you at home already?"

"I need a word. It's important."

She raised her eyebrows and waited.

"Do you want everyone else to hear as well?"

She sighed, surrendered her phone to the others and got up to face me. "This had better be good."

I grabbed her arm and pulled her away from the crowd.

"What are you doing?" she whined.

"Cool it, okay?"

"Just – just hold on," she said, forcing us to stop. "What do you want?"

I made a face. "This is going to sound crazy."

"Just spit it out."

"Mom's here."

"What?"

"Mom. She's here at school."

Rose stared at me. "That's impossible."

Of course it's impossible. But I'm dealing with you, birdbrain. "I know, right?" I said.

"So… what–"

"So, let's go." I pulled Rose away. I made her walk with me.

"You've seen her?" she demanded.

"Yes, she's with Poppy now. She's hiding away out near the back. The cops are looking for her, of course."

"She… she escaped?"

"Real genius, we got here."

"How?"

"Think she had some medical thing, and they took her to a hospital or something and she gave the guards the slip."

"Oh my God."

We walked by the outer buildings.

"What are we going to do?"

I nodded, as if considering her question. "I don't know. She seems super pissed though."

"She would be! We put her in prison!"

"She's talking about some other crazy stuff too. She reckons the cops have found some hidden camera that was in Georgie's room and they're coming after us again."

I added that part in, mostly to just see what she'd say.

"What?" Rose snarled. "Just – do you believe her?"

"How should I know? Ask her yourself."

Walking through the trees now.

"Where the hell is she?"

"I told you, she's hiding out here. Round about that old toolshed."

"Ugh. Gross."

"Well, you don't want anyone seeing her before us, do you?"

"I wonder what Simone's going to say."

"We'll probably have to stop them killing each other."

Rose chuckled, and for a second there, I felt like the whole thing was real. Mom really was out of jail. She really wanted to see us. She was pissed, but all was forgiven.

There would be a new chapter in our lives.

"I don't see them," Rose said.

"The door's open. They must be in the shed."

"It looks dark…"

I waited until we were right at the edge.

"Hello?" Rose called. "Mom, are you there? Poppy?"

I quickly ripped the red band from Rose's hair and gave her a mighty shove into the shed.

"Leanne! Now!"

I pulled the door shut as Rose screamed, lunging back at me.

Leanne forced the chair she'd been guarding underneath the handle and held it in place.

Rose banged and howled and attempted to force it back open.

"Will this hold?" Leanne asked, forgetting we'd just tested it minutes earlier.

"It'll be fine."

I set Rose's headband over my own hair.

"How long do I have to stand here?" Leanne asked.

"I shouldn't be too long," I replied.

"Violet, open the door!" Rose yelled. "This isn't funny!"

"I'm not trying to be funny," I hollered back, applying some cherry lipstick I'd swiped from Rose's cabinet this morning. "I'm taking back what you stole from me!"

CHAPTER 69

Shoulders back. Head straight. Lips pouty. Eyelashes batting. Tits together. Alright, I made up that last one. I don't care how my tits look, or should I say, how *Rose's* look.

It's been a while. But it's all coming back to me. This isn't a mask I'm wearing, except in the sense that my whole body is a mask.

A rose by color. A rose by name.

By the time Rose gets out of that shed, her whole world will be gone.

"Rose! Rose! Over here, Rose!"

I'm looking for my place in the assembly hall. I thought I'd take my usual spot next to the coordinator up front, but no, that wouldn't be right. Rose has all these so-called friends she has to mingle with.

"Rose?"

"Coming!" I called back.

And now I have to look them all in the eye. I have to remember their names. I know that one's Tiffany something, and I think one of them is Barbara or Barbie–

"What did that weirdo sister of yours want?" I was asked by the time there were six or seven of them around me.

"Who? Violet?" I mumbled.

Eyes on me.

"Right… She was just yelling at me for stealing her nomination for school captaincy–"

"Pfft."

"As if anyone would vote for her anyway."

"She's such a know-it-all."

"She is smart though, Violet," I said defensively. "So, she does know what she's talking about."

They looked at each other, jaws dropping.

Groan.

"I mean, got ya!" I squealed.

They nodded and laughed.

"Hey, Rose," a voice piped up behind me. "Do you have my music book? I need it back."

I glanced over my shoulder. Wincing. Shudder.

Poppy was standing there, at first looking confused. And then she didn't know what to say.

"I think I left it in my locker," I said quietly.

"Well, can you please come and get it for me then?" she pressed.

"Uh, I'm not sure there's really time to–"

"Or I can just ask *Violet* to help me."

Okay. She got me.

"Back in a minute, guys," I muttered, and stepped back through the row.

"Aw, Rose, what are you–"

I shirked the hands clawing for me and rushed to Poppy's side. We walked up the aisle and exited the auditorium just as the assembly was getting started.

"Alright, what the hell are you doing?" Poppy demanded, once we were outside. "Where's Rose?"

"Look, I'll tell you," I said, "but you have to promise you won't give me away."

"I promise nothing."

I shook my head. "Alright. I had Leanne help me, and we lured her out to that old toolshed at the back of the school."

"And?"

"Leanne's guarding the door."

"You locked her in there?"

"It's just…" I waited for some kids to go by us. "It's just for the assembly."

"What are you going to do in there?"

"Come and see."

"No, I have Music class." She hesitated. "I'm not happy about this."

"What do you care? You're not involved."

"People find out you're doing this, and no one's going to believe us when we say who we are."

I shrugged.

"Why can't you just let it go?"

"You give them an inch, they take a mile," I said quietly. "This time I hit back. This time she remembers not to mess with me. There's no other way to protect myself…"

CHAPTER 70

I have imagined this already.

"…next item then… We have the results from the student president election…"

I have called it into manifestation.

"…the name of the winner is inside this envelope…"

I have heard this voice in my dreams.

"…Ah yes, of course, boys and girls, please welcome to the stage…"

Violet Greene. Violet Greene. Violet Greene.

Violet Greene.

"…Miss Rose Greene!"

It doesn't matter. It doesn't matter that it's not my name. It's close enough. That's still me walking up here. That's still my shadow darkening the stage.

"Thank you," I said into the mike. "Thank you very much."

They're still clapping. We'll have to give them a moment. And I won't complain, because I have heard this clapping already over and over and over again. It's music to my ears.

"Thank you," I said with a beaming, bright red, realistic smile. "You're all so wonderful. You're all so great."

And what you say is what you are.

"Every single one of you is amazing and fantastic and super-duper excellent for making it to your senior year!" I shouted. "Give it up for yourselves! Give yourselves the applause you deserve!"

And there it is. Louder than ever.

I love this sound.

* * *

Have you been paying attention? Have you been watching me, Rose Greene, on this stage, and understood its implication?

How does our future sit with you?

I've just shown you how I could imagine an audience and then have it come into existence. This is no frivolous desire. This is my sole passion. This is all I have. Nothing else matters. I must be on top.

Front row. First in line. Perfect grades. Complete organization. Power at my fingertips.

What I think is. What I say goes.

I want you to take both my hands now. I want you to close your eyes with me. I want us to imagine my future together. You've already seen where I've come from. Now you can see where I am. So, have you been paying attention? Can you see what the future holds for little, old me?

* * *

I'm halfway into my directive of how we're going to make this the most amazing senior year on earth, when someone shows up at the auditorium entrance and forces both doors open with a loud *BANG*.

"Uh – Uh, yes – uh – as I was saying–"

Their heads are turning. Something's going on. Who is that, who's just walked in here?

"Just a moment."

I looked over my shoulder for the student coordinator and was aghast to see she was hobbling off down the side of the stage already. Students and teachers both were making their way up to the entrance.

"Hey," I said, trembling. "I'm not finished here."

A few moments later, I felt a panic wave through the audience.

One of the teachers came forward and told everyone to remain in their seats, but no one was listening. A couple of Rose's friends moved up through the rows to motion to me, below the stage.

"What's going on?"

"Something's happened with Violet," one of the girls answered. "Everyone's going up to that toolshed at the back of the school."

Uh-oh.

CHAPTER 71

I can see her now. Standing on top of the toolshed. Crowds gathering around her. Rose is telling them everything under the guise of me. She's pretending even better than me. She is, as she's always been, the better actress.

Am I to be condemned as a fraud again? Am I to be called a liar? I had them. I had them right there. I was on that stage. I had their attention. I had the applause.

But as we all know, the red ball rolls.

Out from one cup.

Into another…

"Where is she?" someone's shouting. "Where's Violet?"

I have nothing to hide anymore.

I don't care.

This is me done.

Over and finished with.

"Here she is!" someone else is yelling.

I feel their hands go into my back.

"I've got her, right here!"

I'm being pushed through the crowd. Everyone's making way.

I'm getting closer to the front. The gap is widening.

I'm starting to see… what's ahead…

"That's not her, you moron! That's her sister Rose!"

Oh well, I guess I'm still fooling someone.

"It's okay," I protested. "I'm not going to fight you."

As I'm looking around though, the crowd don't seem to be looking for a fight. In fact, they're barely looking at me at all.

They're looking at–

"Wait," I gasped. "Where is she?"

As I pushed through the last of them, I saw the toolshed's door was wide open. The only people standing in front of it were teachers, keeping everyone else away.

On the floor of the shed. Inside. I see shoes pointing up.

"I'm sorry, Rose, you can't!" the teachers are forcing me away.

"Oh yes, I can!"

I have to see. I have to see what she's done.

So I manage to break through. The sunlight blocked, from this dark cage.

Shoes. Like I said. Shoes pointing up.

I can see her hand too. It's half open, but she's holding onto something. I crouched down, resisting the adults behind me, and pulled the object from her fingertips.

"You can't!" they screamed. "That's evidence!"

My glasses. Dripping with blood. "I dropped them," I whispered in disbelief.

"She's done this, your sister! She was caught in the act! She was seen stabbing this poor child to death!"

Like before.

It's happened again.

"Leanne!!!"

CHAPTER 72

I did this. It's all my fault. I've killed Leanne. I know what happens next. I know how I'm supposed to blame Rose – or blame 'Violet', as now I've taken Rose's identity.

It's not the truth though, is it?

Leanne was *my* friend. I was responsible for her. I knew if she got too close to Rose, something like this might happen.

"Come on now, Rose," one of the teachers demanded. "Give me those glasses."

I wasn't having any of it. Suddenly I couldn't control my feelings. I became swept up in an uncontrollable river of emotion.

Confusion to distraught.

Distraught to anger.

Anger to misery.

Misery to insanity.

I must be insane. I must be insane to have done this to my only friend. If only there'd been some other way…

"She'll pay for this." I seethed, in the arms of adults, being led away. "We can't let her get away…"

But let's be clear. Rose had gotten away.

Somehow she'd broken the lock, and dragged Leanne's body into the dark where she'd been.

I wondered where she'd gone after that.

I wondered what her next move would be.

* * *

Okay. I've calmed down now. No more crazy thoughts. I'm just sitting in the student coordinator's office with a cup of water, waiting for her. Her name's Sarah. Like my mother's name was Sarah. I'd never really thought about that until now. Perhaps it explains some things. Perhaps it's a good omen.

"Oh, Rose." She sighed, closing the door behind her. "Rose, Rose, Rose."

I can see already we're getting off on the wrong foot.

"This is beyond terrible. To think she had us all fooled. You– you didn't know anything about what she was going to do, did you? Honey?"

I swallowed. "Can you please not stand over me?"

"Sorry, my love. So sorry." She pulled a chair from the corner and positioned it on an angle to where I was sitting. "There. Is that better?"

I nodded.

"The police are on their way, as you know. They're going to want to ask you a lot of questions."

"Did you call Simone?"

"Yes, yes, of course, she's also on her way. I can get her on the phone for you now, if you want."

"No," I said. "That's okay. I'll just sit here with you."

Silence. Half a minute went by.

"Did Violet say anything to you?" the woman asked, catching me off guard.

"About that. It's probably best I clarify some things."

Knock, knock.

"Just a moment," the coordinator said, getting up.

I heard her open the door, the sound of the busy corridor sweeping in.

"I'm with someone."

"The police?"

"No, a student. What's wrong?"

"I need to get on record with you before they get here."

"What on earth for?"

"You're aware… I had some sessions with Violet."

"Oh Lord." She came back round to me. "Wait there, Rose. I'll be back shortly."

I found myself nodding.

The door opened and closed, and I was out of the chair.

The voice of the person she'd been with, I recognized. It was Ned, the welfare officer, whom I'd jokingly made advances towards. God only knows what he was saying about me.

I wondered if this time they'd listen.

CHAPTER 73

I'm out of here. She can't help me, so I'm just gone. Feet across the carpet, hand to the door. Down the corridor, the ceiling dips and rises like the ocean's waves. I'm not stable. My thoughts aren't organized. I should have every alibi I need as I was on that stage while Leanne was being murdered. But somehow, I just know it's not going to work out for me.

Hand to the door again. I feel faint. I'm feeling dizzy. I launched myself through the girls' bathroom. And I can't believe it. I'm right there in her peripherals. My figure sliding along the mirror showcase. Running faucet. Water on my fingers and cheeks. Swipe across. Find the app. There's still time. There's still time to–

Snap.

I jumped with a start. She's just closed the make-up case and is setting it down into her carry bag, which lands over her shoulder. I am withered. I am weary. My cheap imitation has deteriorated. Next to me, it's Rose. Without any question or mistake.

You'd know those cherry lips anywhere.

"You're in trouble now." She chuckled. "Everyone's looking for you."

"Well done," I mustered.

"Pardon me?"

"Congratulations."

She rolled her eyes. "Who told you I was pregnant?"

"Okay." I sighed, crossing my arms. "That's a good one."

Rose shook her head and took a few steps toward me. "You know as I was leaving, I saw your glasses in Leanne's hand."

"That was a nice touch."

"Pardon?"

"You put them there to frame me for the murder."

"Yes. All part of my master plan."

"I wonder where you put the knife," I said. "I wonder if it has your prints on it."

"My prints?"

"Or will it have mine?" I asked. "Because you're trying to set me up."

"No one's going to believe that," Rose scoffed. "Don't even bother. I was in the auditorium, remember? Ask anyone."

"You were in the auditorium?" I nodded. "Just like we were both with Jessica the night Georgie was killed?"

A smile touched Rose's lips. "Oh. I get it."

"You get what?"

"You're recording me right now, aren't you?"

A burst of cold air caught in my throat. "No– No, I mean, no, I–"

She reached into my pocket and extracted my cell phone. I kept completely still as she lowered it onto the counter beside us.

"For the record then," Rose said, "Poppy and I have long suspected you were responsible for the deaths."

"Shut up."

"It was *you* who left your bedroom that night. You, who went outside. You, who came back in and went into Georgie's room."

"Lies."

"I just said it was me in court and to the police, because I was trying to protect you."

"You're a complete psychopath. I should have known it was you all along."

"No," Rose said firmly. "That's you, Violet. You're the crazy one."

I picked the cell off the counter and erased the recording.

"Okay? There. You can say the truth now. No one else will hear you."

Rose's eyes fluttered. "Do you really think I killed that boy?"

I decided to answer truthfully. "No, I always thought it was Poppy."

"Well, for all we know Poppy killed Leanne too," Rose said. "One of us was seen – from a distance; one of us was seen fleeing the scene. But really, it could have been any one of us."

"Except me."

"I suspect you," Rose declared. "You suspect Poppy. I wonder – does Poppy suspect me?"

"You'd have to ask her."

"Uh-huh." She lowered her eyes. "I think I'm all out of words, now. It's been nice knowing you, sis. But hey, maybe when you turn twenty-one they'll ship you upstate, and I can knock out seeing you and Mom in one visit."

"I'll look forward to it."

"Goodbye, Violet."

I watched her turn and walk away from me. I figured I had about two minutes before she told a teacher where to find me.

CHAPTER 74

It's not right. It's all wrong. She got me again. She knew I was recording her. And even after that, she couldn't bring herself to admit the truth.

Maybe it's just about playing the part. Getting into character. She needs to keep consistent for her audience. She's still on set after all. The only way to beat a lie detector, is if you believe the lie you're saying.

What lies have I told myself?

* * *

Goodbye, Rose. Goodbye, Poppy. Goodbye, school. Goodbye, Leanne.

I've got to get out of here. No one can help me, so I'm just gone. I've said it before, and I'll say it again.

They're getting smaller. Those buildings behind me. There's a stretch of flat grass going for a while. But if I make it to those trees at the end, they won't catch me. Not today, anyway.

I guess I probably should be running. It will make the journey faster. But I can't speed things up. I've got to slow everything down, I've got to figure out the reality of what's happened, I've got to assess this level of danger. Am I really as screwed as I think I am?

I stopped mid-pace.

"No," I whispered.

No, I'm not. I can prove I didn't kill her. I can prove it was Rose in that shed.

I pulled out my cell and scrolled through my contacts. Poppy's name on the screen.

But I just wonder. I wonder if Rose has gotten to her first. Would Poppy take her side? Would Poppy want to put me away instead of Rose?

"Why would she?"

Of course, she could always take a neutral position, not want to get involved. That was a Poppy thing to do.

"Well. Only one way to find out."

* * *

Everyone to their places. I sit to their right. Rose sits in the middle. Poppy sits on the left. And wherever we sit, whatever the game is, it always ends the same way.

Simone is at the head of this table in the conference room, on my right. At the other end is the school principal, the student coordinator, and two detectives. We've been here before. We've lived through this experience.

All we need to say is our truth.

* * *

An hour later, I've never felt more safe.

"Let's go over this again," the lead detective said, exasperated. "You're Poppy, right? You're the youngest one, aren't you?"

"They're quadruplets," Simone fired back.

"Technically I am the youngest," Poppy added. "I came out last."

"Are you sure?" I asked, leaning over. "I thought Daisy was last."

"No, Daisy was after Rose," Poppy replied.

"I thought Lily came after me," Rose interjected.

"Okay – time!" He glanced at his partner. "How many of them are there?"

"Don't worry," Simone said coldly. "The fourth child is dead."

A moment of silence.

"Walk me through this," the detective began again. "Just so we're clear. Poppy. After Violet locked Rose in the shed–"

"No," Poppy corrected. "Rose locked Violet in the shed."

"Okay, after Rose locked Violet in the shed–"

His partner started grabbing his arm. They looked over some notes together.

"It says here that Violet locked Rose in the shed. That's… according to Violet…"

"That's correct," I said.

"But over here, Rose says she locked Lily in the shed. Why does that name keep coming up? Is she another student here?"

Rose shook her head. "She's our secret sister."

Poppy and I giggled.

The detective took his spectacles off and tossed them on his notes. He pointed at Rose. "You say you were on the stage giving your speech, which everyone was a party to."

Rose smiled.

He pointed to me. "You say you put Rose in the shed and put on her make up to pretend to be her and go on stage."

I smiled.

He pointed to Poppy. "You say after you helped Rose lock Violet in the shed, you put on Rose's make-up and went on stage to give the speech."

Poppy smiled.

"If that's true, Poppy, then why do people say Rose was visited by Poppy before she went on stage? Are you saying that Rose was impersonating you, while you were impersonating her at the same time?"

"Sometimes we switch," Poppy said.

"What does that mean?"

"Right now," Poppy continued, "I could be Rose and you wouldn't know it."

The detective sighed.

I leaned over again. "I could be Poppy."

"And I could be Violet!" Rose laughed.

"Is that what happened, Rose?" the detective asked. "Did you and Poppy switch places?"

"No. I told you already. I went on stage and gave my speech. You can ask anyone."

"That's… that's right after you locked Violet in the shed."

"No." Rose grinned. "After I locked Lily in the shed."

Poppy and I started laughing.

The detective folded his arms. He looked like he was ready for home-time.

"So. We've answered your questions," Simone stated. "Are we done now? Or will I be calling our attorney?"

The detective straightened up. He slowly lowered his hands to the table.

"It's clear you girls aren't being honest," he said. "It's a shame, considering someone's lost their life today."

Simone stood from her chair. "Girls."

We began to stand.

"Not so fast," the detective said. "We're arresting Violet."

"No!" I squealed.

"You've got nothing," Simone scolded. "You've got a pair of glasses in someone's hands. You can't get a conviction on that."

"We have one eyewitness who saw the murder take place – and later we have multiple eyewitnesses that have seen one of the sisters dragging the body into the shed, before fleeing the scene," the partner said.

"But that doesn't prove *Violet* killed her," Simone argued.

"There's also a report from the welfare officer," the lead detective explained. "Without going into detail, it's been claimed that she's a pathological liar."

"Well, he would say that," I retorted. "After he tried to rape me."

"He–" The student coordinator gasped. "He *what?*"

"We didn't have much discourse during our sessions," I said plainly. "Intercourse, on the other hand…"

"That is a very serious accusation, young lady," the principal said. "I hope you know what you're–"

Knock, knock, knock.

The detective's partner got up and went to the door.

No one seemed to know what was going to happen next.

I could see on the detective's face that he wanted to arrest me. But he was also reluctant about it. Sure enough, there would be further problems down the line…

The partner came back from a quick visit to the corridor. He whispered something in the lead detective's ear. He nodded.

"Alright, she's not under arrest for now," the detective conceded. "But there is someone here to see you. I would think it's in your best interest to give them your time."

"Never mind about that," Simone said swiftly. "Come along, girls."

We followed her around the side of the table.

The detective looked at me knowingly as we passed.

I stopped and turned back to him. "Who's here?"

He inhaled sharply and got up. "Your father."

CHAPTER 75

Of course, he wasn't actually here. Not in person anyway. But I'm sure you've put two and two together by now. A familiar face awaits in the corridor. I see Simone flinch immediately, and she's scurrying to put a barrier between us.

"Who called you?" she demanded. "I'll have their badge."

"Relax," Detective Burke reassured her. "I'm just here to bring a message to Violet from her father, Nicholas."

"After what he's done to them," Simone thundered. "After what he's been put away for. You must be absolutely insane."

The prior lead detective came out from the conference room and interrupted. "I thought you said you were their father."

"Detective Gordon Burke. I worked on a case that involved the girls some time ago. I have a recorded message from their father to Violet. A judge has signed a singular exemption to the restrictions that would otherwise prevent the father from making contact."

"Ha!" Simone cried. "You're wasting your time. Violet doesn't want any messages from her father. Come along, Violet."

She grabbed my arm to lead me away.

"No," I resisted.

"What?" Simone snapped.

"I want to hear the message."

She bent her knees a touch so we were on eye level.

"It would be very unwise, I assure you," she hissed. "Don't you forget all I've done for you."

"I just want to hear it," I insisted. "It won't affect anything."

Simone blinked. "Fine. You find your own way home. Maybe the police will arrest you after all." She put her arm around Rose and led the other two away.

I watched her go.

She kept turning back, as though she was expecting me to follow her or perhaps, unsure about her decision to leave me alone with them.

"We'll sit in on this message," the lead detective said to Burke, referring to himself and his partner – maybe even the principal and coordinator as well.

"I don't have a problem with that," Burke said politely. "What do you say, Violet?"

I gave a look of disgust and motioned for Burke to walk with me.

"I'll deal with you on my own."

CHAPTER 76

When a tree falls, it makes a sound. The past is like an ocean of falling trees, crashing underwater. I can cover my ears. I can close my eyes. But we'll never escape the grisly echoes of our dark fable.

"You want a cigarette?" Detective Burke offered once we exited the building.

"No," I said awkwardly.

"Are you sure?" He plucked a silver case from his jacket and opened it so I could see all the smokes lined up.

"I'm not in a… smoking mood."

He raised his eyebrows and extracted one of the cigarettes. He proceeded to light it and inhale.

Snap.

The case returned to his pocket.

"Are you going to give me the message now?"

He shrugged. "I thought we might have a chat first."

"About what?"

"I guess we could start with what happened at school today."

"Oh yeah…" I said, stalling.

Stalling to study him.

Detective Burke had lost some weight since I'd last seen him. He wasn't skinny, but a lot more refined than our previous meetings, years ago. He was also completely clean-shaven and had doused himself in cologne. His appearance was slick. But his eyes were tired.

"I guess you wouldn't tell me if you knew anything about what had happened anyway," he muttered. "Let's go up here."

I followed his lead as we walked towards the staff car park.

"You're taking this personal, aren't you?" I prodded. "You think if you'd got one of us for Georgie, we wouldn't be here now."

"The thought has occurred," he replied casually. "You know, last time we spoke, you were much younger. I wonder if you're able to articulate a clearer picture now you've matured."

"Well, I am only seventeen," I said in a seductive tone. "I'm still a child."

"Not all children are innocent. Not all children… are good."

"One of us has been a naughty girl, hasn't she?"

He stopped.

I saw rage in his eyes for a split second. Then it faded.

He took a puff from his smoke to calm himself.

"Do you have a heart, Violet?" Burke asked. "Or would you say you're heartless?"

"Well, you know, it's not an absolute state. I'm sure everyone has heartless moments now and again. Especially big, strong men like you."

"Your father was strong. He was a big, strong man, wasn't he?"

I swallowed. "Did something happen to him?"

"Why don't we go for a drive?" he suggested. "And I'll tell you all about it on the way."

"Where do you want to drive me, Detective?"

He gave a light smile. Then shook his head. "If you don't come, you'll…" He trailed off and put his back to me walking to the car.

"You'll never know," Burke whispered.

CHAPTER 77

Take it back. Turn back the clock. Reverse the outcome. Experience regret. The universe wants these things from me. The problem is that it invalidates my experience. It invalidates our true reality. There is no other way. Before you judge me, you must first find yourself in my shoes. Until you understand the world from my point of view, you understand nothing.

* * *

I remember the day I fell out of love with my father. For Poppy, for Rose… it could have been a different day. You would have to ask them. But for me, it was during the car ride to the station. I was in the passenger seat next to him. So I got a look up close. He was unbelievably stressed. We'd spent the previous night at his house near the city, but it wasn't until that morning it became clear our mother wasn't going to be free any time soon. He'd already chosen his path. He'd walked away from us. He saw Sarah and his three girls as a package deal, and it wasn't a package he wanted. He'd rather screw the hot twenty-something-year-old receptionist. These may be common actions. These actions may be forgiven by society. They may even be forgiven by the small children he's abandoned.

But cut to me years later. Cut to me when I have the intellectual strength to challenge his decisions. Everyone's already moved on. But now is the time. Ask for my forgiveness.

"Will you stop it?" Dad shouted in the car, breaking me from my faraway thoughts.

I looked up to the rearview mirror and saw Rose and Poppy both shaken. They must have been fighting about something. Trivial, of course. Anything to take our mind off the present moment.

"I'll tell you right now, Jessica won't put up with your misbehaving," Dad scolded. "I don't want to be getting any calls from her, going on about you guys not getting along. Seriously."

So you wait. You wait before speaking. You wait until you think it's safe.

When he's calmed down.

But Dad was in a tough place right now. Every time before when he'd had a problem with us, he could just dump that burden back on Mom, let her deal with it. He could forget us until it was his weekend again.

So that's how we come to him saying, "We only ever wanted one child, you know. That's how it's supposed to work. Have you any idea of the amount of work one child brings? But no. Our few weeks of sexual activity in an otherwise unhappy marriage, were enough to give us four little blessings. Not just the one like normal. Not even double that. Not even triple. Before we knew it, we had four of you, little monsters, to contend with. You know you spend so much time obsessing about what you're going to call your baby when it arrives. You think about that one special girl who is to become your daughter. Or, heaven forbid, a son. But no. Of course not. Your mother fell open like a fat sow in the farmyard and gave birth to a litter. You know, I just pray Jessica has the strength to deal with you. If I ever have to choose between her and you, oh God. Let's just say you don't want to find out what happens…"

But we already know what happens.

We already know who you'd choose.

You've already chosen her.

And I'm sure, I'm sure Jessica is a wonderful lady. I'm sure we're going to have a great time in the big house away from you.

I can see it now.

She'll be like an angel. The mother we always wished we had. She'll show us how to become women. And when it's all over. When you're looking back at your life.

You'll say you're sorry.

"Bye, Dad," Rose said getting out of the car.

"See you," Poppy said, squeezing his hand, before sliding across.

They opened the trunk outside.

"Well?" Dad asked me. "Are you getting out?"

But you're not sorry today.

* * *

It's supposed to break me. This is our earth-shattering moment. Burke's basically an idiot. I can see where this is going. I can see what's ahead. But I'll let this play out some more. This is still important for my rite of passage.

Look down. Into the palm of my hands. I'm holding Detective Burke's phone while he's driving behind the wheel. There's a video playing on the phone. Dad's message, apparently.

It's just some surveillance from prison. Dad's walking out in the yard in his big orange jumpsuit. He seems like he's trying to get near the fence.

Some of the other prisoners are following him.

I looked to Detective Burke to observe his expression. Some of that rage is back. He's all tense. He knows he shouldn't be doing this. He's crossing a line here.

I looked back to the screen and watched my father get stabbed by the men.

"He died a child abuser," Burke stated. "That's how he'll be remembered."

"You condone this?"

He flinched a little. "No."

"You're sure?"

"Aren't you going to ask me why I've shown you this?"

"I take it a judge didn't sign off on it."

Burke let out a wheezing cough. "Uh. No." He straightened up. "I'm no longer working with the police. My career's over. But I still have friends."

I handed the phone back to him.

"You seem to be taking this well," he observed.

"You're a sicko for showing me that," I replied.

He nodded. "I admit, I'm conflicted."

"Do you hate me?"

The question flustered him. "It's… It's not… It's…"

"Why would you show me that footage? Are you trying to give me nightmares? You realize, you can still get in trouble for it. Maybe you think they won't believe me."

"I'm sure you could say all sorts of things to damage me," Burke replied. "It hasn't stopped you before, has it?"

"Just give it to me straight, coach. Stop trying to manipulate me."

"Alright."

The car slowed down.

We were just in a residential street.

Parked outside a house.

"Do you know why we're here?" he asked.

I stared at him.

"We're here, because it's where she would have wanted me to bring you."

I exhaled. "Who's 'she'?"

A pause. "Am I going crazy here? Or did that video have no effect on you?"

"What reaction were you looking for? He died a child abuser, remember."

"But he wasn't, was he? You. And the other two. You *lied*."

"Right. We lied. And now you want me to feel bad because the lies got him killed?"

He shook his head. "How can you justify lying about such a thing? Whatever the circumstances are, whoever you're protecting, you know, there are real victims in this world. Real people who are abused." He swallowed. "Ashley was one of them…"

"Ashley?"

"She used to live in that house next to us. She grew up there. And one morning she woke up. And… She was being raped…" He drew in an emotional breath. "She made me drive here the day she died. She… opened up, told me her secret. That's… why she was helping you. That's why she believed you. Even though the evidence suggested…"

"Am I supposed to know who you're talking about?"

"My partner. Don't even pretend you don't remember her."

Her face appeared in my mind. "Oh yeah… She didn't have such a great end, did she?"

Burke's hand shot out and he grabbed me by the throat.

He threw my head back into the window behind me.

"Stop!" I choked.

He stared into my eyes…

Then released me.

I gasped for air and went to open the door. He quickly locked it.

Then he grabbed my arms. "I know it was you, Violet. I know *you* killed her."

"What?"

"We're done playing games."

"I don't know what you're talking about."

"You heartless Medusa. You poisonous wretch."

I considered. "Take your hands off me and I'll talk."

He let go.

I tidied myself up.

"You killed her," he stated.

"No." I lowered my eyes. "What's your name?"

"My name?"

"Your first name."

"Gordon."

"Gordon. Look at me. I didn't kill Ashley. I also didn't kill Georgie. And I didn't kill my best friend Leanne today at school."

He shook his head. "The welfare officer said he was certain you were the one who–"

I laughed. "That prick knows nothing."

Gordon's lips trembled with frustration.

"Did you love her?" I asked. "Did you love Ashley?"

"As a friend," he answered.

"As I loved my friend, Leanne," I said. "I know what you're going through. But you've got the wrong sister."

"Do you know who is behind it then? Rose? Poppy?"

I nodded. "I didn't always. But I do now."

"So," Gordon pleaded, "tell me who…"

CHAPTER 78

He's been crying. He's as weak as a kitten. The man's so lost, he's forgotten where he is. I let his face rest on my shoulder, and I run my fingernails through his hair. There, there, I say. There, there. His weakness makes me feel stronger.

The car's headlights pour down our darkened street. I should have been home by now. I bet Simone is worried. I bet she's pacing the whole house.

"This can't go on," Gordon declared once we were parked. "She needs to come forward."

"I'll talk to her," I assured him. "Just don't do anything crazy. You need to keep it together."

"I know." A pause. "I'm sorry about earlier. I shouldn't have made you watch that video."

"I'm glad you did."

"Why?"

"He finally got what he deserved."

I went to open my door. Unlocked this time.

"Wait," Gordon said, grabbing my arm.

The door swung open with one of my feet out.

"How can you say he deserved that, if you weren't telling the truth?"

"In a way, I was telling the truth. The suffering he imposed on us was green-lit by our disgusting society."

"Well, he was charged and sentenced."

"You're missing the point. He was allowed to abandon us, his family. We were left impoverished while he got to keep his riches to himself and bang his receptionist. That's abuse. That's what deserves a life sentence."

I stepped out of the car and closed the passenger door.

"You're twisted," I heard him mutter aloud.

He'd be kidding himself if he expected me to explain it further.

And I don't have to. Not to him. Not to you. Not to the world.

What makes you so perfect anyway?

* * *

Home. All cuddly and warm. Resting before bed. Well, it's not that late, I suppose. Dinner shouldn't be too cold.

I opened the front door, and like I guessed, everyone was waiting for me. Simone is at the kitchen bench, holding her wine. Rose is on the recliner of the adjacent lounge. Poppy's on the sofa. I set my schoolbag down in the hallway and walked briskly up to the bench.

"So?" Simone said eagerly. "What happened? What did he say?"

"Where's my dinner?" I replied. "I'll have it now, please."

"You're not getting dinner," Simone said, biting her lip, "until we get some answers."

I looked over my shoulder and saw Rose had gotten up from her chair and was walking towards me.

"If you want to talk about it," I said, "then it's all coming out. Right here. Tonight. No more lies from anyone."

"That seems fair," Simone replied.

Rose stood next to me. I looked to her. "Well?"

She shrugged. "Whatever."

I looked past her. "And *you*?"

Poppy sighed. She got up and went to the side of the counter. "I don't have anything to hide."

I looked across the three of them. "Dad's dead."

"Oh," Poppy said in surprise.

I felt Rose breathe in deeply.

"The detective showed me surveillance from the prison where he got shanked in the yard."

Simone shook her head. "Animal."

"I don't have any regrets," I said. "Anyone else?"

"No," Rose said coldly.

Poppy covered her mouth to hide the emotion.

"Don't even think about crying," I snapped at her. "He was going to leave us in the care of that lunatic, remember?"

Poppy shuddered. "He didn't know what she was like."

"He still left you with her," Simone said. "It could have gone on for years if they hadn't been stopped."

"Am I not allowed to grieve?" Poppy asked.

"Let her," Rose said. "Let her have her sadness. She can't help it anyway. It's biological."

"But do *you* feel anything?" I asked Rose.

She shrugged. "I don't know."

A pause. "Good answer," I said.

"What else happened?" Simone asked me. "What does he know?"

"He knows one of us killed his partner," I said. "I'm not a hundred percent sure, but he said things to make me believe he's seen some vision of the actual murder itself."

"What?" Rose demanded.

"Hold on," Simone said. "What do you mean – killed his partner? What's that about?"

"You remember the woman detective, don't you?" I asked. "From when this all started. Ashley something."

"Yes, I remember her." Simone sipped her wine. "He thinks one of you killed her?"

I shrugged. "It wasn't me."

"Nor me," Rose added.

Eyes turned to Poppy.

"What?" she squealed. "I didn't have anything to do with it!"

"Hey!" I shouted over her. "I said we need to be honest here!"

She shook her head. "I am being honest."

I turned to Rose. "It was you, wasn't it?"

Rose crossed her arms and said nothing.

"Alright, forget about the detective," I said. "Maybe he's mistaken. There's still that other matter we should talk about."

"Which one's that?" Simone asked.

"Who killed Leanne?" I asked. "I seriously want to know."

Silence.

I looked at Rose.

Rose looked at Poppy.

Poppy looked at me.

"Well. You can tell me how you got out of the toolshed to start with."

Rose chuckled. "I heard it happening outside. I heard one of you stabbing her. Of course, by the time Poppy opened the door, Leanne was already dead."

My eyes widened. "Wait – you were there, Poppy?"

Poppy blinked. "No. I was in class."

"She was there," Rose stated. "But she freaked out and ran away when I started dragging Leanne's body into the shed. I was going to call for help, but I was spotted before I could do anything."

"You still had time to plant my glasses in her hand though," I snapped.

She grinned.

"No!" Poppy protested. "I didn't do it!"

"I told you where to find her," I reflected. "Did you go to get that music book you wanted?"

She shook her head. "I went to class."

"There was no class," Rose chimed in. "We had assembly!"

"Oh right. So, I was somewhere else. No big deal."

"What did you tell the detective?" Simone asked me.

"I had to give him something. I told him who I legitimately believe killed Leanne."

"Who did you say?"

I shook my head. "I'm not saying."

"Hey," Simone said. "We just agreed–"

"Well, they're not coming clean, so why should I?"

Silence. I could hear all three of them breathing now.

"What are we going to do about this?" Simone asked.

"I talked him down tonight," I explained, "but Detective Burke will be back. He wants justice for his partner. One of you – whoever is responsible – one of you is going to have to kill him."

"Why don't *you* kill him?" Rose fired back.

"Well, he's not after me anymore!" I laughed. "Besides, one of you owes me for Leanne. You don't see me running around killing your friends, do you?"

"No one's killing anyone!" Simone yelled. "God! Can we all just be sane for five seconds?"

"*She* should do it," Rose suggested, pointing.

"Me?" Simone cried.

"You want to be a good mother to us," Rose continued. "You want to protect us?"

Simone looked at us uncertainly. "Wait. Wait, just now. Did one of you actually kill that girl today?"

"Hello?" Rose sang. "Who do you think you're living with?"

"Yeah," I added. "If you're not careful, we might kill you next."

I looked across to Poppy and saw her wipe her eyes with a smile.

Simone's gaze shifted along the circle. "I think I'm going to bed now. We can talk about this another time."

As she went to leave, I grabbed hold of her wrist. "You still owe me dinner."

"It's in the fridge," Simone said, shaking off my hand. "You can heat it up yourself."

I jumped from my chair and blocked her way out.

Rose moved in from the side.

Poppy came up behind her.

"Look, look, look," Simone said, trembling. "I'm not going to say anything. I love you guys. You're my precious girls."

"Get my dinner, Mom," I ordered.

Simone got my dinner.

CHAPTER 79

When you've slept in a house for long enough, you become adjusted to its sounds. You can tell the difference between a footstep on carpet or tile. You can tell the difference between a window opening or closing. You can judge distance; where a sound came from. You know how each occupant moves, and what their regular timetable is.

It's after midnight, and I'm in bed, staring at the ceiling, trying to sleep. I'm also listening to see if there's anything out of the ordinary going on, if one of my sisters is planning on stepping out. Sure. There could be an innocent enough reason. Maybe they're just going to hang with their friends. Maybe there's a boy they want to run away with.

But I'm thinking about what was said in the kitchen tonight. My sisters know, Detective Burke has to go. Maybe it doesn't have to be tonight. But if I know my sisters, they're swift.

It's a bit after two o'clock, when a car door closes outside. I was half asleep, but I'm awake again. Surely, I didn't miss it. Surely, I would have heard her if she stepped out. Their rooms are right there, after all. Poppy is across. Rose is next to mine. The hallway is ours.

I've been listening, but maybe I–

Okay. There's definitely someone out there. Probably just a neighbor. But I have to go and see.

I pushed my legs off the bed and pulled back the blanket. I shifted over the edge and went to the window, peeling the curtains back.

A flame. A hot, red, burning flame.

It's the cigarette.

I don't believe it, but he's standing there. Right outside the house, where he dropped me off. I know he wasn't there before, because I checked when I came up to the room hours ago. But he's there now. What's he planning?

I kept still in the shadows as I watched Burke finish his cigarette. He's not that dumb. Not as dumb as I hoped. He knows he's a dead man if he goes to sleep. That's why he's here. He's thinking about starting up with us.

I bit my lip.

Burke put his arm to his face. I watched as he sobbed into it.

Jesus. Pathetic.

He stumbled around the side of the vehicle. Probably drunk. He opened the driver's door and sat behind the wheel.

"Pathetic," I whispered out loud. "You're a pathetic person."

Still, I had to be careful. He could have something with him in there.

I swallowed.

His headlights came on.

A sigh of relief.

He started the engine and drove away.

"Pathetic!" I declared.

He wasn't going to do anything. He was too scared to. And he had all those morals to contend with – one of us killed his friend, but he's the bad guy if he does something about it.

Creak.

I immediately turned to my bedroom door in alarm. That sounded like the edge of the hall. But I haven't heard anyone get up.

Maybe I imagined it.

I went to my door and stood beside it.

Thump, thump, thump, thump, thump.

Someone's in here!

Creeeeeeek.

Rose's bedroom door.

I was too afraid to open mine.

"Eeeekkk!"

It's Rose! I pulled open my door and jumped into the pitch-black hallway.

"Help!!!" Rose wailed.

"Die, you! Die!"

Poppy's door opened and she stepped out with me.

No more thinking now. No more fear.

We barged into Rose's room and turned on the light.

CHAPTER 80

It's my fault. My doing. I gave him Rose's name. I don't know if she was the one who stabbed Georgie, but either way she had to pay for Leanne. I never knew it would bring us here.

"Die! Die! Die!" the monster on top of her was screaming. "Die, you sickly little girl!"

I won't tone it down for you. I'll give you the true horror of what I saw. The person on top of her was dressed head to toe in black. They were wearing a poncho of some kind, with all its loose edges and sides flapping about in a frenzy. Long, luscious, dark-as-night hair whirled along with it. I saw the silver blade. I saw the pink handle. Rose's blood was all over the walls. And she wasn't screaming anymore.

Poppy grabbed my arm for support. It was too late to do anything. Too late to save her. But now, it was time to face the devil head-on.

"What's that?" it growled from the bed. "Is there someone else in here?"

She turned, her cheeks saturated in sweat and blood. Snot dripped from her nose. Saliva spilled from her mouth. She put the blade to her lips and licked it. "Brats!" she shouted at us. "You stinking, little brats!"

We heard Simone come in from behind us.

"Get off her," she said.

Jessica. It was Jessica.

She started laughing. It was a repulsive, mutated, rasp.

Simone stepped forward, between Poppy and me. "Get off her, now," she commanded, aiming the semi-automatic pistol.

Jessica licked her lips and stood up on the bed, towering over us. "Foolish woman," she bellowed at her. "You know how these girls treat their mothers, right?"

Bang!

Simone shot Jessica in the belly, and she immediately sprang backwards. Simone hurried forward as Jessica rolled off the bed, howling in pain. The gun went off again, but it missed everything.

Jessica forced herself from the floor and threw herself at Simone.

Poppy and I went to Simone's aide, but it was too late; Jessica had managed to put the knife all the way through her stomach.

"Die," Jessica croaked, falling again. "Die for Georgie…"

"Quickly," I said as Poppy helped to position Simone upright.

Poppy then grabbed hold of the impaled blade and yanked it out.

"Aaareeeegh!!!" Simone squealed. Blood spilled from her torso and mouth.

Poppy stood up and charged over to Jessica on the floor.

"Die, die, die!" she shrieked, stabbing Jessica.

"Stop it," Jessica whimpered. "Just stop–"

But Poppy didn't stop. Poppy shoved the pointy end of the knife through Jess's left eye socket… and twisted.

"Don't," Simone said, trying to stand up. "Please, Poppy, you don't…"

I heard the bones crack in Jess's skull.

I rushed over and tried to pull Poppy away.

Poppy ripped the blade out and handed it to me.

I looked into her eyes.

What? I mouthed.

I followed her gaze.

Our sister. Our most beautiful, special and wonderful sister, Rose. Caked in a dark crimson mess.

There is an exit here.

I turned away from them and stormed towards the bedroom door.

"What are you doing?" Simone screamed as I pounced to attack. "Violet, please! No… Don't–"

PART V

Rose

CHAPTER 81

"Mommy! Mommy!" I squealed. "Look at the ball!"

The ball was red of course. A small, rubber marble. There were all sorts of silver specs giving the surface a shiny glint.

Behind the ball were three emerald cups.

Behind the cups was a blind man seated at a table.

"I love that ball," I said boldly. "What's it for?"

"It's a game," the man explained. "I put the ball under one of the cups to start with. And then I switch the cups around for a minute. Then you have to guess which cup the ball is under."

"Can I play?"

"Sure," he replied. "Five dollars."

I heard Mom's shoes on the pavement.

"Rose! What do you think you're doing? You need to stay with me when we're outside."

"Mommy, look at the ball," I said excitedly. "Isn't it pretty?"

"Ah, yes. Very nice. Now, please can you–"

"I want to play the game. Mommy, can I please play it?"

"Five dollars," the man repeated.

"Heavens gracious, no you may not play the game," Mom said and then bent down. "It's a scam anyway. It's rigged against you."

"I don't care," I said defiantly. "I can win it."

"But you don't have five dollars."

"I do – at home."

"No, you don't–"

"I swear I do!" I shouted. "I have five dollars sixty-five in my piggy bank! I'll pay you back."

"Rose. Darling. I'm not going to let you gamble."

My cheeks started heating up. I stomped on the concrete. "I'm getting very angry, Mommy," I informed her. "If you won't let me play the game, I can feel myself getting a bloody nose."

Mom rolled her eyes. "Good grief."

We approached the man's table.

"Why don't you just let her play for free?" she asked him.

"No can do," he replied. "The magic doesn't work unless there's something at stake."

"I can't believe I'm doing this," Mom said reaching for her purse.

"What do I get if I win?" I asked the man.

"You get ten dollars back," he said. "That's the deal."

"Nuh-uh," I argued. "I want the ball."

"Rose, I think you better take the money," Mom advised me.

I stomped the ground again.

"I'll tell you what," the man said. "If you win, you can have the money *and* the ball. Okay?"

"Okay." I smiled.

Mom reluctantly handed him a five-dollar bill.

"Thank you, ma'am," he said and reached underneath the table for his metal tin. "Now. Are you ready, my dear?"

I grinned wildly. "Let's play."

CHAPTER 82

Bounce, rebound, catch. Bounce, rebound, catch. Bounce, rebound, catch…

It's just me in the chair. The ball hits the corridor floor. It flies up, and rebounds against the opposite wall. Then it comes back to me, and I catch it.

Bounce, rebound, catch.

It's just me and my red ball. No one's going to take it away from me.

"Ssshhh!"

I turned to my left and saw the lady from the front office staring at me crossly. I sighed and put the ball away in my pocket.

Now I can only imagine it.

Bounce, rebound, catch.

Bounce, rebound, catch.

We're still playing. I can see it even if you can't.

The counselor's door opened on my right and Violet stepped out, not seeing me at first.

I leaned forward in the chair. "How was it?"

She turned sharply and then composed herself.

She made a yawning motion with her hand to her mouth.

Then she walked off.

"Hi!" The counselor appeared. "You must be Rose."

I nodded and got up. She held the door back as I entered her room and approached the chair in the center. It was the same as the one outside.

"Sit down," she instructed, shutting the door. "Make yourself comfortable. Would you like a biscuit? Something to drink?"

"Yes, please."

"Is a fruit box okay?"

"Yes."

She went round to her desk at the back of the room. She opened a drawer and produced a fruit box and an open packet of chocolate biscuits.

"Raspberry," I guided her.

"Okay…"

She brought the drink forward and offered me the biscuits.

I took the drink but waved my hand at the food.

"Oh. Alright."

She put the biscuits away and then returned to the center where she took the chair opposite me.

I opened the straw and punctured the hole at the top of the box.

"My name's Simone, and today we're just going to have a nice little chat about how things are going with you."

"You mean at school?" I asked.

"Yes, at school." She adjusted herself. "But at home too. I know we don't know each other, but my role here is to give the students a chance to talk to someone about anything that might be going on, where they might not have someone who would otherwise listen."

I put the straw in my mouth and sucked.

Simone smiled. "I love that little flower in your hair. Is it real? Or artificial?"

I lowered the straw. "It's fake."

"Oh. Well. It looks lovely anyway."

"If it was real, I'd need a new one every two or three days."

"You like wearing it then?"

I shrugged. "I am Rose."

"Yes." She shifted a bit. "You and your sisters are so alike in appearance. You must drive your teachers crazy sometimes."

"Why?"

"I mean, because they won't be able to tell you apart."

I pointed to my flower. "Hello?"

"Right. Of course. I apologize. You obviously have it all figured out."

I put the straw in my mouth again.

Simone exhaled. "So. How are things going with your–"

"It's not such a bad thing," I said, setting the drink to the floor. "Us looking the same."

"There's a few perks then?"

"Sort of. If we just want to be invisible, you know. If we all agree, then we don't have to be ourselves for a while."

"Do you like being yourself?"

I smiled. "They named me Rose and I like roses. So, I like red things mostly."

"Okay."

"See here," I said pulling out my ball. "This is my favorite thing."

"May I see?"

"I'll show it to you."

I got up and held the ball out for her.

"Very nice," she said, humoring me. "I like all the specs on it."

"I like the red."

"Right…"

I took a step back. "I won this, you know."

"Really?"

"From a blind man in the street."

"How did that happen?"

"He was trying to play a trick on me. Thought I would miss where the red went." I shook my head. "I never miss red. Sometimes, it's all I can see."

"What do you mean by that, Rose?"

"Like this." I showed her the ball.

Then I turned and bounced it on the floor.

Simone stood up.

It hit the side wall, and then rebounded, coming back to me.

"Please don't do that," Simone said.

I showed her the ball again. Then put it back in my pocket.

"Thank you," she said, and returned to her chair. "Why don't we sit down again?"

I waited.

Bounce, rebound, catch.

Bounce, rebound, catch.

"Can you see it?" I asked her.

"Can I see what?" she replied.

Bounce, rebound, catch.

"Can you see the ball?"

"It's in your pocket."

Bounce, rebound, catch.

I shook my head. "No, it's not."

"It's not?"

"Take a look."

"Alright."

She got up again and went to my pocket.

Bounce, rebound–

She put her hand in.

Whack.

"Ouch!" Simone cried out.

The ball fell from the back of her head to the floor.

I bent my knees and picked it up.

"What the…" she said in amazement.

"You weren't paying attention," I returned.

CHAPTER 83

I know, right? I must seem pretty smart after pulling off that trick. I'm not, really. Violet's the smart one. If I showed you how I did it, you wouldn't be that impressed. You'd probably go and teach it to your little nephew or niece, and then they can go around impressing their friends with the same thing. They'd get all the credit, if you didn't take it away from them. If I didn't take it away from you.

No one is taking my ball away from me.

I might seem smart at first, and I am also loud. I tend to stand out in a crowd. I don't hide from things, like Poppy. I don't map out a defense, like Violet. So, if something bad was going to happen to us, it would probably happen to me first. I can't help that. I do things I know I shouldn't. I go places I shouldn't go. I can't help it. It's not that I'm not aware of the danger. It's not that I'm not scared. It's more that there's already this momentum behind me. Once the ball leaves my hand, there's already a predetermined path it's going to take that will lead it back. It doesn't get to choose where it wants to go. It can't help it once I've decided where it's going.

Someone's thrown me.

I can't see it yet. It doesn't matter how inevitable it might seem in retrospect. I have no idea what's going to happen.

I live in the moment.

* * *

Adults underestimate children. They think they know us. They think we're like how they were at our age. We're not.

We're not always tougher. We're not always meaner. But how we respond and develop is based on different environmental factors that move through each generation. And there's also a need to understand children as individuals, not just as a collective.

I can see things the adults can't see. I can hear things they can't hear.

I don't think Violet can hear them either. Poppy, I'm not sure. Sometimes, I feel really alone with all my secrets. I know that you wouldn't believe me if I told you.

You have to see it for yourself.

* * *

Sometimes I roll my ball down the middle of the corridor when no one else is around. In this instance, I'm not a hundred percent sure where it will go. It could make a bend here, a turn there. I'm trotting along behind it, to maybe kick it some more if I feel like it.

When you act this way, when you leave it to chance, some awful and miraculous things can occur.

I was shuffling my ball along one afternoon not that long ago, and I happened upon a corridor I'd never been down before. I thought I knew all the places in my school, but some spots get overlooked.

So. One afternoon my ball rolls here. And when I get there, I notice how the inside is getting darker. There's no one in the classrooms ahead, or to the side of me. I'm about to pick up my ball, but I accidentally kick it, and it goes right to the end.

"Oh, drat."

The lights aren't working overhead. The light is disappearing underneath my feet. I know when I get to the doors at the end, I can pull the bars up and push them open. The light from outside will stream in and all of this will just seem like a faraway dream.

But for whatever reason, I decided not to do that. I decided to embrace the fear. I imagined monsters standing at the windows of the classrooms I'm passing by. I could almost see them watching me.

It's just a game in my head. But sometimes games are real.

"What the…"

It's my turn to feel confused. It's my turn to feel amazed. After finding my ball I turn around to face the way I came in, and there's someone standing at the other end, watching me. As I get closer, the confusion mounts.

She's not wearing a purple headband over her hair.

She's not wearing a blue feather clip.
But if I'm not mistaken.
She looks just like me.

CHAPTER 84

It comes along in flashes. It's not a clear picture. I can see this great big house with a gravel drive. Iron gates at the end. There's trees hanging over us. I can feel their shadows protecting me from the sun. Behind the house, there's a vast green lawn that goes on forever. I can see myself running through it. I think the grass is mine. I think I belong here and it's a part of me.

My sisters are here too. They're behind me, and I'm running to get away from them. It's a game, you see. They don't have the same fire I have. But I'm calling them to ignite. Run with me. Run after me. See how light your feet really are…

Now I remember. I stopped and looked back. And of course, I could see all three of them coming towards me.

"Who are you?" I asked the girl standing in the corridor.

She didn't look like Violet.

She didn't look like Poppy.

I would know. We can always tell.

"You don't remember me?" she asked.

I didn't answer one way or another.

In my mind, looking back to my sisters on the lawn that day… I could see Violet's purple ribbon. I could see Poppy's blue ribbon. But the third girl… she was wearing…

"My name was Rose," the girl said and walked off.

* * *

Of course, I tried going after her, but she ducked out one of the exits and jumped around the corner. I lost sight of her. She faded into my imagination. I brought up the encounter with Violet and Poppy later, but they both denied knowing anything about it. I didn't know who she was or what I experienced, only to say that I sometimes saw things other people couldn't. I did wonder whether I would see the girl again. I even went back to that part of the corridor. But the magic doesn't work if you try and force it.

Ding, ding, ding, ding, ding.

The lunch bell.

"Sorry," I gushed. "I talk too much and now I've wasted all your time."

"No, of course not, dear," Simone said, standing up. "I just have to tell the next student to come back so I can see her immediately after lunch."

I waited.

I waited in the chair. My ball in my pocket. My knees knocking about anxiously. I was opening up too much, wasn't I? I was telling Simone all my secrets. She was going to think awful things about me.

But I've already been thrown, like a ball down an empty corridor, or two dice on a board.

The door behind me reopened. Simone walked by and returned to her seat.

She was half-smiling.

"Was it Poppy?" I asked.

She nodded.

"She doesn't mind?"

"She'll be okay," Simone assured me.

Silence.

I shrugged. "Do you think I'm crazy now?"

"Not at all."

"So was the other Rose real? Or is it just my imagination?"

"You said you imagined monsters in the classrooms when you were walking down the corridor towards this girl," Simone said. "So, if you did imagine her, why would you know that you were imagining monsters, but not her?"

My eyes fluttered. "You're making me afraid now."

"I am?"

"You're making me think she's real."

Simone moved to the edge of her seat. "If she was real, why would that be a bad thing?"

"Because I took it from her," I whispered.

"You took what from her?"

The name the color the ball the face the mother the family the life.

"I took everything."

CHAPTER 85

A lot can go wrong in an afternoon when four girls are on the loose.

Mom was busy in the kitchen making dinner for tonight. I thought I was helping her, but I was probably just getting in the way. Meanwhile Violet was on the sofa reading a book. Poppy was in the corner with her coloring crayons. I saw my other sister playing with our small white dog – Sparky – in the living room.

That's how it was.

A constant moment, frozen in time.

The next time I looked to the living room, the front door was wide open, and my sister was just standing in the middle of it looking out. Dad's car pulled in a minute later. I heard the car door slam. He was ranting and raving about something outside.

Eventually, he came in, holding Sparky in his arms.

"Sarah! Sarah! Where are you? Why is this door open?"

"What's that, Nicholas?"

Mom put down whatever she was doing and walked by me through the living room archway. I followed her in.

"I just found Sparky here in the middle of the driveway," Dad exclaimed. "Did you leave the door open?"

"No, of course I didn't," Mom answered.

"It was Rose," Violet said from the sofa.

"Rose?" Dad thundered.

"She opened the door and let him out."

Our eyes searched. Rose was sitting at the table with Poppy, not looking at us.

"Is this true, Rose?" Dad demanded. "Did you let Sparky out?"

Rose started trembling, tears bubbled in her eyes.

Dad rushed over, picked up the entire table in front of them and hurled it across the room.

Poppy shrieked and ran away.

Rose backed up against the wall.

"What the hell is wrong with you?" Dad yelled.

"Nothing," Rose cried.

"Why are you so disobedient?"

"I'm not."

There were no more words after that.

He took her by the hand and led her away to another room and shut the door.

I sat on the floor, patting Sparky. Violet continued reading her book.

Rose screamed in the other room.

* * *

It might have been a few days – maybe a few weeks, maybe months – I'm not sure. But it was another afternoon where us girls were in the house, occupying ourselves as usual. This time Mom was cleaning the bathroom. Poppy was playing in the backyard. Violet was using the computer for something.

I walked into the living room and found Rose standing there, looking lost. Behind her, the front door was wide open.

"What happened?" I asked.

"He's gone," Rose replied. "He ran away."

I went to the open doorway. Breathed in the grass, the garden, and the road.

There was no sign of Sparky.

But there was Dad's car, coming up the drive.

I turned around and saw Rose was already crying.

"Don't," I whispered, trying to comfort her. "It's okay…"

"*I'm scared*," Rose moaned.

Dad's car door slammed, and she shuddered.

I suddenly felt an impulse rush through me, and I plucked the gold ribbon from my hair.

"Here," I said. "Give me your one."

Rose plucked out her red one and handed it to me.

"Go," I said.

She took off.

I turned around and saw Dad's enormous figure already bearing down on me.

"Rose?" he demanded. "Why is this door open…? Where's Sparky?"

I shut my eyes and didn't say anything.

I knew what was coming.

CHAPTER 86

I'm not ready. I'm not ready to look at it. These memories are coming back to me, and they're destabilizing. I make up stories. I make up people. I make up things. An entire world comes to life when I fall asleep. Please don't tell me any part of it is true.

Ding, ding, ding, ding.

"I'm sorry," I said. "I've taken all your lunch."

"It's fine," Simone said briskly. "We can continue this tomorrow. In the meantime, I want you to do something for me. Tonight, if you have a chance, I'd like you to write down three things you'd want to change about your life."

"Like what?"

"It can be anything, big or small. Just think about it, and then we'll have a look tomorrow to see what you've written down."

"Okay." I nodded.

I got up from the chair and Simone led me to the door.

Before she opened it, I beckoned her.

She bent her knees. I put my arms around her.

I squeezed.

"Are you okay, Rose?" Simone asked, comforting me.

"I don't know," I whispered.

"It will be okay," she said. "Don't worry…"

Will it, Simone?

Will it, really?

* * *

I remember one time I was in the car with Mom and the others, and we had to stop for some ducks who were crossing in the middle of the road.

"Oh!" I cried, jerking forward in my seat. "What are they doing there?"

"Aren't they lovely?" Mom said quietly.

"Very pretty." Poppy smiled.

I could see the mother duck was leading the way for her babies. She kept going back to check on the stragglers, to make sure the group was staying together.

"A cat will get them," Violet said from up front.

"What?" I gasped.

She looked back at me. "That's if someone doesn't drive over them first."

"Hey," Mom scolded her. "Cut it out."

Violet shrugged and turned back to the front. "The blind leading the blind…"

* * *

The school is hiding enemies. I can't see them. They're here. They're in the shadows somewhere. But there's this veil blocking me from seeing the danger. Poppy is stressed in the chair. She doesn't seem her usual self. Her hair is messy, and her feathers are displaced. She seems shaken.

Out of Simone's office, I am crossing the corridor towards her. "What's wrong?"

Poppy didn't answer. She was off somewhere else, in a daze.

"Poppy?" Simone called behind me.

Poppy got up and moved by.

I looked back and watched her go into the office with Simone.

Simone didn't look at me once.

* * *

I didn't get a chance to speak to Violet later in class. She sits at the front, where I sit in the middle. I was waiting for Poppy to come in, but she was taking a lot of time with Simone, just like me. This made me anxious. There was a growing fear that my sisters knew my secrets and would reveal them before I had a chance to. I couldn't even face this concept myself. A part of me was completely certain we had a fourth sister, but that ran in contradiction to so many things.

And if that was her in the corridor…

Ding, ding, ding.

That was fast. Home-time already. The crowd of students exiting blocked any chance of me meeting up with Violet at this point. We had a spot at the center gate, where we had to wait anyway. Mom didn't like us walking home by ourselves. The town was full of strangers.

“Where’s Poppy?” Violet asked, as I came to our spot at the gate.

I looked over my shoulder. “I haven’t seen her since…”

“Since when?”

I turned back. “She went into Simone’s office.”

Violet groaned. “I’ll wait one more minute, and then I’m leaving.”

“That’s not fair. You have to wait for Poppy.”

“Unlike some people, I have study to do when I get home,” Violet snapped. “Were you even paying attention at the end there? Or were you just playing with that stupid ball?”

“Shut up about my ball,” I said defensively.

Violet chuckled. She checked her watch. “I have to go. Seriously, I have to go.”

“Well, go then.”

“You’re waiting for her, are you?”

“Uh, yeah.”

“Don’t take forever then. I don’t need Mom blaming me for you two going missing.” Violet walked off.

I crossed my arms. Leaned against the gate.

Waited.

* * *

I didn’t have a watch, so I didn’t know how long it’d been. I was comfortable for probably another five minutes. I was getting annoyed approaching ten minutes. A bit after that, I started to move around some more.

I couldn’t stray too far. I had to keep the gate in sight. If I walked back to the school grounds, and went into the building looking for Poppy, there was a good chance I’d miss her. Now, the last I saw of her was in Simone’s office, but that didn’t mean she’d been in there the entire time. She could have been let go early and allowed to walk home by herself. I’d be pretty mad if that’s what happened. She knew we were supposed to meet here. There have been times though, where that doesn't transpire the way it's supposed to. The world had a way of shuffling us around. Any one of us could be here one minute and gone the next.

I reckon twenty minutes to half an hour had gone by now. There were still a few kids around, but those numbers had thinned significantly.

"Oh, the hell with this."

I turned around and walked through the side gate, back towards the grounds. Before I made it to the building, however, I saw Simone carrying her things in the adjacent car park. I waved and called out to her. "Simone?"

She looked up and waited till I reached her.

"Hi, Rose. Why are you still here?"

"I was waiting for Poppy," I said. "Have you seen her?"

"Well, yes. I saw her earlier. But that was a while ago."

"She never made it back to class."

"Oh dear. Shall we phone home to alert your parents?"

I considered. "She's probably gone home already. I guess I better be going again."

I turned my back to her and began retracing my steps to the gate.

"Rose?" Simone called out.

I glanced back.

She forced a smile. "Would you like a ride?"

CHAPTER 87

No one thinks it's going to be them. No one thinks they're going to be the one who is taken. Mom and Dad did a good job of trying to scare us though. It was right before Dad's cousin's wedding where they first sat us down and explained the realities of the world.

"Now you're going to see a lot of people here today," Dad said outside the front entrance. "Most of them are friends, family. But not all."

"You need to stay together," Mom said. "All four of you. You're responsible for each other."

"What happens if one of us gets lost?" Violet asked.

"You come and find us," Mom answered.

"No," Violet pressed. "What are you scared of happening?"

"There's a lot of bad things that can happen," Dad explained. "You could fall over, have an accident, get hurt, or a stranger could take you."

"Nicholas, are you sure–" Mom began.

"Look, if you want them to go off on their own today, then there's certain truths they need to realize."

He moved through each of us, and sat down on the steps to reach our eye level.

"Don't trust anyone you don't know," Dad said. "Only trust your mother and me. If anyone tries to get you alone from your sisters, you run away from them. You get us. If anyone tries to take you by car, you refuse."

"Why would they try and take us?" I asked.

"There are bad people in this world. That's all you need to know."

I shook my head. I still didn't understand. "But wouldn't we come back?"

Dad smiled. "Did Sparky come back?"

* * *

Some lessons stay with you. Others slip away. Or it could be argued that it wasn't a real lesson. It was just a reading of the rules. The lesson happens later…

I'm riding up front for a change. Usually, Violet's riding up front or all three of us are in the back. Today I'm in the front. There's no one in the back. It's just me and Simone – my new friend I found today.

But I don't recognize this way.

"Do you want some candy?" Simone offered. "There's some stuff in the glove box."

I leaned forward and pushed the button below. The cover fell open. "Hey, it's real candy," I said. As in candy canes. "But it's not Christmas."

"No, but I keep it there," Simone returned.

I plucked one of the canes out and tore off the plastic. I started sucking on it.

"I don't suppose you've had time to think about the assignment I gave you," Simone said. "If you could change something about your life, remember?"

"Oh right. Yeah, I probably need tonight for that."

A pause. "It's out of the textbook, that question."

"What do you mean?"

"I'm trained to ask that. It's a very general question, used to get the student to open up."

"Okay…"

"There's a lot of other things I could ask you, but they might border on inappropriate."

I glanced out the window. I still didn't recognize where we were going.

"Are you sure you know where my street is?" I asked.

"We're stopping off somewhere first," Simone replied.

"Where?"

"My place."

Sensing my awkwardness perhaps, she added, "I have to get something."

"What?"

"Why don't you let me ask the questions, dear? That's what I'm here for."

I nodded, and continued sucking on my candy cane.

"You know, I spoke to Poppy about some of the things you brought up in our session."

"Oh."

"She remembers Daisy too."

Just hearing the name sends a blast of white air through my chest. My vision blurred. I dropped the candy.

"Did you hear what I said, Rose?"
I shook my head.
"I said Poppy remembers Daisy."
"I didn't say that name," I whispered.
The car was slowing down. We were in a busy neighborhood. No houses – just shops, office buildings, apartments. Things of that nature.
"Why are we stopping?" I asked. "Is this your house?"
"I've got something to show you," Simone said firmly.
"Just take me home."
Simone stared. "Are you scared, Rose? Are you afraid of me?"
I stared back. "I don't know what I'm afraid of."
Simone shook her head. "I'm trying to help you. I'm trying to help all of you."
She pushed her door open and got out.
She came round and opened my door. "It's just over here."
"No."
"Rose."
"Let go of me."
"Rose!"
My red ball escaped during the struggle and started bouncing across the road.
"Oh no!" I yelled. I quickly ripped off my seat belt and rushed past Simone after it.
Two cars screeched to a halt and blew their horns as I went by.
Bounce, bounce, bounce.
Bounce, bounce, bounce.
It was rolling about like crazy.
I made it across to the opposite footpath and saw someone get up from a bench near the ball.
They bent over to pick it up.
"Hey!" I cried. "That's mine! That's my ball!"
I rushed over, out of breath, to confront the person.
They got back to their feet, the ball in hand.

My face fell.

"Hello, Daisy," the girl said. "Remember me?"

CHAPTER 88

I can see the playground. I don't want to look at it, but it's there in front of me. And it's in my mind. I can see ourselves that day. Running about. Laughing. Dancing around. I wasn't looking at Mom or the strange lady, but I was standing still, catching my breath. And I could hear every word.

"You have four, I want one. Now, which child will you give me?"

It took a moment. But then I realized. This was one of those bad people we'd been warned about.

"You can't catch me!" Rose was singing. "You can't catch me!"

She crawled into the playground's tunnel. I went after her, but my feet moved slowly.

"Daisy." Mom's voice. "You can take Daisy."

My insides turned to stone.

"Which one is that?"

"The one with the gold ribbon."

Time to run now. Time to run as fast as I can. I charged into the tunnel and found Rose lying on her back halfway down. She giggled and turned to escape. I grabbed her leg. "Wait. Wait, Rose." I unraveled the ribbon from my hair. "Here. Give me yours."

"What? Why?"

"Dad's here," I said. "You're in trouble."

"But I didn't do anything!"

"He's angry about Sparky."

"No! It's not fair!"

"Quickly," I urged her. "Quick before he comes."

I took her red ribbon.

And she took mine.

* * *

I wish I could leave it there. I wish that was the end of the memory. But the worst part was recalling what happened after Rose crawled back outside.

"Daisy! Daisy, come here!"

"What? No, Mommy–"

"I won't ask you again, Daisy."

"She's… She's–"

"Do you see this nice lady here? She wants to talk with you. Be a good girl, please."

"But… But–"

"Come along, Daisy. She has some candy for you in her car. You like candy, don't you?"

"But she's in the tunnel, Mommy!"

"That's okay, we just need you."

"No, no – she's back there!"

"I'm sorry, Daisy. I'm just so sorry…"

My face was pressed against the dark plastic of the tunnel. I heard my sister cry for our mommy as the stranger led her away.

CHAPTER 89

You can't undo it. You can't take it back. It's who you are. It's how the planets have aligned. Sure, I'll escape judgment from those whose lives weren't affected. But stop thinking about what you'd do if you were me. Start thinking about how you'd feel if you were Rose. I know that's all I can think about. And now she's all I can look at.

"Well, you found me," the girl said. "Congratulations…"

Simone caught up behind me. "I'm sorry, Rose. I didn't know she'd be here."

I glanced over my shoulder. "What's going on?"

The girl poked me. "Don't play dumb."

I swallowed. "Are you… are you okay?"

She laughed. "Am I okay? Did you just ask me that?"

"That's enough," Simone said.

I took a step back from them.

"Look, I'm sorry, Rose," Simone went on. "I was trying to help you remember gradually. Not all at once like this."

I pointed. "Do you two know each other?"

"I've been looking after Daisy," Simone confessed, "for a while now."

The girl glared at her. "That's not my name."

"I'm just trying to make it easy for the both of you."

She saw my eyes drifting back to her hands. "You want this, don't you?"

I nodded.

She tossed me the ball. "Take it then. Take my whole identity. What do I care?"

She stormed off, sulking.

"Daisy!" Simone called after her. "I mean…" She turned back to me. "Can you just wait here a minute, dear?"

I sighed and went to the bench where my sister had gotten up from. It was facing away from the road to a fenced-off clearing.

Sitting down. Facing it.

It still took a few moments.

It was the playground.

CHAPTER 90

There's the past. There's the future. Then there's what's right here and now. I don't know, maybe this is the future. I don't feel like I've ever grown up. I'm still in that tunnel somewhere, facing the dark plastic below me, listening to those screams. I was supposed to be out there. I was supposed to be with that woman. Mom chose me because I was the strongest.

But I chose Rose. Because she was the weakest.

"Everything alright, Rose?" Mom asked from the opposite side of the table. "You've hardly touched your plate."

I gave a small smile and pushed my fork into the peas.

I looked to Poppy on my left. "Where were you after school? I was looking for you."

"Simone said I could go early," Poppy answered.

"Simone?" Mom asked.

"Just a teacher at our school," I added.

"That allows you to call her by her first name?"

"She helps with the sports program," I improvised.

Violet chuckled.

"What's funny?" Mom asked.

"There's no need to lie to her," Violet said. "She can't do anything."

"Just shut up, Violet," I snarled.

"Yeah, shut up," Poppy joined in.

Mom put down her cutlery. "Who's lying? Are you lying to me?"

I put my fork down and stared at her.

"What?" Mom demanded.

"Do you remember Sparky?"

Her eyes fluttered. "Who?"

"Sparky? Our dog?"

Searching. Darting. Displaced. "We never had a dog."

"What about you?" I asked Violet. "Do you remember Sparky?"

She paused a moment, then turned to Mom. "May I be excused?"

"You may," Mom answered.

Violet started to get up.

"Hey!" I yelled. "I asked you a question!"

"No, I don't remember your stupid dog," Violet said. "Now let's keep it down, okay, everybody? I have homework." She left the table.

I turned to Poppy. "What about you? Do you remember him?"

Poppy was watching Mom.

Mom was watching Poppy.

"Well?"

Poppy shrugged. "I don't know."

"You see?" Mom said, rising from the table. "Now, you heard your sister. You all have homework so, get to it."

Poppy left the table and Mom started to clear it.

I remained seated. My eyes didn't leave her as she moved back and forth.

"I know everything," I whispered.

"What's that?" Mom said innocently, her back to me.

Silence.

She turned around and we locked eyes.

"Nothing."

CHAPTER 91

My room is in the middle of the hall. Violet's is on my left. Poppy's is on my right. Mom's is opposite. You could ask anyone. There are no secrets in this house. Except that isn't true at all. My whole life is a secret.

Daisies are pretty, but Roses are beautiful. I reject the sunlight. I reject the sweeping yellow decay. Her memory is a stain on all of us. Her existence challenges my own. There's only room for three flowers in this house. She will not be a threat to me.

Knock, knock.

"Go away!" Violet yelled.

I stepped away from her door. I turned and saw Poppy peering out from hers at the end. I approached her.

"We need to talk," I said.

She moved away from the door and let me inside.

It's a blue room, full of oceans and skies. The coolness of the colors both calms my anxiety and thickens my depression. Poppy sat on the edge of her bed and made herself as small and gentle as could be. I looked away from her, not knowing where to begin.

"Simone didn't let me go early," Poppy confessed. "I got chased."

"Chased? By whom?"

"The bullies. You know who they are."

"How many of them?"

She shook her head. "A lot."

"What were they going to do to you?"

"One of the girls had a bottle of paint." She got up and went to the cupboard. She pulled out a crumpled school sweater and handed it to me.

Two bright-blue blotches stained the sweater.

"Have you shown Mom?"

"I'm too afraid to," Poppy said. "She doesn't have a lot of money. And if she does replace it, then they'll just do it again."

"Are you going to tell a teacher?"

She nodded. "I'll tell Simone."

She took her sweater back and put it away.

"That's a bad idea," I said.

"Why?"

"Look, I gotta tell you some things."

"About our old dog?"

"Do you remember him or not?"

Poppy walked back to the bed. "Mom doesn't like talking about when Dad was around."

"You ever wondered why that is?" I pressed. "That maybe it's more than just… hurt feelings."

There was a moment of silence. I could see Poppy was starting to think, starting to remember. Then she lowered her eyes and sat down. "Just tell me what's going on."

I sighed, sat down next to her.

"Do you remember Daisy?" I asked.

Poppy didn't respond. She looked at me vacantly.

"We had a fourth sister who wore yellow and gold. Do you remember her?"

"That's you," Poppy said softly.

"You do remember."

"Mom gave her away. The Rose before you."

"That's not exactly how it went down."

Poppy shrugged. "So?"

"Does… Violet know? Did you ever…?"

"We always pretend," Poppy said. "If we remember her, then she's imaginary. I play along. That's how it works."

I nodded. "Daisy's living with Simone now. I saw her today after school. And once before as well."

"What?" Poppy gasped.

"She blames me. I'm sure she blames Mom too."

Poppy swayed, her head moving involuntarily.

"Poppy? Are you okay?"

I put my hands around to stabilize her.

Her face fell to my shoulder. "What are we going to do, Rosie?"

I quivered, overwhelmed with emotion.

"I don't know," I whispered. "I just don't know…"

CHAPTER 92

You savor breakfast. You savor the sleep. You savor your shower. You savor all the tiny moments between you and the unknown. School is an unknown. I can't keep track of everyone. I can't get a grip on the frenzy. Around any corner, behind every door, my sister is waiting for me. She wants my life, but I cannot negotiate. I am Rose. Say it with me now. There's nothing artificial about me.

"Rose," Simone called from the classroom doorway.

It's nine thirty. She's barely waited around at all. She hasn't even called Violet first. Violet, who curiously looks back at me from the front of the class.

I look over my shoulder to Poppy in the back.

Poppy nods, giving me strength.

Yes. I can do this. I can face the dragon. I can make this sacrifice.

I got up from my table and shifted around the chairs until I was walking up to the door. Simone waited until I was in the corridor, and then we walked together.

"Are you okay, Rose?" she asked me. "You look pale."

I shook my head.

"I must say, I'm really sorry about yesterday. I honestly didn't know she was going to be there."

"You're a liar," I said.

"A liar? About what?"

"You let me say all that stuff to you and you never let on about her."

"I suppose that's fair," Simone conceded. "You have to understand, I wasn't sure what the best way to reunite the four of you would be. Involving your parents was out of the question."

"Why's that?"

"Daisy's never forgiven them. It took a lot to bring her around about you as well."

"Are we calling her Daisy now?"

"That's what she's always been called. Since…"

Simone paused as we reached her office. She opened the door and my jaw dropped as I was confronted face to face with Daisy on the other side.

"Oh, it's you," I whimpered.

Simone pushed her away from the door to give me enough room to slide in. She closed it after us and resumed her stride.

"Take a seat, both of you."

The chairs were set in place opposite her.

I took the chair nearest to me, on the left.

Daisy moved round to the one on the right.

"What's going on?" I asked. "I don't want any trouble."

"No, we couldn't have that," Daisy said sarcastically, crossing her arms as she sat down.

Simone waited until everyone was seated before responding. "This isn't what anyone wanted, to find ourselves here. The main thing is, Daisy, you're okay. You made it through your shocking ordeal. And, as I've been saying, Rose isn't to blame."

Daisy turned to me. I noticed she was wearing my old yellow ribbon.

"I'm sorry for what happened to you," I said. "I'm sorry for what I did."

"If you had any idea what I've been through," Daisy replied, "you'd still make the same choice. If you had to do it over again."

"No. I'm not sure I would."

"Why don't you tell Rose what happened?" Simone asked.

"I don't know if she wants to hear it," Daisy said.

My eyes darted nervously. "Is it really bad?"

She grinned. "You have no idea."

CHAPTER 93

She was right. I didn't have any idea.

I don't even have to say what it is. I'm not going to repeat those words. Everything Daisy's talking about gives me a dizzy feeling. I don't know if I'm afraid or paralyzed.

I mean, I know what sex is. I'm aware that things go on in private between adults. But what Daisy is describing, I can hardly comprehend.

"Where are those people now?" is all I can say in the end.

"Back at the building, I guess," Daisy answered. "If they haven't left the country."

"Surely you've got to go to the police."

"If we get them involved, they'll put Daisy back with your family," Simone said. "We can't have that. She needs to stay with me where it's safe."

"Are you thinking they'll be back for you?" I asked.

"Our father was the first one who touched me," Daisy said. "Don't even say he hasn't touched you."

"But… he hasn't."

"You probably don't remember," Simone said.

"How would I forget a thing like that?"

"That's what it does," Daisy explained. "It messes with your head. I have to… like… not be me a lot of the time."

"She means disassociation," Simone clarified. "She has spells where her emotions become unbearable so she either blacks out or reverts to an alternate personality. Typically, it occurs when the abuse starts at a very young age. As it did with Daisy."

I shook my head. "I don't know what to say."

"We need you on our side," Simone stated.

"Me?"

"You let me down before," Daisy said, wiping away her tears. "You betrayed me. But I'm willing to forgive if you help us now."

"What do you want me to do?"

"Tell the truth," Daisy said.

"You've got to start talking about the abuse in your household," Simone said.

"Huh?"

"It's mostly Dad," Daisy said. "But the others are also complicit. We want to get all three so there isn't any confusion."

"Who are you talking about?"

"Mom, Dad, and Jessica, who is Dad's girlfriend."

I stared at them. "Dad has a girlfriend?"

"She's an enabler, just as your mother is an enabler," Simone pressed. "We've written a statement on your behalf that is going to be forwarded to the police but, of course, we need your cooperation."

"Slow down," I said. "I'm not understanding what you want me to do. I don't know what you're talking about with Dad's girlfriend or abuse in the household."

"Well, that isn't true," Simone said crossly. "Are you going to sit there and lie in front of your sister? After all she's been through?"

"I have no idea what you're on about," I argued.

"Dad did that stuff to you," Daisy said. "Just like he did it to me."

"No." I shook my head. "Nuh-uh."

"Stop disassociating and face the truth!" Simone shouted.

I stood up and backed away from them. "You're crazy. You're both…"

"Where are you going?" Simone said, rising from her seat. "Get back here, at once."

"What did you expect?" Daisy sulked. "I told you she's a traitor. Once a traitor, always a traitor."

"Sorry," I muttered, and left the room.

CHAPTER 94

It's not right. It's not right what they're asking. Honestly. They can't expect me to go ahead and say those things. None of it's true. Why would it be? I can't guarantee nothing happened to Daisy when she was still with us, but all this stuff bringing Mom into it and Dad's 'girlfriend'. What's going on here? Seriously. That Simone is trouble.

I walked up the corridor and turned right to approach the school's administration. I was going to come clean alright. I was going to tell my story. The story of the craziness that just happened back there.

"What are you trying to tell me, Rose?" the office lady asked from behind the glass screen. "Did your dad do something to your sisters?"

"What? No!" I exploded. "I just told you, Simone is making me say that."

"I don't know why she would," the lady argued. "She is a licensed doctor, you know. They're not exactly the ones who make up stories. Little girls, on the other hand…"

"I'll prove it. I'll show you. She's in there with Daisy right now."

"Daisy? Is this the sister who disappeared?"

"Yes."

"Oh, okay." She sighed. "Alright, let's see what she says."

The lady came out from the reception and stepped through to meet me in the corridor. We proceeded along until we reached Simone's office, which was closed.

The lady knocked on it. "Are you in there, Simone?"

I glared at her and forced open the door.

Simone and Daisy were as I'd left them.

"I'm sorry to barge in here when you're with someone," the lady began. "But little Rose here has said–"

"That's her–" I said, pointing. "That's Daisy."

Daisy turned from the chair. The yellow ribbon was gone. It had been replaced with a red one.

"I'm not Daisy," she said. "I'm Rose."

"No!" I yelled. "I'm Rose!"

"I'm Rose," she repeated and faced Simone.

"Well, this is a bit of a conundrum," the office lady exclaimed. "How are we supposed to know which is which?"

"May I speak to you outside?" Simone asked.

"I guess you better," the office lady replied.

They went out together, leaving me with Daisy.

"What's she saying?" I asked.

"Who cares?" Daisy shrugged.

"Why are you trying to make me say all that stuff about Dad?" I demanded. "You know it's all lies."

"They owe us."

"Who does?"

"Mom and Dad."

"Well, maybe if you just get away from her and come see us–"

"Ha! They never wanted me, don't you know that?"

"No."

"That's why you don't talk about me, *ever*."

"How do you know that?"

"Simone knows you. She knows Violet. She knows Poppy. Pretty soon, we're all going to go live with her. She'll be your new mom."

I stared at her. "I don't know who you are anymore."

She stood from the chair. Approached me. Plucked a strand of my hair.

"Ouch!" I cried.

"She did that to me every time I said no," Daisy said.

"Who did? Simone?"

The door reopened. "Sorry about that," Simone said cheerily.

The office lady was beckoning me. "Rose, come on."

I glanced back at Simone. "You might have convinced her," I said, "but I'll be telling Mom and Dad everything tonight. I know what you're trying to do."

Simone gave a cold, relaxed smile.

The office lady pulled me away.

* * *

"So?" I demanded, a minute later. "What did she tell you?"

"That's little Poppy in there," the lady answered. "She borrowed one of your ribbons to fool the bullies who are after her."

"Alright," I said. "Come with me."

"No, darling. I have to–"

"I'll show you!" I squealed, stamping my foot on the ground. "I'll show you that's not Poppy!"

"Um… Uh…"

I led the lady down the corridor till we reached our classroom. She was tall enough to peer through the windows, and I went to the door, just to make sure.

"You see?" I hissed.

Right there. Violet at the front. And Poppy at the back.

The lady turned away from the window. Her expression had changed. "What game is this?"

"I already told you," I gushed. "We used to have a sister named Daisy but she got kidnapped. That's her in the office, pretending to be one of us. Simone knows everything. She's trying to make me say bad things about Mom and Dad so she can force us to live with her."

"Come here, Rose."

I went to the lady's side.

She bent down to my level, and asked, "Do you swear every word you said to me is true?"

"I swear."

She touched her lips anxiously. Then she stood back up and went to the window. I rocked back and forth, waiting for her.

"I have to check," she said. "I have to be one hundred percent certain."

"What do you mean?"

She sighed. "Follow me."

* * *

We walked down the corridor again, for one last time. As we passed the administrator's office, she told me, "Wait here." Then turned. "Don't move from where I can see you."

I remained frozen. I watched her go back to Simone's office. She didn't knock this time. She just went right in. I fumbled around for my ball. I moved around the side of the corridor till I was facing the opposite wall.

Bounce, return, catch. Bounce, return, catch.

And there it was. A cry of alarm. It was faint, but I heard it.

Of course, that was ridiculous. Simone wouldn't do anything on school property. There were cameras and staff around. At least… well, maybe not in this part of the corridor. In fact, I'm not sure how many cameras there were around here to be truthful.

You imagined it. Your mind's playing tricks on you again.

I put the ball in my pocket and shuffled along the hallway.

The door to Simone's office opened. It was Simone, not the lady.

"There you are," she purred. "Now why don't you be a good girl, and come in here?"

I backed away.

"I just want to talk to you. That's all I want, Rose."

I shook my head. "I don't believe you."

CHAPTER 95

I don't trust the teachers. I don't trust the faculty. I don't trust the principal. Simone's anticipated my every move. She's already spoken to them about me. My name is ringing out over the PA system. I'm being called to the front office. They need to speak to me. They need to explain how Simone's right and I'm wrong.

And then they need to shut me up.

I'm not shutting up. I'm going to scream about this till my lungs burst.

I'm on my way home. At first Mom seems like the obvious answer. She'll listen. She'll protect me. But then I realized something else. I saw how she could be manipulated. I imagined Daisy, her long-lost daughter, reuniting after all these years of pain and suffering. Daisy would seem weak, like Poppy. Her words would carry the same blood and fire that mine do. And behind all of it, she'd puppeteer things with Violet's cunning intellect.

Love her as I might, Mom wasn't ready to deal with this.

And so I knew, I had to put my father to the test.

* * *

Dad's work was three towns over from our neighborhood. I'd been there a few times. Figuring out how to get there wasn't the easiest, but I did remember us driving past a train station on the way there. I sketched out a map in my mind of where I would walk once I reached the station… and it seemed too far. I wasn't sure. It was hard to tell.

"Drat."

I had to be cleverer than this. Of course I could always phone his office… if I knew its number. If I had a phone. I thought about going into a gas station or café and asking for help first… but it seemed a bit awkward. Then I thought about going to the public library, but even though it was probably nearby, I wasn't exactly sure where to walk to get there. In fact, after I deviated from my usual route home from school, I was sort of lost.

I spied an old lady on her knees doing some gardening, and decided to approach her.

"Hi there."

She glanced up at me. "Good morning."

"Yes, good morning." I smiled. "Uh. Excuse me."

She stopped what she was doing, and wiped her forehead with a cloth. "Yes, dear?"

"I need to call my dad at his work. Can you help me?"

"I suppose so." She took off her gloves and got up. She produced a cell phone. "What's your name, dear?"

"Rose."

"Lovely name… Do you know his number?"

"We have to look it up." I gave her as much information as I had about my father's building.

"Does that look right?" she asked, showing me a picture.

I nodded. "Think so."

She punched in the number and handed me the phone. I put it to my ear.

"Braxton and Greene Financials, Jessica speaking."

"Uh. Nicholas Greene, please."

"Mr. Greene isn't available at the moment. May I take a message?"

I sighed. "This is his daughter, Rose. I need to be put in touch with him urgently. It's an emergency."

Silence.

"Hello?"

"How is your mother, Rose? Keeping well?"

"What business is that of yours?"

"Haven't you ever been told it's rude to talk back to your elders?"

"Just put me through to Dad. Or I'll get you in trouble."

The old lady motioned to me. "Give it here, dear."

I reluctantly handed it over.

"Who is this?" my new friend demanded. "Never you mind who I am – you just put this young lady's father on the phone immediately, or there'll be serious trouble coming to you…" She nodded to me. "We're on hold now."

I smiled. A minute passed.

"Yes. Yes, I have Rose right here for you, sir." She handed me the phone.

"Rose?"

"Hi, Dad. Something's happened at school. I can't say over the phone. But I need you to pick me up."

"I'm sorry, honey, but that's completely out of the question."

"But it's an emergency."

"I've already spoken with your principal. I've been informed of your antics this morning and I must say I was not impressed in the slightest. We are going to have a very serious chat when I see you next."

"What part of emergency don't you get? Are you really abandoning me right now?"

"I'm not abandoning you. Go back to school. I'll see you on Saturday."

"Dad!"

"One last thing, Rose. Don't be rude to Jessica. She deserves better. Alright? Okay. Bye, honey."

I stood there, dumbfounded.

The lady took her phone away.

"No luck, huh?"

I started crying.

"Oh goodness me–"

"He doesn't get it! No one gets it!"

"It's alright, angel. Please. Calm down…"

"Sorry."

I wiped my eyes. I reached into my pocket for a tissue. But once my hand was in there, I realized something else was missing.

CHAPTER 96

No, no, no! This cannot be happening!

Can you even believe this? How did I lose my ball out here? Did it just fall from my pocket? Wouldn't I have noticed it? Wouldn't I have heard it, felt it, seen it, knew it the moment it happened?

I want to stop running. I want to catch my breath. I'm going over the ground too fast. I'm going to miss it.

No, you won't.

My ball is so red I'll see it coming a mile away.

Red is all I can see.

"Aw! Where is it?!"

That's me getting angry. My thinking is distorted. I'm trying to remember the last time I did have my hand on it, would have been all the way back at school. Between here and there is where I must have lost it. Now did I come in here from the left? Or was it the right?

Why do all these streets look the same?

* * *

Hours pass. Morning becomes noon. I'm going around in circles out here. I'm tired, hungry and dizzy. I don't know if I'm any closer to my school, or if I've just gone completely away from it. I don't recognize these roads. I don't know the people. I'm going to have to ask for help again. But all these faces are so unfriendly.

"Daisy."

The sound of her voice makes me shudder. I don't want to turn. I don't want to look. I'm caught up in the hopelessness of it all.

"Looking for something?"

Well, now I have to turn.

It's Simone, in the driver's seat of her car. Pulling up slowly beside me.

I can see the ball. It's in the palm of her hand.

"Give me that," I growled at her.

She pushed open the passenger door. "Come and get it."

"No!"

"No?"

She reached over to pull the door shut.

"Wait," I pleaded.

I stepped in to stop her from closing it.

"Well?" she beckoned.

I reached for the ball.

She grabbed me by the throat and pulled me into the car.

"Give it! Give it! Give it!" I yelled. "It's mine!"

She kept it away from me. "Shut the door."

I made a face. Then yanked it shut.

She pulled away from the curb.

"Ball. Now," I ordered.

She tossed it to me.

I turned it over in my hands to make sure it wasn't damaged.

Not a blemish in sight.

"Things have changed," Simone said. "Listen to me carefully. You had your chance to go along with our plan, and you've refused us. You've also stirred up a bit of trouble for us at the school. We'd hoped you would be more understanding. You do owe your sister a great deal, after all. What we wanted from you, wasn't too much to ask."

I quietly stroked my ball. "Just let me out please."

"It's not that simple. I'll show you why."

A few moments later, the school came into view. Turns out I wasn't so far away from it after all.

We drove around the perimeter, until we reached a view of the grass oval.

"Straight through there," Simone advised.

"What?"

"Just look. You'll see."

I followed where she was pointing. It took a moment, but there they were. In the distance. Three familiar faces walking together on the track. Violet, Poppy and...

"She's still wearing that ribbon."

"It's hers now," Simone said. "You're going to wear this."

She put the yellow ribbon into my hand.

"The hell I am."

"Look at me. Come on. You *are* Daisy. You've always been Daisy. She's Rose and she's always been Rose."

I looked on at my sisters walking together.

It was as if Violet and Poppy didn't know that she wasn't me.

"You're not getting away with this," I said defiantly. "There's no way you'll pull it off while I'm alive."

Simone stared at me. "You don't think much before you speak, do you?"

I kicked the interior with both feet and tried to force open the door. "Let me out of here!"

"No," Simone resisted. "No, Daisy, I will not."

"Stop calling me that!"

"It's your name, honey. You are the yellow child. Or the golden child. I saw you that day, when your mother spoke your name. I saw you quickly scurry away to the tunnel where you could have Rose switch places with you. Of course, I didn't know that wasn't you who crawled out the other side. I didn't know that you were still in that dark tunnel, just staring down at the plastic. Listening. Listening to her screams as she tried to explain what you'd done."

My face had fallen. "You were there?"

"Of course, I was. Who do you think took your sister away?"

CHAPTER 97

Once a stranger, always a stranger.

I had to get out. I had to get help. But the car is moving by the school. We're heading into the road at full speed. I can't escape from her so easily.

"Just sit there and be quiet," Simone said in an authoritative tone. "I'm going to tell you everything now. All the stuff Rose glossed over. It's time you learned the truth."

I stopped fighting. My emotions were switching. The ribbon was having an effect. My true identity, staring right back at me.

"I'm not who you think I am," Simone said. "I know you, Daisy. I know what you're going through. I know how you're seeing things. You're afraid of me. You think I mean you harm. It's understandable. You think I won't let you out of the car now because I'm going to hurt you. Wrong. I just have to tell you my side of the story, so you don't go charging after your sister. I couldn't bear it. After all she's been through…"

We were making a turnoff, highway rolling up ahead.

"So, you took Daisy?" I asked.

Simone glared at me.

"I mean… you took Rose?"

"Yes. Of course, I didn't want to. But I was made to see it was the only way."

"How's that?"

"Maybe you remember, maybe you don't. I was with you at your father's cousin's wedding that day. It was a few weeks before it happened. I saw the four of you playing on the grass. I helped set you up for the photo. Afterwards, I gave you some cake."

"I thought we just had family there," I said.

"Family, and friends. I was… a friend of your father's. I was his girlfriend before he dumped me for Sarah."

"So, this was all about revenge?"

"Absolutely not," Simone said.

There was a pause. I found myself turning towards the window. Fields of grass passed by without end.

"Your father paid me to take Rose," Simone continued. "It wasn't a lot of money, but I thought I was doing the right thing. He said he wanted to pull you away from your mother. He wanted you to move into his big house in the country, where the wedding was held. He was going to take each of you, one at a time. And then he was going to leave your mother and be with me. We'd live happily ever after…"

"But that didn't happen."

"He had no intention of having me move in. He just used my love to manipulate me. All your father wanted, with… every fiber of his being, was to have one of you to himself."

I shook my head. "No…"

Simone continued, "I thought she might have died. I thought some accident must have occurred. I just didn't understand why Rose never came back to your family, why everything just carried on as usual with Nicholas. I couldn't figure it out. I confronted him about it… five years or so after our relationship had deteriorated. He said Rose was doing fine and he was just seeing his secretary or something now. But when I asked Jessica about it, she had no idea what I was talking about.

"I looked up various schools that Rose may have been attending. There was no record of her enrollment anywhere. I was sure she must be dead. I had to know. I had to know if I'd killed her. So, I got friendly with some of the servants at his place… and none of them knew about Rose either."

She looked at me. "But they all heard a child's screams late at night," she said.

I bit my lip. I didn't want to believe it.

I didn't want to make the leap my mind was racing towards.

"All that stuff about the sexual abuse that Rose described to you," Simone explained, "all of that really happened. It was your father, Nicholas. It was his friends. The parties they held at that house… One night I drove up there and saw for myself what was going on. And then I came back, broke in. I found where Rose was living…"

"Stop," I said, tears in my eyes. "I don't want to hear any more."

"I rescued her – Rose, Daisy, whatever she was to be called. I'd always wanted children with Nicholas. When Sarah gave birth to so many of you, I thought it unfair she should get you all, because I had love to give. I wanted you, and she didn't."

I wiped my eyes.

So much horror. So much pain.

How could he have done this to us?

"I tried to make Rose forget about Sarah and the three of you. I thought about taking her overseas, but it would also be difficult. Nicholas knew someone had taken Rose from his dungeon, but he didn't know it was me. Nevertheless, I had to keep Rose safe. She kept talking to me about you and Violet and Poppy. She missed her sisters so much. I couldn't just let her go live with you, as Nicholas would obviously intervene. No. If she was going to see her sisters again, I would have to bring them to her…"

Outside, we were slowing down. Our destination was near.

I tried to poke holes in her story. Tried to see where she could be lying or wrong. But the more I thought about my father, and my memories of him living with us, the more it was adding up.

"Do you understand now why I asked you to tell the story about Nicholas? Do you see now why I need to bring you girls to safety?"

I found myself nodding. "I get it now. But… why not just tell Mom? Go to the police?"

"I was too afraid to face your mother again," she confessed. "After what I'd already done to her, she wouldn't believe a word I'd say."

"But she'd believe Rose, wouldn't she?"

"Yes, Daisy," Simone whispered. "Maybe. Maybe she would…"

CHAPTER 98

We have now arrived.

Simone has a spacious five-bedroom residence in a middle-class neighborhood. Everything is clean and properly furnished. She has a pot of fresh daisies on the desk waiting for me. The walls are yellow. The carpet is white. The bedspreads are gold.

"This is her room, isn't it?" I asked, standing in the doorway.

"It's yours now," Simone said ominously.

There's a bunch of boxes in the hallway. My sister's just moved out.

And I'm moving in.

"Have a look in the cupboard," Simone said, walking in with me.

I went to the glass door and pushed it across.

Her clothes. Her dresses. Her shoes. Her accessories.

Daisy's.

"Want to try them on?" Simone asked.

I closed the door. "Simone."

"Yes, sweetie?"

"I want to go home."

A pause. "Turn around."

My feet shifted on the ground.

"To the side. There."

I was facing the dresser mirror.

Simone stood beside me in the reflection.

"Who is that in the mirror?" she asked. "What are their names?"

"It's Daisy," I said. The golden ribbon couldn't lie.

"And who is standing next to Daisy?"

I swallowed. "Daisy's mother."

"That's correct. I am your mother."

"Is that what you want me to call you?"

"Well, we don't need to lose all sight of reality. You can keep calling me Simone."

A moment passed.

"Simone?"

"Yes, honey?"

"What happens now?"

"You're going to live here now," she said. "Come on. I'll show you."

I followed Simone back into the hall.

She began to open the bedroom doors. "This is for Rose. You can see."

I peered in.

A red room, just like mine at home.

"Over here we have one for Violet."

A purple bedroom next door.

"And over here, back next to you. Poppy's room."

A blue room.

She'd spared no expense.

"Well?" Simone said proudly. "What do you think? You're impressed, right?"

I lowered my eyes. "You're mad. Completely, totally, mad."

SLAP.

Simone's hand came out of nowhere and swiped across my tender cheek.

"Don't you say that to me!" she shouted. "I am your mother! You will treat me with respect, young lady!"

"Ouch," I moaned. "You didn't have to hit me."

"Go to your room. You can think about what you've done."

She ushered me in, and before I knew it the door was closing.

"Wait–" I began.

Click.

The door was locked.

CHAPTER 99

I don't know what's happening. I don't know why I'm here. Is this my fault? Have I been stupid? I hate Simone, I'm afraid of Simone, but the things she says just break me apart. I can no longer argue with her. It is useless.

I sit in front of the dresser mirror. I look at the girl in the reflection. I'd said her name was Daisy, but I'm not Daisy. That's not me. That hasn't been me for seven years. So, technically, I've been Rose longer than I've been Daisy, and Rose has been Daisy longer than she's been Rose. You can't just make us switch back. I don't care about what's right. I don't care about what's fair.

"Yes, this is Dr. Archer. Who is calling?"

I heard Simone's voice echoing from down the hall. I got up from the bed and crouched by the door.

"Yes, I did see her earlier this afternoon. She came to see me in my office."

Has Mom raised the alarm? Did she see Daisy wasn't me?

"Oh goodness! No, I had no idea. That's terrible."

Please help me, Mom. Please, please, please.

"Yes, she was awake when I left, she just said she needed to lie down. I let her have a rest on my sofa. You're saying she…"

Wait. Are they talking about me?

"That's just awful. Who would have thought? If I'd known she'd had heart problems…"

Oh. It's the lady from the office they're talking about. The lady who believed me.

"I'll be right there, yes."

I heard Simone's footsteps moving back up the hallway. I backed away from the door… holding my breath.

"Daisy?"

I hesitated. "Yes?"

"I'm going out for a little bit. Don't try and escape, please. You know what happens to people who get in my way."

"Okay," I moaned.

When she didn't immediately move from the door, I realized she may have been having second thoughts about coming in. Or second thoughts about taking me.

"Love you, Mom," I quickly added.

She sighed with relief. "I love you too, Daisy."

CHAPTER 100

Bounce, return, catch. Bounce, return, catch. Bounce, return, catch…

Fear not, my friends. I'm not giving up.

I'll get what I want. I'll take it back.

I could break the window and run right now. But I think it's just leading to the backyard, and I want to be sure I can get to the front.

That door will unlock soon. It has to. I'll pretend to be Daisy. I'll pretend everything's fine. Simone will be fooled. She'll put her back to me, and then *bang*. I'm gone.

I'll go to Mom, as I should have at the start. I'll tell her everything. She'll know it's me. She'll know it's her little Rose. That other one is a screwed-up mess. Her nature will come out if provoked. It will be there for all to see.

Goodbye Simone.

Goodbye Dad.

Goodbye Daisy.

You can all burn in the fire as far as I'm concerned. I never had three sisters. I only had two sisters. I made the third one up. Just like the dog Sparky. He was imaginary too. As was the open front door, and the screams in the other room.

My screams.

My screams weren't real either.

He never touched me. No, no, no. He did not. My father loves me. He can still burn, of course. The main thing is that I'm not violated. Not in body. Not in mind. Not in spirit.

Click.

Gosh. Took her long enough. It's almost dark now.

The door swings open slowly but it's not Simone standing there.

It's Rose – I mean Daisy – I mean Rose – I mean…

"Enjoying your room?"

"This has to stop," I whispered.

"What has to?"

"Give me my ribbon."

She smirked. "Fat chance."

I stepped out into the passage and saw Violet and Poppy appear from the archway.

"What are you doing here?" I demanded. "Is Simone back yet?"

"She's asleep," Violet answered, glancing over her shoulder.

"You know she means to keep us all here."

"They know," Rose assured me. "I'm just showing them their new rooms."

I stood back while Violet and Poppy came down the passage, following Rose. I grabbed Poppy's wrist. "What are you doing?"

"What?" Poppy replied.

"Do you actually want to live here away from Mom?"

"I don't know."

"Wait till you see your room, Poppy," Rose called.

Poppy went along to see the room.

I backed out of the passage, looked to the kitchen, the living room sofa. I walked over and saw Simone sleeping.

It was time for us to go.

I hurried to the front door, made sure it was unlocked and open. Then I raced back to the hallway.

Violet and Rose were going into the purple room, while Poppy was just sitting in the blue room by herself.

"It's just like at home," Poppy said.

I hurried over and grabbed her arm. "Come on."

"I'm not ready to go yet."

I put my hands on her shoulders. "Listen to me. We're in danger here. Simone is a mad woman. She kidnapped me and had me locked in that room all day. I think she also might have killed a woman at school."

"What woman?"

"She works in the front office. She was trying to help me…"

Poppy shook her head. "I don't believe you."

"But why would I–?"

"I believe Rose."

"That's not Rose," I hissed. "I'm Rose."

"I know. You used to be Rose."

I shook my head. "Please, Poppy. Don't be stupid."

"I'm not stupid," she said. "But it's safer here than at home. It's never safe there…"

I know what she's talking about. But I can't think about that right now.

"If we tell her," I whispered, "Mom will protect us."

"She doesn't listen," Poppy said sadly.

"Mom can't help us," Rose said from the doorway. "With Simone, we have a chance."

I turned around and saw Violet behind her.

"So, you're just going along with this as well?" I asked.

Violet shrugged. "Simone reckons we can get money from Dad if he's found guilty. Maybe even enough for private school."

"Who cares about that?" I exploded. "Am I the only sane one here?"

"Daisy," Rose said sternly. "Daisy, calm down."

"Shut up," I snapped.

I went to push by her in the doorway, but suddenly there was a pain in my side.

"Whoa," one of my sisters exclaimed. "What did you just do?"

I could feel the knife was still in me.

I staggered along the passage, the walls dissolving in front of my eyes. I couldn't see properly, I could barely hear. A warm trickle lined the path below.

"It's for the best," one of them said. "She would have talked."

I collapsed to my knees. Simone was standing in front of me.

"Daisy?" she cried. She put her fingers to my cheeks. "Daisy, are you alright? What's wrong?"

I am here. And I am not here.

I am Daisy and I am Rose.

"Well, I guess we better finish her off," one of my sisters cackled.

"No," Simone said. "I won't let you!"

She was pulling me back up, helping me to stand.

"Who did this?"

There's my ball. It's rolling out to the living room floor.

"Which of you was it?"

"It was Rose," said Violet.

"It was Poppy," said Rose.

"It was Violet," said Poppy.

All I see is red.

PART VI

Poppy

CHAPTER 101

I don't know what time it is. I don't know how I got here. I don't remember a thing.

In a way, I shouldn't be surprised. Life keeps fading in and out.

What happened back at the house… it's already gone.

"Poppy…?"

A voice in the dark behind me.

"Poppy, is that you…?"

Yes, it's me. I wish it wasn't. I wish I was someone else. I can't handle this world. I can't handle it… much longer.

"Poppy."

I glanced to my left and saw my friend, Zowie, sitting down beside me. We were on the edge of a long wooden dock, reaching out into the ocean. Back on the beach, I could see a campfire, flickering in between the silhouettes of the others.

I should have been with them tonight.

"Are you hurt?" Zowie asked. "Is that your blood?"

"No."

I lifted the flower from my pocket. Rose's flower. The artificial clip. I held it out in silence. A gentle breeze came by and sent it floating away into the water.

"What happened?"

"Rose is dead," I said softly. "It's all my fault."

CHAPTER 102

I didn't go home that night. I slept on the beach with my friends. We stayed up till sunrise, telling stories, and singing sad songs. They didn't quite know what to make of my ordeal… the little that I told them. But they knew I was a good person who belonged with them, so they looked after me. Until the new day was here.

I returned home around midday, Zowie came with me. She was probably my best friend at the moment. The story with her was – her mom had recently thrown her out because she had borrowed some of her jewelry. She stayed with her sister for a bit before moving back. I don't know how long it will last.

Zowie's boyfriend, Mark, had been arrested for possession of narcotics… I didn't know the specifics. I'll be honest – he wasn't a great guy. I'd only met him a couple of times, and I think once I felt him touching me while I was asleep. I didn't tell Zowie though. I didn't want to break her heart.

"It was self-defense," Zowie was saying to me as we walked up my street. "That's all you need to say. Don't say anything else."

"Why not?"

"The cops will twist it," she said. "They don't care about the truth – they only care about getting a result. Look at what happened to Mark."

"But he wasn't innocent."

"Those drugs weren't his – they were planted. He swears it to me."

"If you say so."

She stopped me. "I don't do drugs. Not after what they did to my sister. You know that, right?"

I nodded. Zowie's sister was in more trouble than she is.

"It's going to be okay, Poppy. Come here."

We hugged.

* * *

Zowie had a point. As much as I'd blacked out some of last night, I knew things had gotten away from me in the end. Lines had been crossed. Or maybe just blurred.

Maybe it really was self-defense.

After all of it though, there was no telling what Violet had told the cops. Violet, who'd stayed behind.

"Where are you going?!" she'd demanded as I fled from the house. "Poppy! We're in this together! Come back here!"

But I'd left. I couldn't deal with it.

I... I...

"I killed someone," I said out loud.

"Shut the hell up," Zowie hissed at me. "Your house is right there."

And I could see it. Three cop cars parked out front. Two officers talking at the foot of the drive. Police tape everywhere.

I suddenly felt sick.

"What's the matter?" Zowie asked, as I came to a halt.

"Maybe I shouldn't go back," I said. "Maybe we should just run away together."

"Ooh, Poppy," Zowie moaned. "You know I love you. But I have Mark as well."

I swallowed.

"We have to face this. We can do it."

"But I don't know if I can."

She grabbed both my hands. "*We* can."

CHAPTER 103

My heart is racing as we approach the house. I don't want to be here. I want to run away. But I know Zowie's right. I do have to face this. I have to face what I've done.

"We can't let you in the house."

"My clothes are in there," I argued. "And I need a shower."

"We can't let you in."

And now we wait, the officers standing over us. We wait for the higher authorities to arrive.

"You don't need to be here," one of the officers advised Zowie.

"Yes, I do."

"She does," I affirmed.

"Were you here last night?"

"No, I was at the beach…"

"Where I went afterwards," I added.

"Okay, you can come down to the precinct with us," the officers decided. "We will have some questions for you… what's your surname, Zowie?"

I grit my teeth together as Zowie gave her details. I hadn't meant to get her involved in this.

"Do I need to call my mom?" she asked. "She's going to be mad."

"How old are you?"

"Seventeen."

"Yes, your mom needs to be present for the questioning."

"She hasn't done anything!" I interrupted. "Leave her alone! You just want me, don't you?"

"It's okay," Zowie said. "I just want to help."

I lowered my head in shame.

"Okay, just hang tight," the officer said. "The captain will be here soon."

It was happening then. We were both about to be taken in. My freedom was on the line.

"Are you okay?" Zowie said, leading me away. "We'll get through this."

I shook my head. "I'm sorry, I don't know what I was thinking last night."

"Careful," she whispered.

She was right. I couldn't say too much. The men were listening.

* * *

Captain Frank Roper showed up about fifteen minutes later. We were in another town, so this shouldn't have been his investigation. But of course once it was known that it was us again – the Greene Girls – he must have been called down.

He was looking at me the moment he got out of the car. The last time I'd seen him was not long after Dad's trial. He stopped by Simone's old house to congratulate us.

"Hi, Poppy." He waved on approach. "Remember me?"

I waved back. "Yes."

"I'm sorry about Rose. She was a lovely girl."

"She never liked you."

He gave a pained smile. "Yes. I was a fool to begin with. I should have listened to her and Dr. Archer. But… we can't change the past, can we?"

"No."

"This is Zowie," I said, introducing my friend. "She was with me last night, after it happened."

"Hello," Zowie said.

"Hi, Zowie," Roper replied. "Listen, I want you to know you're not in any trouble. No one's upset with you for fleeing the scene like you did. It would have been a hell of a thing to witness."

"Witness…?"

What's he talking about?

"Where's Violet?" I asked.

Maybe she took the fall for me.

"She's staying with one of our therapists," he explained. "A short-term solution, of course."

"Did she tell you what happened?"

"Yes." Roper sighed. He glanced back at the house. "She told us about the break-in with Jessica. How Jessica attacked poor Rose. How Simone tried to stop her."

I closed my eyes.

It was the next part I had to live with.

"And then finally… how they killed each other."

CHAPTER 104

It's gone then. It never happened. Violet covered for me. She didn't tell them what I did to Jessica. I, myself, don't know what happened. It was like I wasn't me anymore. I was somebody else.

"Rose," I whispered, in the back of Captain Roper's car. "Where are you?"

I saw his eyes look at me momentarily in the mirror. But then he pretended not to hear.

I didn't want to believe it. I didn't want to believe she was gone. And I don't care what they want to say about her. I don't care if they're saying she did some awful things.

Rose was my sister. And I love her.

"It will all be over soon," Roper said quietly. "This is the end now. It has to be…"

I wanted to believe him. But a part of me knew, some things followed us forever.

* * *

Captain Roper had sent one of the officers into the house to pack some of my clothes to take with me. They'd taken Zowie to the precinct, but driven me first to where Violet was staying so I could shower and change.

"We need a statement," Roper advised me before we got out of the car. "It doesn't have to be today, if you're not ready."

"I'll be ready," I said. "Once I talk to Violet. That's okay, isn't it?"

He sighed. "As long as the therapist is present."

"What's her name?"

"Trisha."

"Okay."

* * *

Trisha was a nice lady. She was young – late-twenties, maybe. She was slender with dark skin and frizzy hair. She had a really caring, angelic smile whenever she spoke to me, that made me feel safe. I don't know why it was so important – it's just I didn't know if I was going to trust her after everything we'd been through with the mother figures in our life.

"Where is she?" I asked Trisha, after I'd changed.

"In her room," Trisha replied. "I mean, the room where she's staying."

I nodded slowly. I could see from the window that Captain Roper was outside on the phone with someone.

"Can I talk to her alone?"

Trisha hesitated. "For a few minutes, I suppose."

"Thank you." I followed where she gestured down the hall.

"I'm right here, if you need me," she said.

"I'll keep that in mind."

* * *

Violet was sitting near a flowerpot by the window. For a moment, I thought it was the same as the one she kept on her desk at home… but it was different. "You're back."

"Yes," I replied. I walked over and sat on the bed.

She was still looking out the window, away from me. "Why did you leave me there?"

I shook my head. "I… I… I just couldn't deal with it…"

"We're supposed to be sisters," Violet said coldly. "We're supposed to count on each other."

Silence for a moment.

"Thanks for not telling on me," I said.

"You're welcome."

"They really ate your story up, huh?"

"It was the truth." She swallowed. "To some degree."

"What's wrong with me?"

"Huh?"

"Why did I do that to Jessica?"

Violet glanced back at me. "It wasn't you. It wasn't you who stabbed her–"

"Yes, I did–"

"No," she said firmly. "It was Lily."

"Lily?"

"Our secret sister."

Images flashed in my mind.

The pink necklace.

The pink handle.

Dad.

"Don't tell, please," I begged her.

"I'll never tell," Violet stated. "Your secret's safe with me."

CHAPTER 105

I took a few steps and stood outside Trisha's house, the sun's rays bearing down on me. Captain Roper hadn't seen me yet – he was still on the phone. I looked up into the vast, blue skies. They were so beautiful, so infinite. I just felt like I wanted to soar all the way up there. Disappear in the foreverness.

Thinking back to Violet. Thinking back to dark houses, with dark rooms, and people screaming. I couldn't do it. At a certain point, the fear becomes too much. I fall out of myself and become the very thing I'm trying to forget.

I never wanted any of that. I'm trying to be a peaceful person.

Aren't I?

"You ready?" Roper hollered. "Everything okay?"

My childhood was ending. I realized that now. The world would only let me stay in my imagination for so long. Until one day, I'd look up. And I wouldn't see the sky at all.

* * *

"Did you speak with Violet?" Roper asked when we were driving again. "Was Trisha there?"

"I saw them both," I answered nonchalantly.

"Is Violet okay?"

"I don't know. Not really, I guess. She has a different way of processing things, I think."

"How about you?"

"I'm fine."

"Poppy?"

I exhaled. "Look, no offense. I don't really know you. I can't let it all out here."

"Fair enough." He tried a different tact. "How about Trisha? Did you get on well with her?"

"She seems nice." I reflected. "But they all seem nice at first."

"All?"

"Moms. People in general, I guess."

"What was Simone like? Wasn't she…"

"She was okay."

He made a face. "Just okay? She gave her life for you."

"Simone had a whole other side to her. She was capable of a lot of things."

"What sort of things?"

"I think she had someone killed for us in the beginning. Daisy said…"

"You spoke with Daisy? When was this?"

I was talking too much. I had to remember this man was in charge of the police. "It's nothing. Forget it."

His eyes watched me in the rearview mirror. I knew he wouldn't be satisfied with that.

"Were you with your mom, Sarah, when Daisy was killed?"

"Mom never killed Daisy."

"She didn't? Who did?"

"It was Lily," I said.

CHAPTER 106

She's still with me. The buildings come and go on the road beside us. The people. The cars. The sights and scenery. It doesn't matter how fast I'm going. It doesn't matter how far I run to. Lily is chasing me through the fog. She wants to show me something. The truth behind all things–

"Poppy?"

I looked up to Captain Roper.

He smiled, aware I was far away for a minute there.

I looked around outside the car, and saw we were in the precinct parking lot.

"Let's get this over with," I muttered.

* * *

The precinct was busy as hell. I could barely stand or move around the main entrance without brushing into someone. Captain Roper eventually led me to the elevator, and we went up to the third floor, where there was an empty conference room.

"I do apologize," he said, "there will be a wait. I thought we'd have someone from child services to sit in on your interview, but some wires got crossed apparently. So, we're just waiting for Trisha."

I brushed my fingers along the side of the table as I moved around it.

"Can I get you something to eat or drink?" he offered. "Have you had lunch? Or… breakfast?"

"A blueberry muffin would be nice."

"Blueberry?" He chuckled. "Sure. I'll see what I can do."

As he left, I walked to the watercooler at the back of the room and filled a paper cup.

* * *

Twenty minutes went by and nothing. No Trisha. No muffins. I could feel myself getting restless. I knew Roper was going to ask me about Lily when the questioning started – I shouldn't have said what I did back there.

It's like, I'm still figuring it out.

Who Lily is. What she became.

Violet knows more than I do. Maybe, Violet can see the truth more easily. Everything's a fog for me. I haven't thought about Daisy's death in such a long time. But I was right there when it happened.

We all were.

I opened the door where we came in and looked out of the conference room. At this point, I was so hungry I'd settle for food that didn't have blue stuff in it. That was really a childish thing we had – being obsessed with our colors. Obsessed with… being seen for who we are.

I followed the corridor round and noticed a door ajar on my left.

I thought I heard Captain Roper's voice from within.

"Uh, excuse me…?" I called peering in.

"…Let's go over it again. Where did you go after dropping Violet off last night?" Roper was asking.

"To my house. Home, where I went to bed and went to sleep and that's the end of it," Detective Burke replied.

But they weren't in this room. They were both in the next room, and I could see everything through a two-way mirror. Burke was sitting at the table, his sleeves rolled up, his eyes puffy, his hair a mess. Captain Roper was standing right next to him, while the detective who asked us questions at the school yesterday was sitting directly opposite.

"You know how this works," the detective said. "We have your cell. We're tracking your calls, your location. You know your story won't stand up."

Burke shrugged.

"Why carry on the charade?"

"This is such bullshit," Burke muttered.

"And why's that?"

"You pricks know I haven't done anything. I never set foot in that house."

"No one's saying you did," Roper rebutted. "We just want the truth, that's all."

"What do you think happened?"

"Alright," the other detective said. "After dropping Violet off, you proceeded to call Jessica Hart, and tell her of the Greene sisters' whereabouts."

"And why would I do that?"

"Ashley," Roper answered. "You always thought they were to blame for Ashley's death."

Burke shook his head.

"It's true, isn't it? You came to me repeatedly at the time–"

"Yeah, you remember what I said. And I don't take it back."

"What did Mr. Burke say? Just so we're all on the same page," the other detective asked.

"He said the killer called him, right before Ashley was being murdered. Isn't that right, Burke?"

"Yeah, that's right."

"The killer? What did they say?"

"I don't know!" Burke shouted. "I just heard Ashley crying out..."

"The killer said something though," Roper added.

"Yeah. They did. But not to me."

A pause.

My heart had started to race again. I looked at the door, wondering if I should leave. This was getting too real.

"They just called me and put the phone off the hook, so I could listen in to Ashely screaming. But before she died, I heard Ashley – she was saying who was in the room with her..."

"And who did she think was there?" the detective asked.

"Violet? Rose? Poppy? She was calling out all their names. And the killer answered her. It was one of them. It was a little girl's voice."

I swallowed hard.

"She said, 'You'll never know...'"

CHAPTER 107

Rose's death was revenge for Ashley. But did Rose really kill her? Was it possible? We never talked about what happened to Ashley. I remember her in Simone's house while Rose was telling her story – the story about how Jessica really killed Georgie. Was it possible Ashley didn't believe Rose? Because if she believed her, then why kill her?

Detective Burke must be wrong. There must be some other explanation. I hadn't figured it out yet. It was staring me right in the face, but I didn't want to believe it. I turned away from the mirror and walked back into the conference room before Captain Roper figured out what I'd witnessed.

"Are you ready, Poppy?" he asked, peering through the doorway a few minutes later. "It's time."

I stood up. "No muffins?"

He shook his head. "No muffins."

* * *

I originally thought we'd be talking in the conference room, casual-like. Not at all. I was taken to an interview room, only a few doors down from where Detective Burke was being grilled. Three chairs, a table, video equipment. Glass behind me. People watching, presumably.

Trisha had now arrived and sat in the room with me while Roper went outside for a bit. She wanted to make sure I was comfortable and happy to give my statement today. I said that I was. Truth be told, I just wanted to get out of there… but a part of me *was* curious. I wanted to understand more about what Rose had done.

I wanted to understand what *I'd* done.

When Captain Roper did return and sat opposite us, I was grateful that it was just him, and not that other detective from school. I knew that one didn't like us.

"Everything okay then?" Roper asked.

"Poppy is here to talk about what happened last night," Trisha said. "As long as we keep things simple and don't stray too far, it should be okay. Right, Poppy?"

"Sure," I said.

I had to give some basic details like my name, address, date of birth, and all that stuff about reading my rights. We passed through that swiftly and the questioning began.

"Before we talk about what happened last night," Roper began, "I think it's important we touch on the death at school yesterday. Violet's friend."

"Leanne," I said.

"Yes. Leanne Lu." He paused. "You know I've spoken with her family. It's been absolutely devastating for them, losing their child. Were you close with Leanne?"

"She was Violet's friend." A pause. "No."

"But you saw her often."

"We went to school together."

"She was in your class?"

"A couple this year."

"How would you describe Leanne and Violet's friendship?"

I hesitated. Looked to Trisha.

"If you don't know, honey, just say so," she said.

"They were friends," I mumbled.

"Right…" Roper replied.

"They were… good friends." I closed my eyes. "I don't know."

"Were they as close as you and Zowie?"

I inhaled sharply. "No."

"No?"

"Leanne visited the house once over the holidays. But I think Violet was away that day. So… it was a bit weird."

"Would it be fair to say, you were all friends in a way?"

"Sure. Why not?"

His head tilted sideways. "Is that not accurate?"

"No– I mean, yes, it's accurate." I turned to Trisha. "We were friends."

"Who do you think killed her?"

"Leanne?"

He nodded.

"I'd rather not say."

"Because it's a bit interesting how at first it seemed like Violet killed her; Violet's reading glasses were nearby anyway." He drew in a breath. "But Rose was really the one locked in the shed, wasn't she? Leanne was Violet's friend – they locked Rose in the shed together, didn't they?"

"I wouldn't know."

"Captain, we're here to talk about the events of last night," Trisha interrupted. "This is exactly the line of questioning we were hoping to avoid."

"It's important we get to the truth, though. Do you agree, Poppy?"

"You don't have to answer him," Trisha advised. "Just say 'no comment' if you don't want to."

"The truth is," I said slowly, "Violet locked Rose in the shed. I saw her when she went up on stage, dressed as Rose."

"Did you go to the shed then?"

"Me?"

"Did you go there?"

I stared at him. "I don't want to lie to you."

"I'm not asking you to."

"Don't make me lie!" I shouted.

"Alright, I think we're done," Trisha said. "If you can't stay on topic, Captain, Poppy and I would like to terminate–"

"Did you go to that shed?!" Roper demanded.

Tears rolled down my cheeks. "Yes. I went there."

"And what happened next?"

"I… I let Rose out–"

"Who killed Leanne?!"

"It was… it was… it was Lily–"

"There is no Lily!"

"There is, I swear. She's a real person."

Captain Roper got up abruptly. He went to the door and knocked on it. The door opened and the other detective entered, holding an evidence bag. He put it on the table in front of me.

"Do you recognize that?" Captain Roper asked.

I stared down. It was a knife, a knife from our kitchen at home.

"Don't answer him, Poppy," Trisha advised. "Don't say another word."

"I do," I whispered.

"It was found in the bushes near where Leanne was killed. Leanne's blood was on it. There were fingerprints on it too."

I stopped breathing.

"As you know, we fingerprinted you and your sisters after George Hart was found. We tested the prints, and we came up with a match."

"Whose prints were on it?" I asked.

Roper chuckled to himself. He removed the knife from the table and handed it back to the other detective.

"Whose prints?" I repeated.

CHAPTER 108

Captain Roper was reluctant to answer. He thought by withholding that information, he could hopefully get more out of me. But as Trisha was about to pull me out of there, he relented.

"We found Rose's prints," he said. "So, unless you and Rose killed Leanne together, what you've said today is a lie."

A lie.

Was it? Was I deliberately misleading him? Because every time I went back to the shed, I kept seeing one of my sisters, in the pink necklace. There was blood on my hands…

Was it Leanne's?

"I think we're done now," Trisha said. She looked at me. "Are we done?"

I nodded.

"Come on then."

We both stood up.

"Don't bother asking to see Poppy again unless she's under arrest," Trisha said. "You crossed a line – not only with her. But with *me*."

"I apologize," Roper said. "It had to be done. We still need answers." His eyes were on me squarely, as Trisha and I proceeded to the open door. Once there, I turned back to him.

"Rose didn't kill Leanne," I declared. "Like I said before, it was Lily."

* * *

"Poppy, I have to be honest with you," Trisha said as we walked the halls of the precinct. "It's better to say nothing, than to lie to the police. I'm sure you had nothing to do with Leanne's death, but they're going to be asking questions about you now. You just admitted to being present when the murder took place, and you refused to give an honest account of what happened. You're going to need to get proper legal representation."

"Okay," I said tonelessly.

"Poppy?"

I couldn't hear her. She was fading away into the background.

I was going back in my mind. I was trying to see what happened.

To Leanne. To Ashley. To Georgie.

To Daisy.

There she is again.

The girl in the pink necklace. I can see she has the knife in her hand. She's doing something with it I wouldn't dream of doing.

And for a split second, I can see her walking away from Dad's car.

"*Poppy?*"

I stopped.

I can feel a sickness now. It's warning me from going further…

"Poppy!"

I looked over my shoulder for Trisha. Somehow we'd been separated. "Sorry."

"This way."

* * *

We were going down two flights of stairs. The faster we got out of here, the better. I needed to see Zowie again. I had to tell her the truth about everything. She would be the first person I'd told. I know, in my heart, she would accept it.

It's not all in my head. There is a reason these things happen.

"I have some papers to sign," Trisha said as we neared the ground floor. "Are you okay to wait outside for a few minutes?"

"Yeah, I guess."

"You won't run off on me?"

"No." I sighed. "It'll be okay."

"Yeah, I hope so."

Not as convincing as I'd like, but I'll take it.

I could see Detective Burke standing at the reception, waiting in line to talk to someone. I guess his interrogation was finished.

Were they letting him go too?

"Poppy?"

I turned to Trisha. "What?"

"Do you know that man?"

"Who?"

"He's staring right at you."

Looking up again, I could see she was right. Detective Burke was staring at me. And this was no normal stare. His eyes were growing wider and wider in horror.

Self-consciously I lifted my hand from the banister and put it in my pocket. "What?!"

He didn't say anything.

He just kept staring.

CHAPTER 109

"Poppy! Poppy!" Zowie was calling to me the moment I exited the precinct. I ran across the parking lot to where she was, at the side of the road.

"Oh, Zowie." We embraced. "What happened to you?"

"They full-on interrogated me. It was disgusting," she declared. "I'm so glad they couldn't get hold of my mom. She'd kill me."

"Did you have one of those child-services people...?"

She nodded. "My sister's coming to get me now. You should come with us."

"Yeah, okay. I have some woman following me, but..."

I could see Zowie looking over my shoulder. There *was* someone coming our way... but it wasn't Trisha.

"*You*," Detective Burke roared. "You're the killer."

"What?" I mumbled.

Zowie stepped in between us. "Get the hell away from her, you psycho."

"She's the psycho!" Burke taunted. "How many people have you killed, Poppy?"

"No people," I said weakly.

"I know of at least two. First Georgie. We always knew it was the sister who dragged her hand along the banister when she came down the stairs. But then the boy wasn't enough. You went after my partner, Ashley, who was just trying to help you–"

"I didn't! It wasn't me!"

"Who else have you killed? Was it you who killed that girl at your school yesterday? It might as well have been. What about your sister Daisy? Did you kill her too? What about Jessica and Simone last night?"

"I had to – you don't understand!"

"So, you admit it," Burke declared triumphantly.

Zowie turned to face me. "What's he talking about?"

"You don't understand," I sobbed. "It wasn't me. It wasn't ever me. I didn't do it. Not really. It was Lily."

"Right, Lily," Burke scoffed.

"She's our secret sister."

"You're scaring me, Poppy," Zowie said. "Tell me you didn't really kill those people."

I couldn't deny it. I just kept shaking my head.

"Poppy? It isn't true!"

"I've got you now," Burke declared. "Nowhere to run. Nowhere to hide. Your reign of terror is over. At long last."

CHAPTER 110

I'm silent in the car with Trisha on the way back. I'm not going to talk about what just happened. I don't care if she believes Detective Burke. He's wrong about me. He doesn't understand how it works.

Zowie. I wish I didn't have to leave her behind. She doesn't understand either. But it's not her fault. If I told her, I know she would. On the other hand, there's still a lot *I* don't understand. A lot, I don't remember. But yes, it's true. Lily is a part of me.

And I'm a part of her.

* * *

The clock is ticking. I can feel it counting down. I don't know how long it's going to take for Burke to convince Captain Roper they pinned Leanne's murder on the wrong sister, but not very long, I suspect. Even with Rose's prints on the weapon.

"Do you want some lunch?" Trisha asked upon arrival.

"Yes, please."

She opened the fridge and we both peered inside.

"I can make you a sandwich if you like," she suggested.

I pointed to the yogurt. "What about that?"

"Alright. Strawberry or blueberry?"

"Strawberry."

* * *

I wound up taking both and went to see if Violet wanted any. I found her still in her room. She was on the bed, reading a book.

"Yogurt?"

"Gimme." She tossed the book aside and snatched the tub off me. "How'd it go?"

"About that…"

Violet sighed with disappointment. "Oh, Poppy. What did you say?"

"Nothing."

"Literally – nothing?"

"No, not literally."

"You moron."

We ate together in silence. I knew I had to tell her. I had to tell her what happened to me last night. I had to tell her what's been happening with me for a long time.

Of course, I'm sure she already knows.

"I'm a bad person," I said without thinking.

"In what way?" Violet replied.

"I've done terrible things." A pause. "It's out of my control."

"Specifics."

I closed my eyes a moment. "They know about Lily now. I told them…"

"What?"

"They know I'm her."

"That's it?"

"I'm sure the pieces are falling into place. They'll figure everything out."

"The cops are stupid," Violet said scornfully. "They can't comprehend anything complex. They just want it served up good and simple."

"I think I killed Leanne," I confessed. "I think she made me do it."

Violet stared inquisitively. "Who did? Rose?"

"No. Lily."

Silence.

She set her yogurt aside. It was hard to keep looking her in the eyes.

"I'm not buying it." She exhaled. "You're not that crazy, are you?"

"Maybe I am."

"Well, did you kill her or not? It's a simple question."

"It's not always simple," I whispered. "Sometimes… it's complex…"

Violet nodded slowly. "Leanne was my friend."

"So do you hate me now?"

It was a fair question. And I didn't know how she'd respond. Violet seemed to be taking this all in her stride, without giving away too much emotion. But for a brief moment now, I thought I did see some pain in her eyes. Perhaps it was grief. Whether it was for the passing of her friend, or that she was about to lose the only sister she had left, I wasn't quite sure…

"Well. I'm upset with you," Violet said finally. "Really, I always thought you might have done certain things… But Rose was fairly convincing too. I think she wanted me to believe she was the one who was behind everything."

"No, she wasn't."

"You're sure?"

I swallowed. "It was me."

CHAPTER 111

I knew Violet wouldn't approve of my next move. It amazed me how she was so willing to accept and forgive my actions. Furthermore, I don't think she fully recognized the gravity of what I've done. I guess when you grow up around so much tragedy and violence, you become sort of desensitized.

What I wanted was for her to be okay. I wanted her to be safe. She's not to blame for my actions. There are people – people close to me – whom I do hold accountable. But Violet isn't one of them.

She has suffered too.

"Trisha," I called, coming from down the hallway. "Trisha, where are you?"

Violet and I stood in the empty living room. I noticed numerous religious paintings and ornaments decorating the interior. I suddenly felt even stronger than before.

"Coming," Trisha called back, and came out from the laundry room.

I waited till she was with us. "I have to confess something."

"Alright."

"To the police. I'm going to tell them what I've done. Starting with last night."

"What happened last night?" Trisha asked.

"After Jessica attacked Rose, my mind went into meltdown. I was there, but I was not there. Simone fired a gun, and somehow I got hold of Jessica's knife. I saw myself… I… I stabbed her. I killed her."

"Is that really what happened?" Trisha turned to Violet.

Violet rolled her eyes in frustration and sat down over by the sofa. "I don't want to say anything that incriminates anyone."

"But I'm doing this," I said to her. "I *need* to do this. It's my fault those people are dead."

"Which people?"

"I killed Jessica," I repeated. "And then, I remember, Violet was trying to pull Simone away from me. But I blacked out, and I killed her too. The same thing happened with Leanne. It happened with Georgie too."

"Wait. Georgie? You mean that little boy that your stepmother went to trial for–"

"She wasn't our stepmother," Violet corrected. "She was just some woman Dad was sleeping with."

"I didn't know what I was doing," I said. "I didn't know. Lily comes in… She comes in when I'm afraid… She comes in when I need help…"

"Oh God," Trisha gushed.

I could see she was terrified now. But she has nothing to fear. I'm coming clean. I'm owning up. I'm ready for the punishment.

"You understand what this means," Trisha began. "You understand what I have to…"

"Please, tell Captain Roper, I am willing to make a full, detailed confession of my actions. For all the murders. There's only one request he has to honor, before I'm ready."

"What's that, Poppy?"

"I want to see my mother," I said defiantly. "You tell him, I want to see Sarah Greene."

I looked over my shoulder to Violet. She was shivering.

"One last time."

CHAPTER 112

Violet and I are sitting on the porch outside Trisha's house. We're both aware this might be the last we'll see of each other, for a very long time.

I'm not crying. She's not crying.

I'm not sad.

I feel almost… at peace.

"It didn't have to be this way," Violet said, in dismay. "I would have kept your secret. I would have kept it till I died."

"I know you would."

"I don't understand how this helps anyone."

"There's something wrong with me, Violet," I tried to explain. "I know you'll say there isn't. Or you'll say there's something wrong with all of us. But this is different. There's something *really* wrong with me."

"I think, in your own way, you were always looking out for us," Violet reflected. "Rose and I."

"We looked out for each other."

"We did." She hesitated. "I wish there was something I could do. But I think we're past that now…"

Captain Roper's car pulled up along the sidewalk.

"We have to make amends," I said. "Leanne's family. You need to do something for them."

"Like what?"

"You need to let them know what happened, it wasn't her fault. Leanne didn't do anything to us. She just got in the way…"

The driver's door opened. Roper began making his way around the car.

"What about Mom?" Violet asked. "What are you going to tell her?"

"Everything. Of course."

"And what do you think she'll say?"

"I don't know yet."

Roper took a few steps from the car and stood directly opposite us.

A cold breeze went by.

He didn't say anything.

"Say goodbye to Zowie for me," I instructed. "I left her in a bad way. Let her know I'm sorry."

I stood up.

"Sure, no problem." Violet hesitated. "Did you go see her last night after…?"

"Yeah."

"Did you tell her what happened?"

"I tried to," I whispered. "I was so out of it. I don't think she took it seriously. But she will now."

"Poppy," Captain Roper called. "Say goodbye."

Violet stood up.

We turned to each other.

"You survived," I said to her. "You made it through. Not all of us did…"

We put our arms around each other.

"You made it too," Violet whispered.

CHAPTER 113

Mom's prison was a two-hour drive away.

"You understand, that after this, there will be no going back," Captain Roper said while we were on the road. "There will be no more games. No more requests. No more lies."

"I know," I replied stiffly in the back seat.

"We need the truth this time."

"That's what I've promised."

"Yes."

I could tell part of him didn't believe I was going to confess. He thought there was a high likelihood I was pulling his leg.

"I'm not going to waste anyone's time," I reassured him. "I regret my actions. I need to be punished for what I did."

"But… why did you do it then?"

"Because I'm not well. Obviously."

He didn't seem satisfied with that answer. But he would have to wait. There was something I had to be sure of first. Something… only Mom would know.

* * *

We finally reached the women's penitentiary where Mom was being held. Captain Roper had said she'd been a model prisoner since her incarceration. She was apparently well liked by the other inmates, despite the nature of her conviction. She helped teach some of the classes there, and participated in a lot of the recovery programs.

Roper organized a visitor's pass for us, and we both made our way through the administration building to the visitation center. There was a process where I was searched and asked a lot of questions by the prison officials, a little taste of what was to come perhaps. I wasn't looking forward to it – I knew that much.

But it's what I deserve.

"Through here, Captain."

We passed through the last set of doors which opened to the visitation room; it was completely empty. The blinds were all down and the lights were on, although they probably needn't have been.

Mom wasn't here yet.

We were taken to one of the tables and told to wait for her.

I wasn't too thrilled about Roper's immediate presence at the table, but I figured it would be useless telling him to go stand somewhere by himself. He was the reason I was here, after all.

"What happens to her?" I asked, suddenly feeling nervous. "If I confess to killing Daisy?"

"Be careful what you say to her," Roper cautioned. "You don't want to get her hopes up."

I knew Mom was innocent. She had nothing directly to do with Daisy's death.

Indirectly, though…

Suddenly the door ahead of us open.

Mom and I were about to meet for the first time in six years.

CHAPTER 114

She was already in tears. Tired, haggard, gaunt, Mom staggered towards our table, overwhelmed with emotion.

Captain Roper got up anxiously and moved away from us.

"Poppy?" she gasped. "Poppy, is it you?"

I didn't get up. I didn't know if I wanted to touch her or not. "It's me, Mom. Please, sit down."

"Yes, yes." She lowered herself into the chair.

"Fifteen minutes," one of the guards hollered from the corner.

Mom winced.

We would have to make them last.

* * *

"So, you're looking well," she said, before I could really collect myself. "You're all grown up. You're practically a woman now. How old are you? Are you seventeen…?"

I nodded.

"The time flies," she went on. "Life passes you by, in here, anyway. I always wondered though. I wondered how you were getting on."

"I've thought about you too."

"What about your sisters? Why didn't they come with you?"

"Mom." I bit my teeth together. "I'm afraid I have bad news."

"Yes, I know. I already found out. I wish things had turned out differently with your father. He wasn't a terrible person, he just got some things wrong. I know you set him up, the same as you set me up." She chuckled. "Naughty girls… The four of you…"

I couldn't break it to her yet. It was going to destroy her.

"Mom. About Dad…"

"It's okay, if you don't want to say."

"Rose wasn't lying. Not entirely. He… did things… He had Simone take Daisy…"

"Simone? Who's that?"

I stared at her. "Dad's woman on the side, before Jessica. She took Daisy at the park that day. You don't remember her?"

"I remember the woman in the park. But I didn't know what her name was." A pause. "Have the police caught her?"

"Simone's dead," I said. "There was an incident last night… Jessica found where we lived. We were living with Simone. She tried to protect us, but…"

"I don't understand," Mom said slowly. "I feel so lost. I'm not supposed to know things about you. And…"

She looked away.

"Mom. I have to ask you something. It's important."

"Yes, dear?"

"Who is Lily?"

"Lily?"

"Who is she?"

Mom looked down at the floor. "I don't know what you're talking about."

"Mom. Do you remember when Daisy died? How the police said one of us was with her? In a pink necklace?"

"They said some ridiculous things back then, didn't they?"

"Do you know where the necklace came from? Think."

"No."

"Mom," I growled.

"You and your sisters like to play games," she said dismissively. "Children's games. You're all just making things up. Pretending to be… other people."

"Mom. Lily was real."

"Lily? No."

"She was a real person."

"You were just pretending. We were all just pretending. Once there were four, and then there were three and… What you don't know, won't hurt you. I'm not responsible."

"Mom, look at me."

She didn't want to. But the tension in the room forced her to lift her gaze from the floor to meet my eyes.

"I was Lily," I stated.

"Your name's Poppy."

"We were *all* Lily."

CHAPTER 115

It's night when I close my eyes. It's day when I open them.

Never listen to parents who say they don't play favorites.

"I'm going to tell you a story," I remember our father saying one evening in the lounge room. The TV was muted and he had our pup Sparky resting on his lap.

Us girls were sitting cross-legged on the floor in front of him.

"There's four of you," Dad said. "I have four daughters. Violet. Rose. Daisy. Poppy. My girls. Would it surprise you then, if I were to tell you there's one more?"

He watched us intently. Patting the dog.

"Oh yes. It's true. There's a fifth daughter running around here some place. Have you seen her?"

After a moment of confusion, Violet spoke up. "That's not true. There's just us four."

"It seems that way, I understand," Dad said, smiling. "But she's not like the four of you. She's different, in every way."

"What do you mean she's different?" Daisy scoffed at him.

"She doesn't sleep for one thing. No. She… she hides a lot during the day. But after all you four are asleep, that's when she's really awake."

"She lives here?" I asked. "In the house?"

"She does," Dad replied.

"Then why haven't we heard about her before?" Violet asked.

"Do you know why?" Dad said mysteriously. "Do you know, Daisy?"

"No," Daisy said.

"What about you, Poppy? Do you know?"

I shook my head.

"Rose? I'll give you a hint. It's because she's a sssssss…"

A pause.

"She's a secret?" Rose exclaimed.

"That's right!" Dad grinned. "She's your secret sister. You girls are very lucky to have a secret sister watching over you, while you sleep."

"What does she look like?" Violet asked skeptically.

"Oh, she just looks exactly the same as you," Dad said, putting Sparky on the floor. "Only there is one little difference."

He looked to each of us.

"She doesn't have a purple ribbon. Or a red ribbon. Or a yellow ribbon. Or a blue ribbon. No. Do you know what color she has?"

We shook our heads.

He then reached into his pocket and plucked the ribbon.

"She wears a pink ribbon. Like this," he said.

He handed it to me, and looking at it I passed it along the group.

"Her name is Lily, your secret sister. She's the most special out of all of you. I bought her a magical pink necklace to wear. Only, it's been a while since I've seen her. I leave it out every night in this room, if she wants to come and find it. Do you know what happens then?"

We waited for the answer.

"When Lily puts on the pink necklace – she turns into a princess. Yes, she's all grown up while she's wearing it, and we get to do all sorts of wonderful things together."

"How would you know it's her?" Rose asked.

"What do you mean?"

"What if one of us puts it on?"

He shook his head. "The magic only works when Lily's wearing it, I'm afraid. And the necklace will know it's her because Lily always wears the pink ribbon in her hair. Speaking of which – where did that ribbon go?"

We all silently shook our heads.

One of us smiled.

"That's alright," Dad said standing up. "I'm sure it will turn up. Now… let's see how Mom's going with dinner…"

CHAPTER 116

Blue is my color. Blue is my soul. The colors of our flowers represent where we feel safe. Whether it's a bedroom. Or a house. Or a ribbon. Things have happened to our poor Lily. Things have happened to our secret sister. We know, because we are her.

"That's a horrible story," Mom said coldly when I was finished, "and not a word of it is true."

"It is true," I replied. "I was there. I was in that room when he told us what to do."

"You couldn't remember it even if it were true – you would've been too young to remember!"

"But I do remember, Mom. I remember you were in the kitchen when he told us about her. You heard every word."

"Oh, what hogwash," Mom snapped, disgusted. "And what difference does it make anyway? You got what you wanted. I'm in here, and he's dead!"

"Rose is dead," I whispered.

"What?"

"As I said, Jessica broke into our house last night. She went after Rose. She stabbed her to death. Revenge for Georgie."

"Oh no… You're still lying…"

I looked at Captain Roper.

"She's not lying," he muttered.

"Oh no! Oh God!" Mom screamed.

"You have to take responsibility for what happened to us," I stated. "We're not to blame for who we are. You should have protected us from him."

"Just stop it, Poppy. Just stop…"

"Admit it at least. Admit you knew what he did to us."

"I didn't, I didn't." She shook her head. "I would never have thought…"

"Rose is watching us, Mom. She's on the other side. She's here with me now. Are you really going to keep on lying to us? To yourself?"

And then she went still.

"Alright, time's up, Mrs. Greene," the guard in the corner said. "Say your goodbyes."

"Mom?"

"I'm sorry," she said and got up.

I grabbed her arm to stop her leaving. "Admit it."

She looked back at me. Her spirit decaying.

"Admit you did this to me!"

Her jaw fell open. "I'm sorry, Poppy, but I can't. I just can't…"

CHAPTER 117

I am dead inside on the drive back. I thought after all this time, after all the progress she'd supposedly made while away – I thought she'd finally be ready to face up to what she did.

"Don't take it personally," Roper said, trying to ease my disappointment. "I'm sure what you said tonight will leave a great impression."

So what then? I wonder. Am I to return for my apology on another day? In how many years' time will it be? What if she still won't admit it, all the way up to her last breath?

"You're not having second thoughts, are you?" he asked. "On holding up your end of the bargain?"

"No," I replied. "I don't want to be like her. I don't want to run anymore."

"Thank you." He sighed with relief. "Are you hungry? We'll have time to stop once we get back to the city, if you like."

"Yeah, sure," I said, watching the endless trees go by the road. "Nothing beats a last meal."

* * *

I let him pick where to eat. Nothing too fancy. Just an ordinary, discount pizza place. We each got a couple of slices on a plate, and cupful of soda and ice. I looked inside the beverage before I took a sip. Blue lemonade.

Believe it or not, I'd never tried it.

"There's something you should know," Captain Roper informed me, as we took our seats at the back of the restaurant. "I haven't told anyone about how you mean to confess. I know you probably think I'd just be happy to tie up all the loose ends and get the easiest conviction – but that isn't the case. We've made mistakes over the years. Mistakes of which, I'm personally accountable. I don't want to make any more."

"I'm not going to lie this time," I said. "I know what I've done."

"Gordon – formerly Detective Burke – is certain that you killed Georgie, because of something he and Ashley found on the cameras – something about you sliding your hand down the banister when you go up or down stairs. But I want something more concrete than that. I want proof it was you who has done this."

"What proof?"

"There was something we could never figure out with Georgie's death. How after the girl came up the stairs and went into his room, she left the house again, leaving the knife in the sink, and never came back. For so long it looked like there really was a fifth child. We went as far as looking into your birth records."

"But there was no fifth child, was there?"

"No." He shook his head. "But if it really was you, Poppy, then you should be able to tell me; how did you get back into the house without being seen?"

I thought carefully. So much of that night I'd blocked from my mind. I didn't want to look at it.

Because it was so painful.

"It's okay," he murmured. "If you can't remember… it's fine. We'll work it out…"

"No, I want to remember."

He nodded slowly. Put his hand next to mine.

"I have to. I need to."

Deep breath now.

"I will."

CHAPTER 118

Chantley House is cold at night. It's so cold I'm shivering. The lights don't work, so it's after 9 p.m. There's very little space in the room. All my bags are propped up in the corner. The dessert bowl Jessica gave me is resting on the floor beside it. I ate mine. Even though it didn't feel right. I feel like I'm going to get in trouble for it later.

Knock, knock.

The door opens. Rose and Violet silently tiptoe into my room. There isn't much light. I'm just sitting, huddled-up in the corner of my bed. I don't know what they want.

"Dad's here," Rose said, holding out a cell phone.

"Where did you get that?" I cried.

"He gave it to me. Dad wants to see Lily."

"Tell him no," I pleaded. "Tell him to go away."

"Simone thinks it will be better if we just kill him," Rose continued. "It's the only way to win for sure."

I shook my head. She couldn't be serious.

"Do you have the poison?" Rose asked Violet.

"What poison?" Violet replied.

"I thought Simone gave you some poison to take care of him peacefully."

"Oh right." Violet turned to me. "We decided to use this instead."

She lifted her sweater up, and produced a long, shiny dagger. There was a pink handle at the end of it.

"Are you ready?" Rose asked me.

"I'm not doing it!" I yelled. "I can't!"

Violet put the dagger on the floor between us. "I've already done my part, okay?"

We then turned, as the sound of a grand piano echoed throughout the halls of Chantley.

"What's that?" I mumbled.

"Jessica," Violet said disdainfully. "She likes to play."

"She's still awake?" Rose asked with worry.

"I'll go keep an eye on her." Violet pointed to the knife. "One of you needs to do this."

I kept shaking my head as she left.

"Rose," I pleaded. "I really can't. He's our Dad."

"He's not a man. He's a monster." She shuddered. "You'd know that if you were locked in his dungeon with me."

"But I really don't want to. I'm scared."

"I'll take the blame," Rose promised. "Whatever happens. We'll tell Violet it was me who did it."

"Why are you making me? Why don't you do it?"

"Because I need to know you're on my side. I need to know you really care about our new family." She lowered her eyes. It was dark, but I could still see the tears. "Violet has already proved it. It's just you now. And then we'll be sisters forever…"

* * *

I can see what happens next. I can see Lily leaving the room and putting on her pink necklace. Downstairs, everything is pooled in shadow. I can feel the knife under my sweater. It's tight. One wrong move, and it will go into my skin.

But I have to remember, this isn't happening to me.

This is all for Lily.

I guide her. She guides me.

We protect each other.

* * *

The man we see in the car is not my father. He's a monster, just like Rose said. He has done things now, I cannot put into words. Everything around me starts to change. I can't see properly. I feel my hand on the stairs. And the piano is still playing.

I'm walking up. I'm walking forward.

I'd dropped the knife earlier before I reached the car. Too afraid to do what I needed to. And now, it's somehow found its way back to me. I feel it pricking at my skin.

Every second or so, I see the inside of the car again. I see the monster.

"You want to be a good girl, don't you? You want to be a princess. Princess Lily. Don't make me ask you again–"

And that's it.

That's the end.

Lily is outside of me and walking into Georgie's room.

He doesn't struggle. He doesn't scream.

He doesn't even wake.

It just happens, like it just happened to me.

The child in us has died its death. Our innocence has been taken.

We didn't see Georgie when we stabbed him.

I thought it was me in the bed.

CHAPTER 119

"The next thing I knew, I was wandering the grounds outside Chantley," I told Roper. "It was still night, but I felt like I'd been asleep for hours."

Roper shook his head, moved by the tale. Sickened by it. There were still things I hadn't said. But he knew what they were. "And then?"

"The ground fell out from under me. I slipped and fell in a hole in the middle of the yard. I would have injured myself, but I grabbed hold of the ladder just in time." I closed my eyes and I was there again. "I climbed down. It was a narrow cavern of sorts. But there was a big door at the end. It was halfway open." I swallowed. "I went inside, and suddenly there was light. Not a lot, but enough. I didn't know at the time, but where I was walking into… it was Dad's dungeon."

"Dungeon?"

"He held Rose prisoner there. Of course, he thought it was Daisy. Everyone thought Daisy was the one who was taken, but it wasn't. It was Rose all along. And then, years later… when we were eleven, she came back to us. Through Simone."

"She escaped?"

"Simone rescued her. Simone was the one who originally kidnapped her for Dad." I took a chug of my blue lemonade. "Eventually I made it out of there. There was another ladder, leading up to our bedrooms in the house. I pushed open the trapdoor and lifted up the rug which was hiding it. And then I was back in my room, right where I started…"

"Wow."

There was an awkward silence.

"We'll have to check that out," Roper said.

"I'm sure it's still there."

He nodded. "And you're prepared to go into the same detail with the other murders, as you have done with Georgie's?"

"I guess so."

"Well, we can save those for the station."

I looked down at my pizza. I'd hardly touched it.

"Finish up," Roper said. "We have to leave soon. They'll be waiting for us now. We have a long night ahead of us."

"Sure," I said, and picked up a slice. "I'll just eat this one, okay?"

"Okay, Poppy. When you're ready…"

CHAPTER 120

I don't want to say I'm relieved to have finally told my story, because that isn't fair. Georgie deserves better than that. So, I'm not relieved. For the rest of my life now, I have to live in this suffering. It's the only path ahead for me. Because as much as I want to blame my parents for who I've become, ultimately, I'm responsible. I did this. Not them.

"Are you crying?" Captain Roper asked as we drove to the precinct. "Do you need a tissue?"

I shook my head. "I'll be okay."

"I almost feel bad," he muttered. "I have to keep reminding myself of what you've done."

"You don't have to feel bad for me. I deserve what's coming."

A pause. "For what it's worth, I think you're taking it bravely."

"Thank you."

"There'll still be a life for you inside. I know it probably doesn't seem that way, but what you do now still matters."

"I hope so."

* * *

Ah, Captain Roper. Such a gentleman. He was being perfectly nice to me now, but I knew it would change. As soon as I gave them what they wanted, the act would fall away. I'd just be a murderer in their eyes. A student. A sister. A child, no more.

"Hi, Trisha."

"Hello, Poppy."

Roper had left me alone in the interrogation for about twenty minutes. I knew we were about to get started.

"Since you're cooperating, they want a statement from you first," Trisha explained. She set a notepad and pen on the table in front of me. Then she took the chair opposite. "The whole truth, as you remember it."

I swallowed. "What if I forget something?"

"They will question you afterward. The point is to get the main stuff out now. Your confession, to all the murders."

"I think I'm afraid," I whispered. "I don't know if I can do this."

"No one's forcing you."

"That's true." I stared at her. "How can you even look at me anymore? I'm just a monster now."

"What you went through is unspeakable," Trisha replied.

"But what I've done is even worse."

"I don't think it works that way. I don't think you're a bad person."

"So, what am I?"

"I can't answer that." Trisha sighed. "Only you know what is in your heart." She looked at the notepad. "Until you decide to tell us."

EPILOGUE

I have imagined this already. I have called it into manifestation. I have heard this voice in my dreams.

It's a voice, that tells the truth.

A voice, that tells a story.

Even as I write this now, I know I may never say these words again. Once they're out of me, I no longer own it. I no longer identify with it.

I want to say, once it's out, I will never kill again. Because I'm not that person anymore. I'm just someone who told a story.

* * *

We'll start at the beginning. Our parents were good people, on the surface. It goes without saying, they weren't ready to look after four girls, all at once. I think our birth sped things up in their relationship. They fell out of love a lot faster.

I want to say, I didn't really know them. I can't explain what they've done. At some point, it became apparent… our father was abusing us. I don't like to think about it. I don't like to talk about it. Most of it's a blur. There are some things I want to say though…

I saw the dungeon. Where he took Daisy to live. He brought me there a few times. I saw other men there. They were drinking and smoking. Now that I think about it, there were other girls there too.

I was so young. And it was so awful, you just push it down. You pretend it didn't happen. You pretend it's not a part of you.

I think what I most felt, was that I was betrayed. Not just by him, but by Mom too. She turned a blind eye. And she knows it. I have seen her since. I can't forgive someone who doesn't ask for forgiveness.

* * *

My sister, Daisy, was first. I remember killing her. All it was, was a single, hard thrust. I was aiming for her heart. I don't think I hit it squarely.

Because it was so quick, I never felt bad about killing her. In the weeks leading up to it, Rose came to visit me. Rose, who had been living as Daisy since her abduction. I sat with her and Simone and learned the truth about what had happened to us. Since the other two had never witnessed it, I knew they wouldn't understand. Later I'd realize, that up to that point, our father hadn't touched them either. I think I was jealous.

In the end, Rose wanted her old life back, and Daisy didn't want to give it to her. She was going to ruin everything. So I just did what I did to solve the problem.

Afterwards, my sisters weren't the same with me. I tried to convince them it wasn't me who stabbed her. It was Lily. I knew if I could make them believe I thought Lily was holding the knife, then I was one step closer to them believing they held the knife. In the end, we all killed her. Only I confess.

* * *

Ashley was the one I really enjoyed killing. I hate all police, but I especially hated her. She was so naïve. She bought every word of Rose's false confession, while I had to sit there, knowing the truth about Georgie. Why he really died.

Dad gave us a phone to correspond with him in secret. We had it the night Georgie died. I kept it hidden from the cops. But I wound up dropping it in Ashley's car during the ride back to Simone's, because I needed to keep track of her.

It was later that afternoon, as Ashley was leaving, that she found Daisy's red ball. I knew in that moment, when she looked at me, she'd found me out. Maybe she didn't realize how, exactly. But it would come to her.

I later tracked Dad's phone on Simone's computer and found the motel Ashley was staying at. I caught a bus there in the middle of the night when everyone was asleep. The motel was so cheap they didn't have any CCTV installed to catch me peering in the windows till I found her room, and let myself in.

* * *

Lily is not to blame for Ashley's murder. I was very conscious of what I was doing. And I enjoyed it too. I enjoyed getting away with it.

Leanne's murder was less pleasant. Despite her affiliations with my sisters, I considered Leanne to be a friend. That's why it hurt so much to see her go the way she did, but friendship meant nothing to her. It had to be done. And I'm not going to blame Lily for that one either.

There have been times though, where I have seen Lily in action. After Jessica killed Rose, for example. That whole room was filled with terror. I could hardly breathe. I wasn't completely present.

But Lily was there, on top of Jessica as she lay dying from Simone's bullet. She was stabbing her eyes out. I remember turning from them to the door, where I saw Simone cowering. I looked back to Lily, and realized there was an understanding.

Where you go, I go.

Lily, dearest. You have confessed to more than you have done. Because now we come lastly to Master Georgie. Where you have walked away from our father's car, and up those dreaded stairs to Georgie's room. You have stabbed that little boy as he lay in his bed. And then you have fled, while your sisters remained.

You have confessed.

You have pleaded guilty before judge, jury and executioner.

Of course, it never occurred to you that little Georgie was dead before you got to him.

I shall explain. Jessica killed Georgie.

Jessica killed Georgie when she handed him his last bowl of ice cream.

Simone's original plan was for one of us to poison Dad, rather than stab him to death. She'd given us a syringe filled with cyanide.

"For Georgie. I'm not hungry."

I'd given my bowl back to Jessica with a little present attached. Serves her right for treating us that way.

Later, I sent word to Simone and fearing it would lead back to her, she managed to get inside the precinct and alter the coroner's report. So Georgie was stabbed to death, and the poisoning never happened.

But I know the truth.

And now since you're reading this, so do you.

Yours sincerely,
Violet Greene

***

It's after 3 a.m. by the time I finish my confession. I collect the pages from my desk and step into the hallway. The house is quiet; Trisha is sleeping soundly in her bedroom at the end, and her door is closed. I walk in the opposite direction, through the lounge and kitchen to the front door leading outside, and sit down on the porch, the pages in my hands.

I haven't decided what I'm going to do with them.

I could take them with me when I go visit Poppy in prison on the weekend. I'm sure they would make interesting reading. Or I could just bury them in the yard.

I pull a cigarette lighter from my pocket, and spark the flame. Its golden torch brings the words to life below.

"I'm sorry, Poppy," I whisper. "Will you forgive me, sister?"

A gentle breeze drifts through the night.

And just for a moment, I think I'll take the pages with me. I'll tell the truth about who I am and what I've done. I'll give her back her freedom.

"I wonder what that'd be like," I muse, as the pages catch light.

I guess we'll never know.

If you enjoyed this book, please let others know by leaving a quick review on Amazon. Also, if you spot anything untoward in the paperback, get in touch. We strive for the best quality and appreciate reader feedback.

editor@thebookfolks.com

www.thebookfolks.com

More fiction by the author

GONE BUT NOT

One girl
Two mothers
Someone is lying

The new psychological thriller by Shane Spyre

To be released in Spring 2024

Follow us on Facebook or Instagram for more details

Other titles of interest

LIES WITHIN ME
by Vanessa Garbin

After being taken speed-dating by her friends, Alice wakes up in a stranger's house. She can't remember the night before, but thinks she has been drugged and assaulted. Worse, however, is the man responsible is found murdered. Was it her? If not, who killed him? Finding the culprit might be the only way to get herself out of the frame.

FREE with Kindle Unlimited and available in paperback!

THE IDEAL COUPLE
by Anna Willett

Detective Veronika Pope heads to an old mining town in Western Australia, tasked with the cold case of a couple who went missing there some three years previously. Everyone in the town seems to be hiding something and she gets few leads. But the more she probes, the more cracks appear, and if she can avoid falling into one, just maybe she can get closure for the couple's family.

FREE with Kindle Unlimited and available in paperback!

THE PIPER'S CHILDREN
by Iain Henn

A boy is found wandering in the woods, dressed in medieval clothes and speaking a strange language. When another child turns up, it doesn't shed any more light on the mystery for FBI agent Ilona Farris. Only by digging into her own past will she begin to work out what is going on, and who these children are, seemingly lost in time.

FREE with Kindle Unlimited and available in paperback!

THE
BOOK
FOLKS

Made in the USA
Columbia, SC
19 April 2024